MONSTER AND ME

THE COMPLETE COMICS COLLECTION

STORY BY ROBERT MARSH

ILLUSTRATED BY TOM PERCIVAL

STONE ARCH BOOKS
a capstone imprint

MONSTER AND ME

STORY BY ROBERT MARSH

ILLUSTRATED BY TOM PERCIVAL

DESIGNER: HILARY WACHOLZ
EDITOR: CHRISTOPHER HARBO

Stone Arch Graphic Novels are published
by Stone Arch Books, an imprint of Capstone.
1710 Roe Crest Drive, North Mankato, Minnesota 56003
www.capstonepub.com

Library of Congress Cataloging-in-Publication Data is available
on the Library of Congress website.
ISBN: 978-1-4965-8730-5 (library binding)
ISBN: 978-1-4965-9319-1 (paperback)
ISBN: 978-1-4965-8734-3 (eBook PDF)

Summary: Like every kid in town, twelve-year-old Gabby has
a pet monster. However, Gabby refuses to keep her monster,
Dwight, in the closet. Instead, she brings him to school!
Soon Dwight gets into all sorts of shenanigans--from playing a
part in the school play to taking the field in a baseball game.
But even with Gabby's best-laid plans, things don't always go
smoothly for Dwight. Can Gabby find ways to help her loveable
monster fit in at school?

Printed and bound in China.
2493

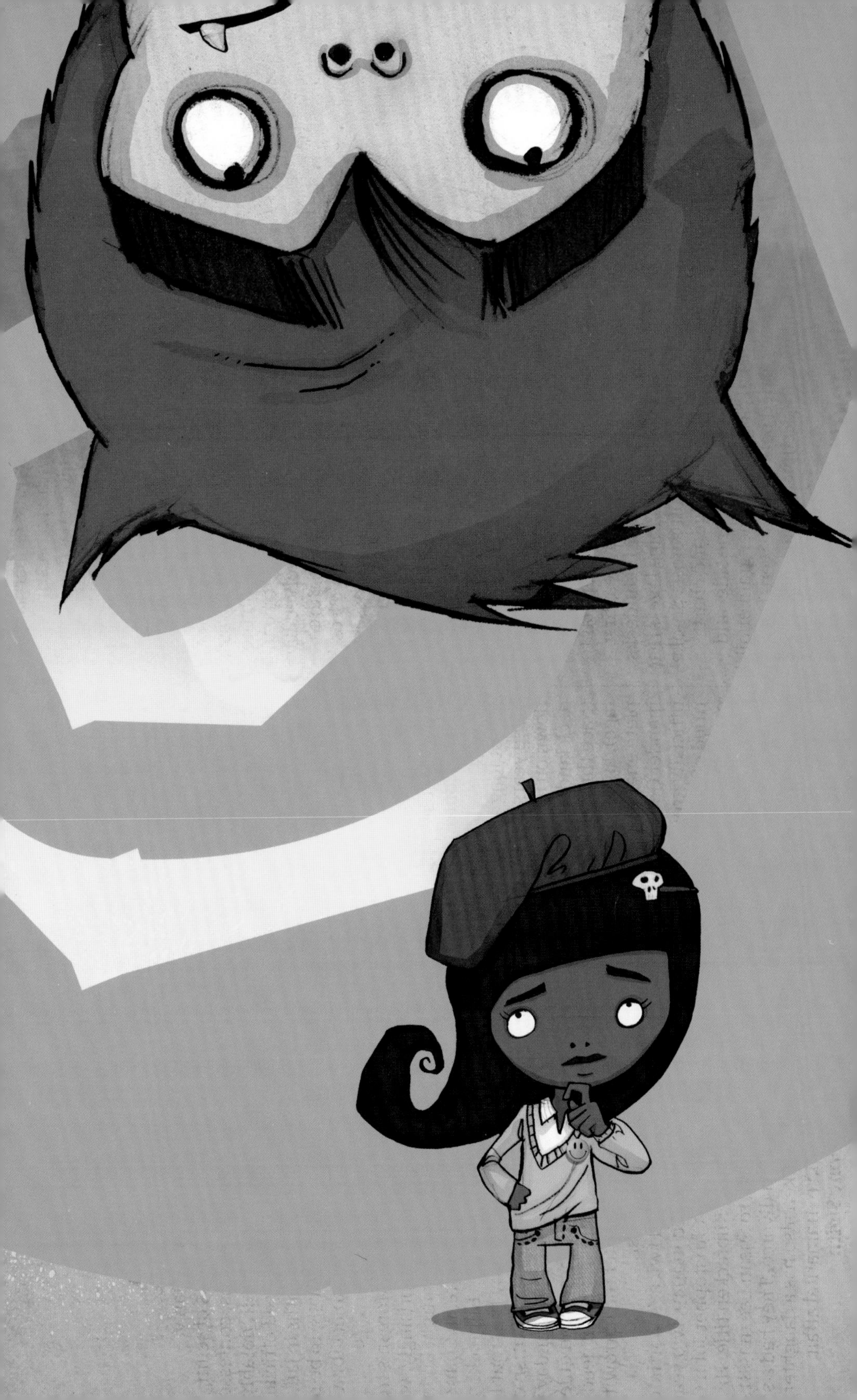

CONTENTS

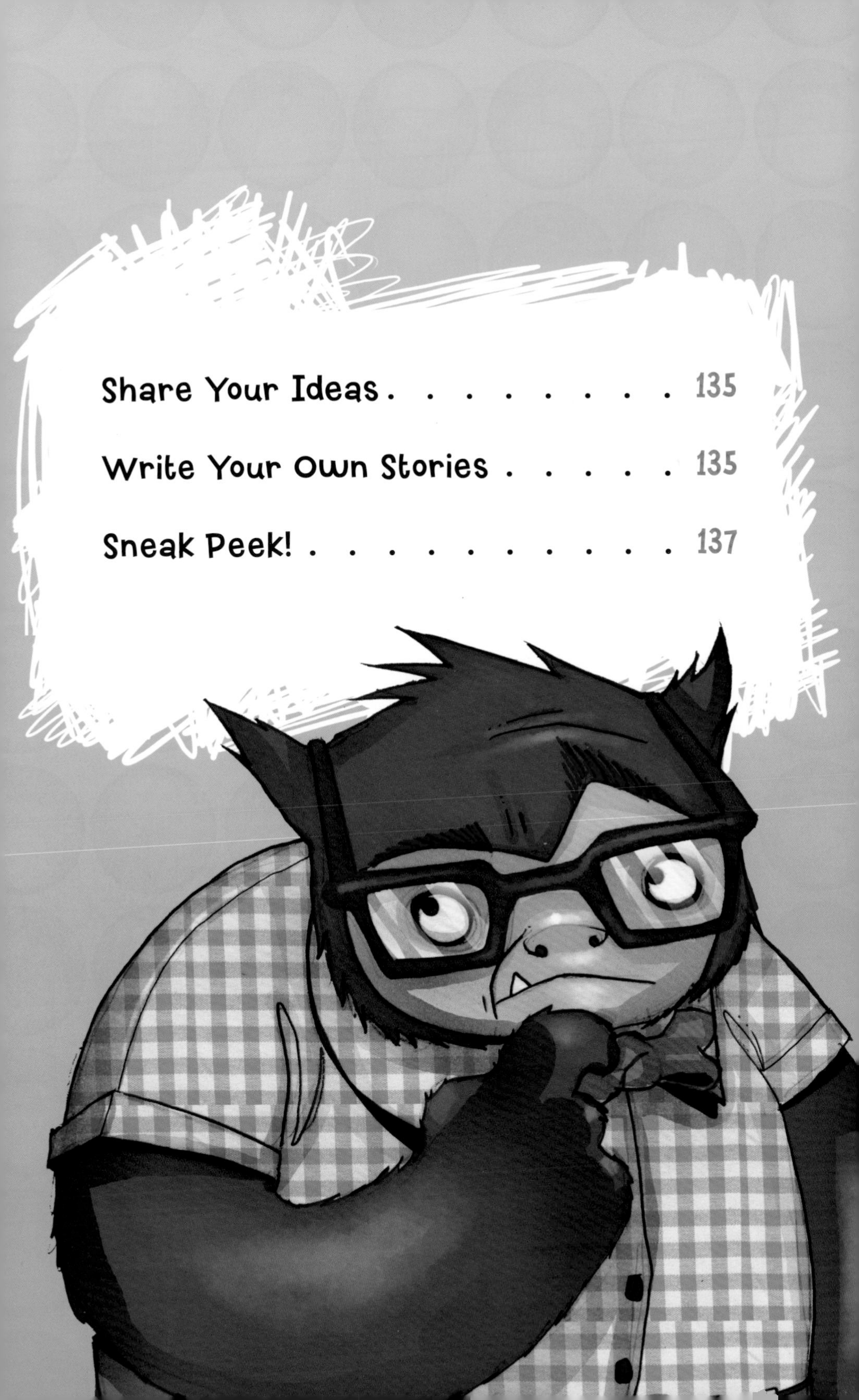

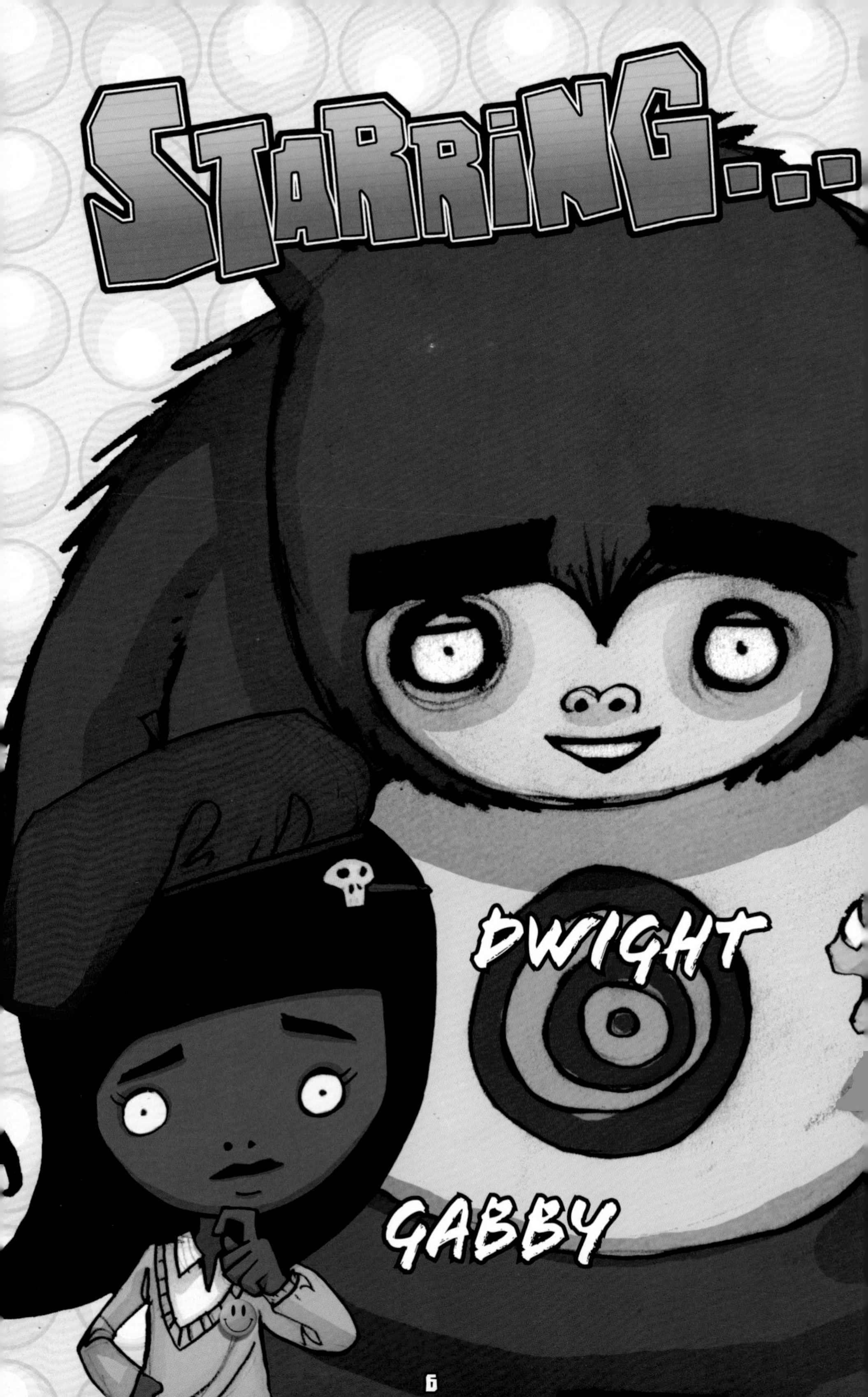
STARRING...
DWIGHT
GABBY

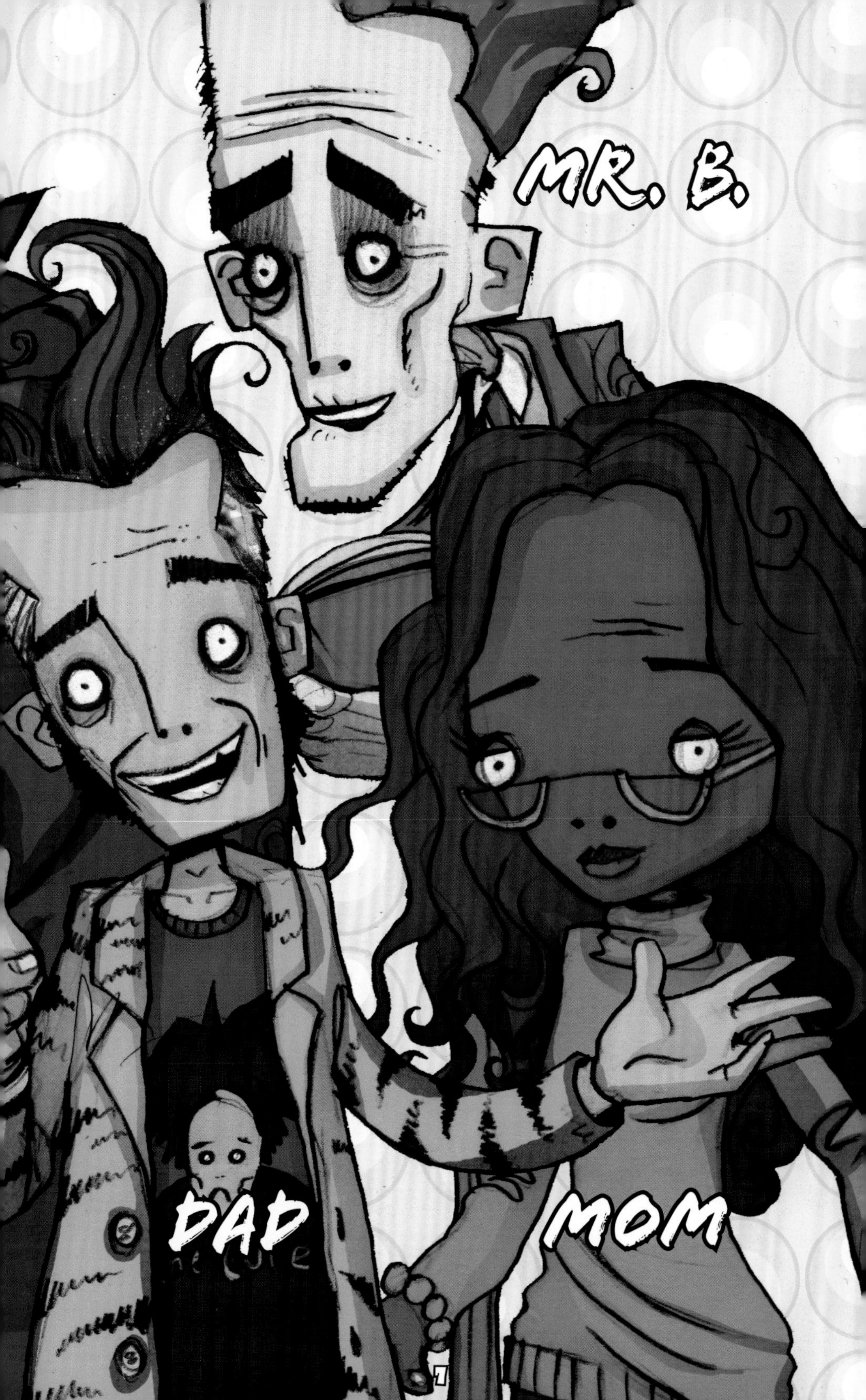
MR. B.
DAD
MOM

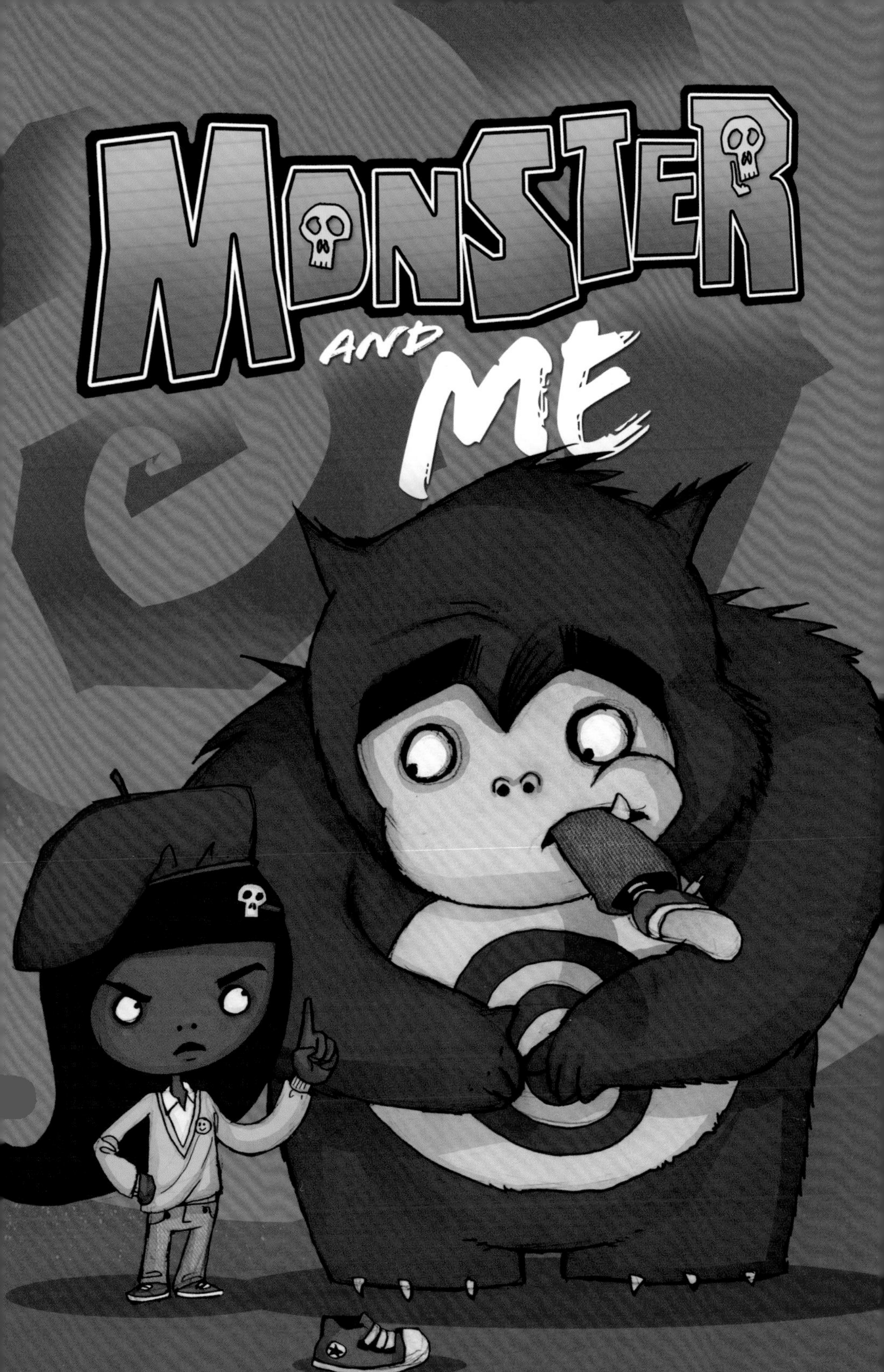
MONSTER
AND
ME

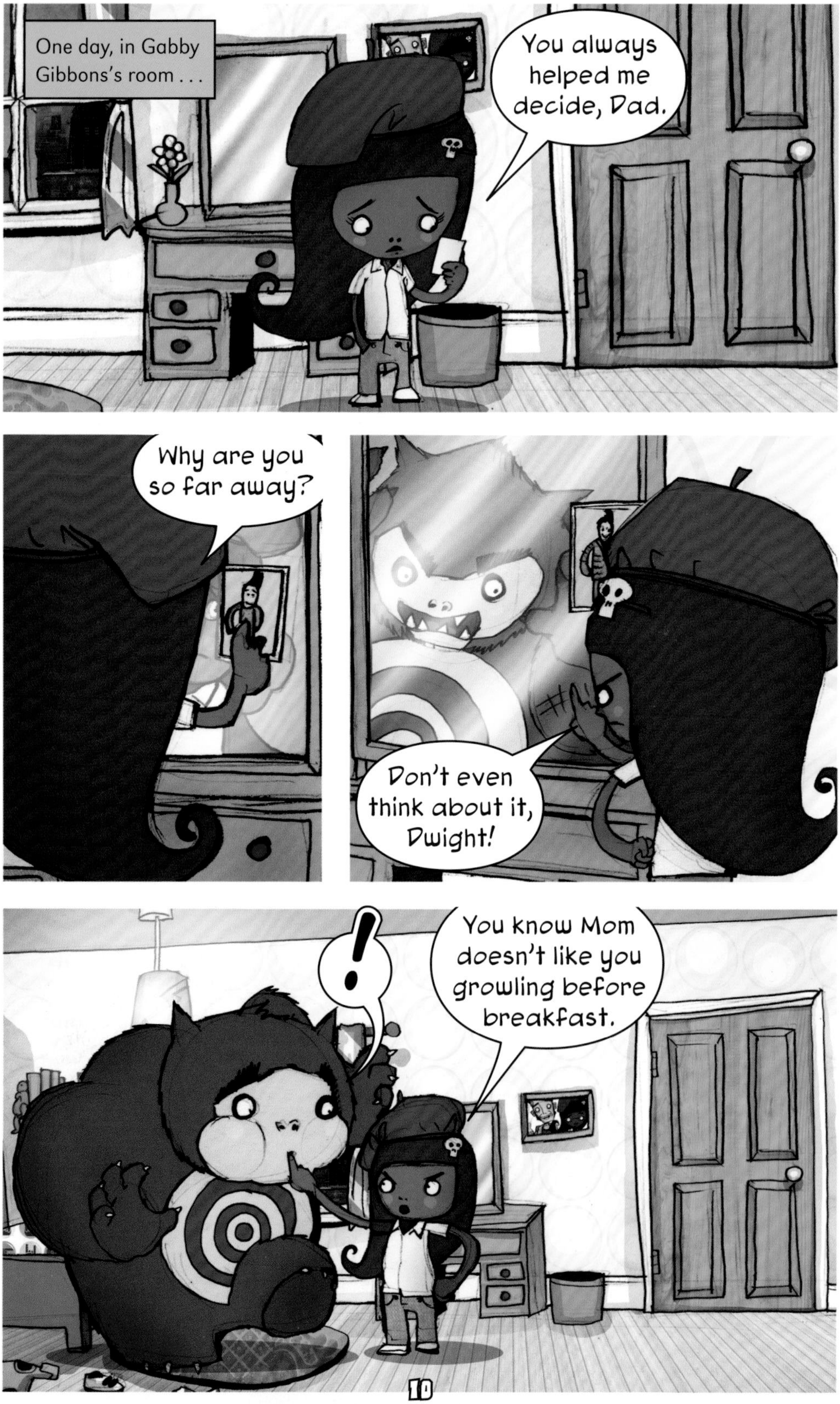
One day, in Gabby Gibbons's room . . .
You always helped me decide, Dad.
Why are you so far away?
Don't even think about it, Dwight!
!
You know Mom doesn't like you growling before breakfast.

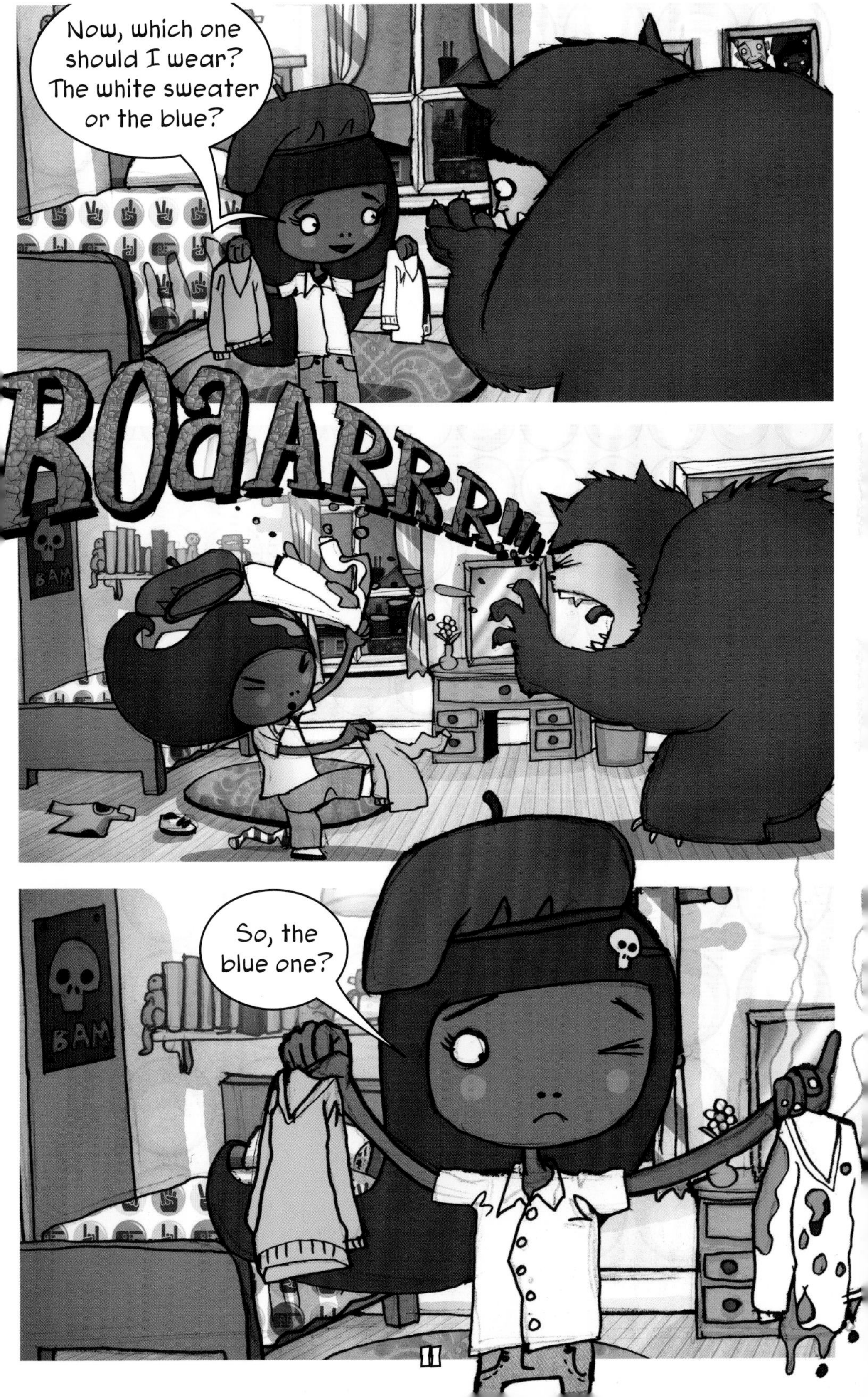

Now, which one should I wear? The white sweater or the blue?
ROAARRR!!!
So, the blue one?

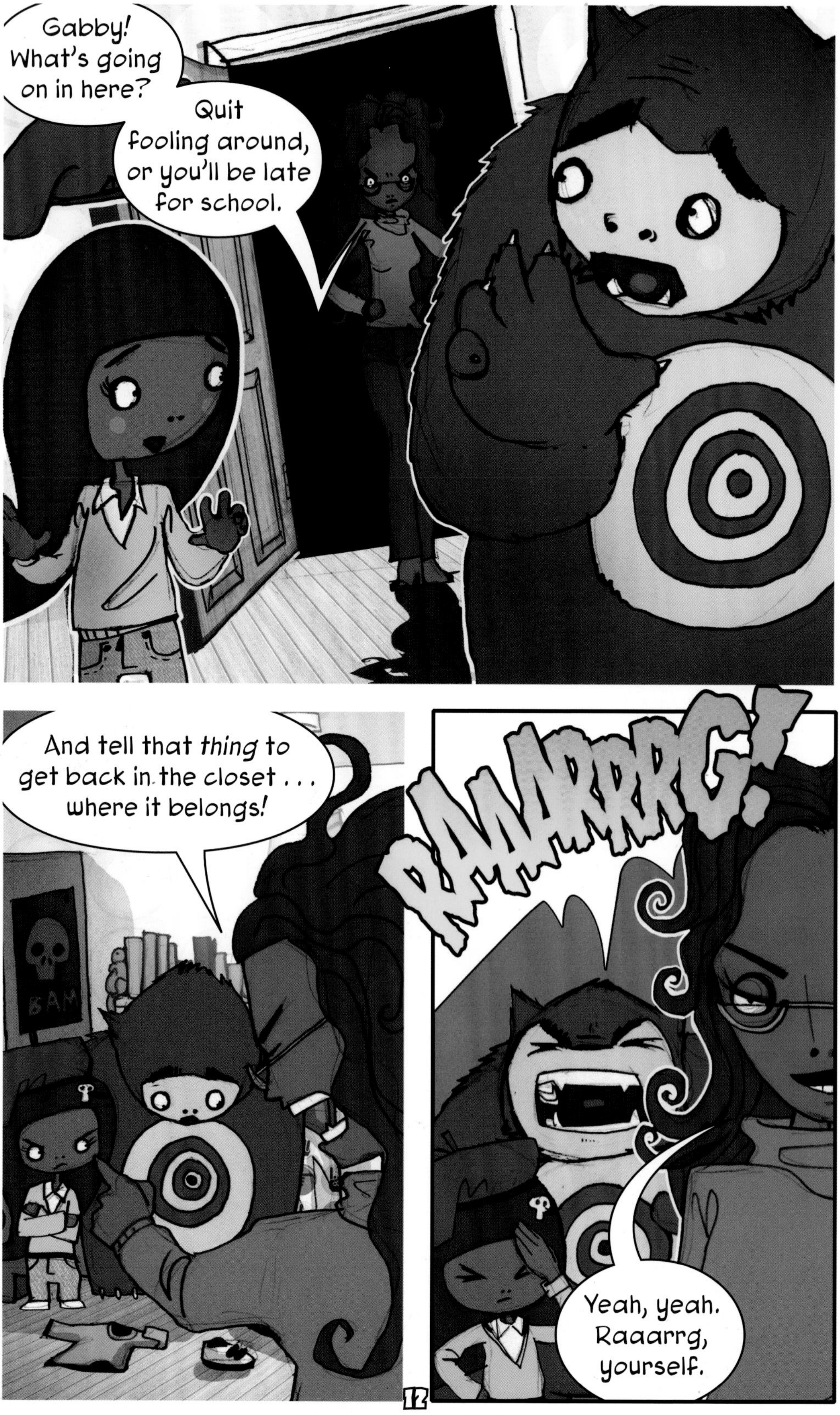
Gabby! What's going on in here?
Quit fooling around, or you'll be late for school.
And tell that *thing* to get back in the closet . . . where it belongs!
RAAARRRG!
Yeah, yeah. Raaarrg, yourself.

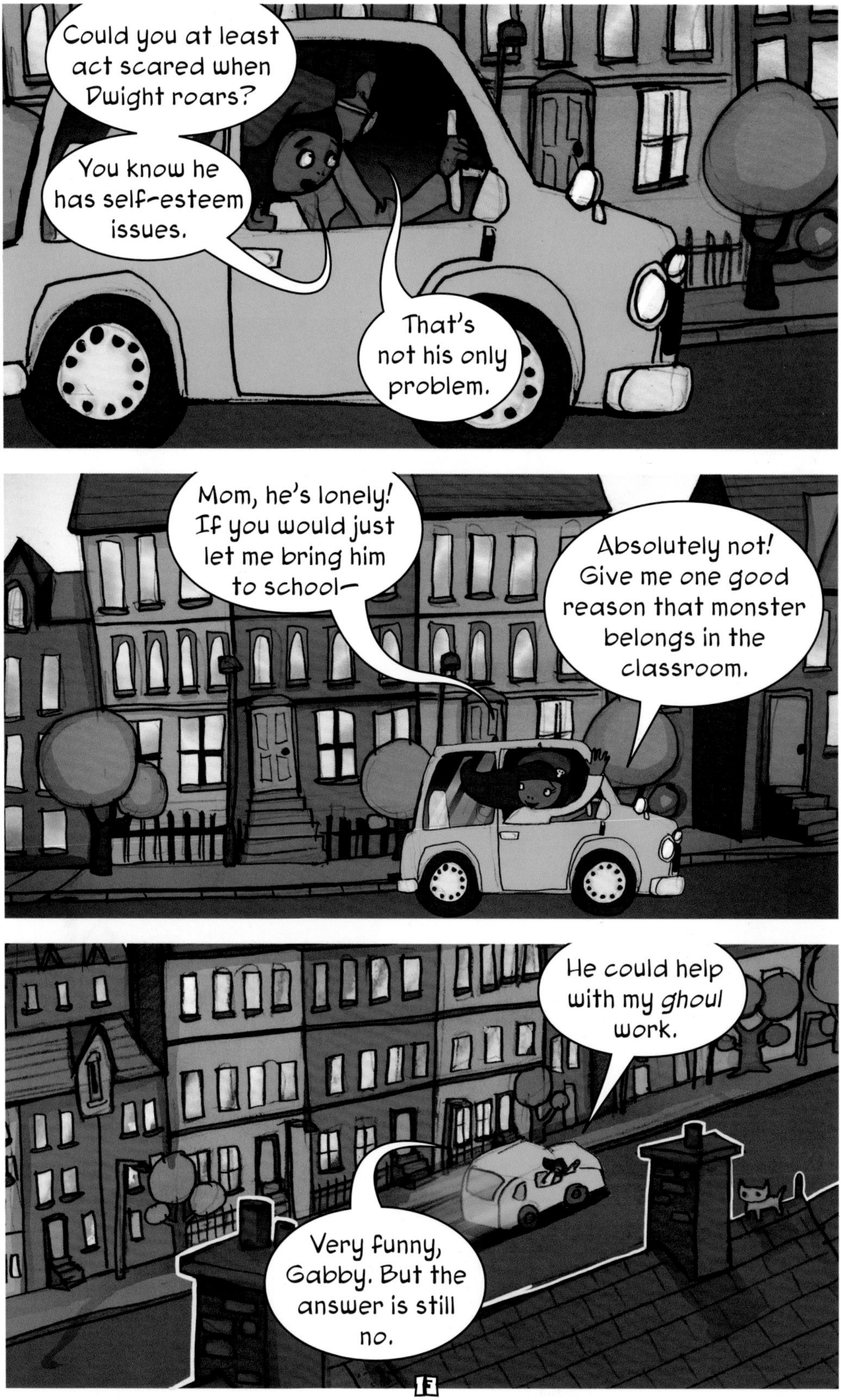
Could you at least act scared when Dwight roars?
You know he has self-esteem issues.
That's not his only problem.
Mom, he's lonely! If you would just let me bring him to school—
Absolutely not! Give me one good reason that monster belongs in the classroom.
He could help with my *ghoul* work.
Very funny, Gabby. But the answer is still no.

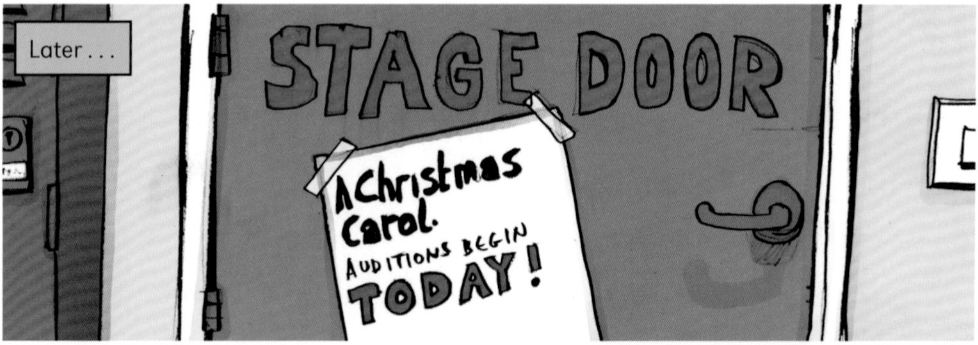
Later . . .
STAGE DOOR
A Christmas Carol.
AUDITIONS BEGIN
TODAY!

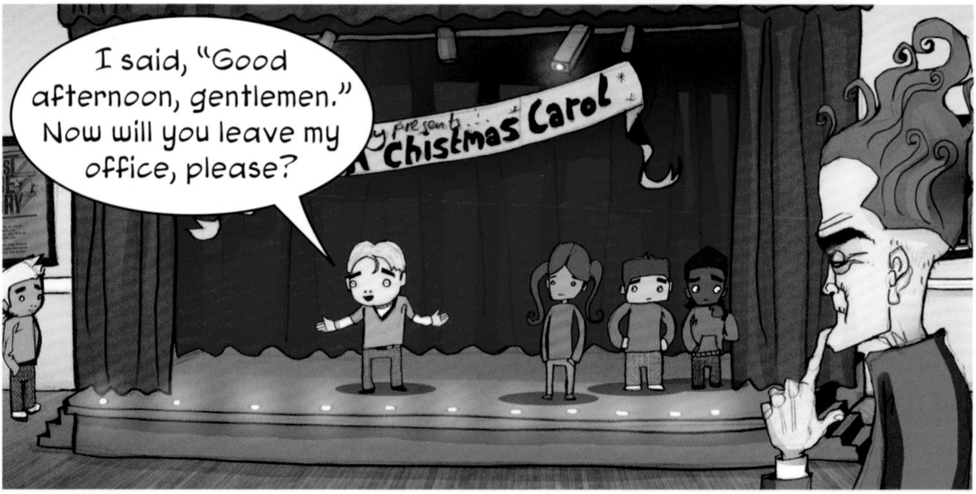
I said, "Good afternoon, gentlemen." Now will you leave my office, please?
Chistmas Carol

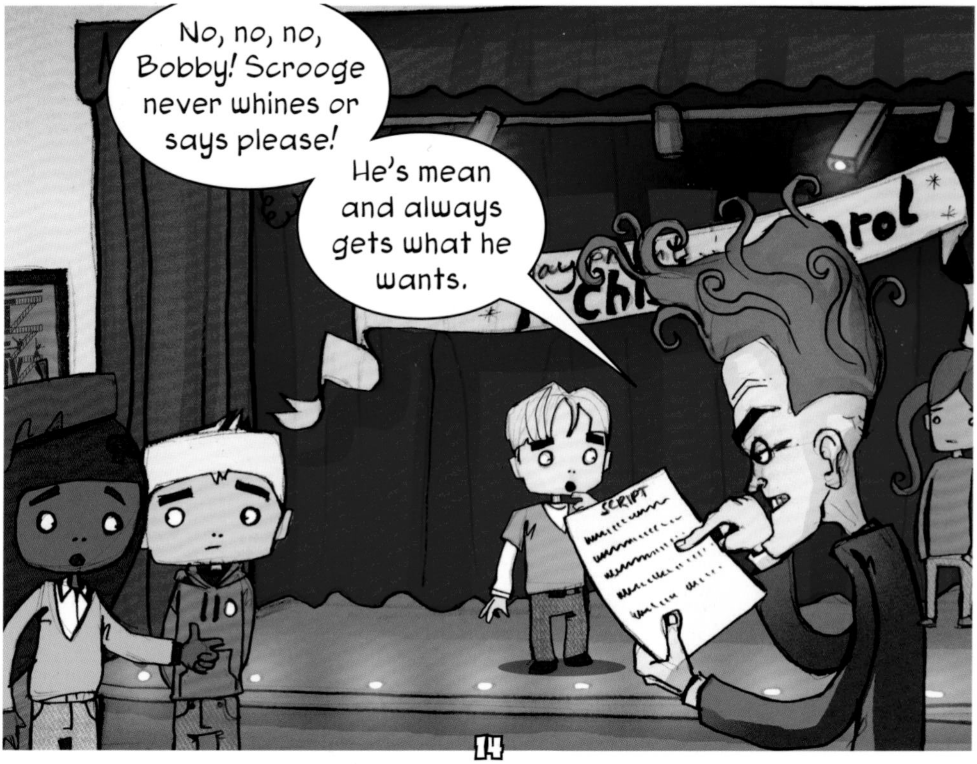
No, no, no, Bobby! Scrooge never whines or says please!
He's mean and always gets what he wants.
SCRIPT

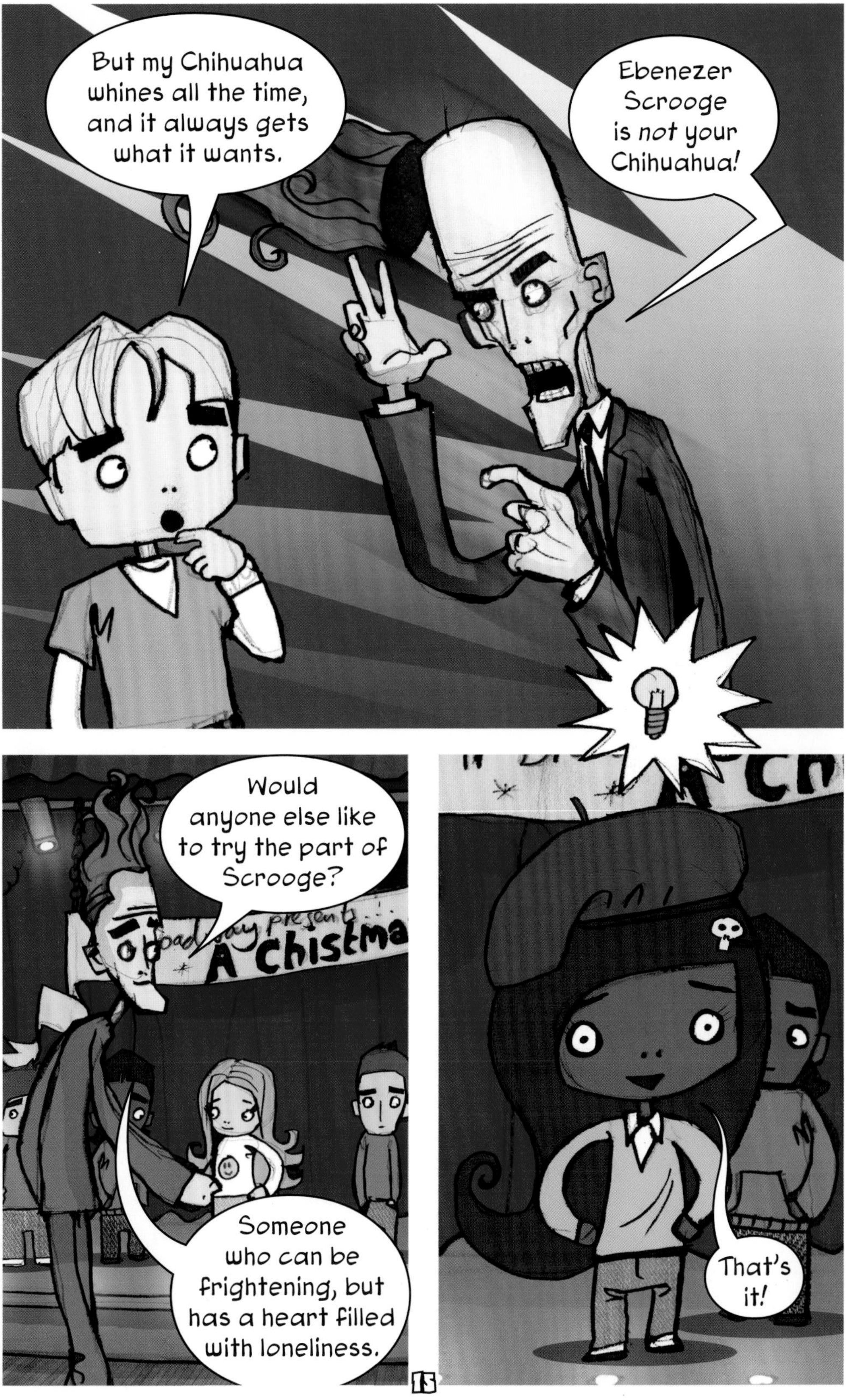
But my Chihuahua whines all the time, and it always gets what it wants.
Ebenezer Scrooge is *not* your Chihuahua!
Would anyone else like to try the part of Scrooge?
Someone who can be frightening, but has a heart filled with loneliness.
A Chistma
That's it!

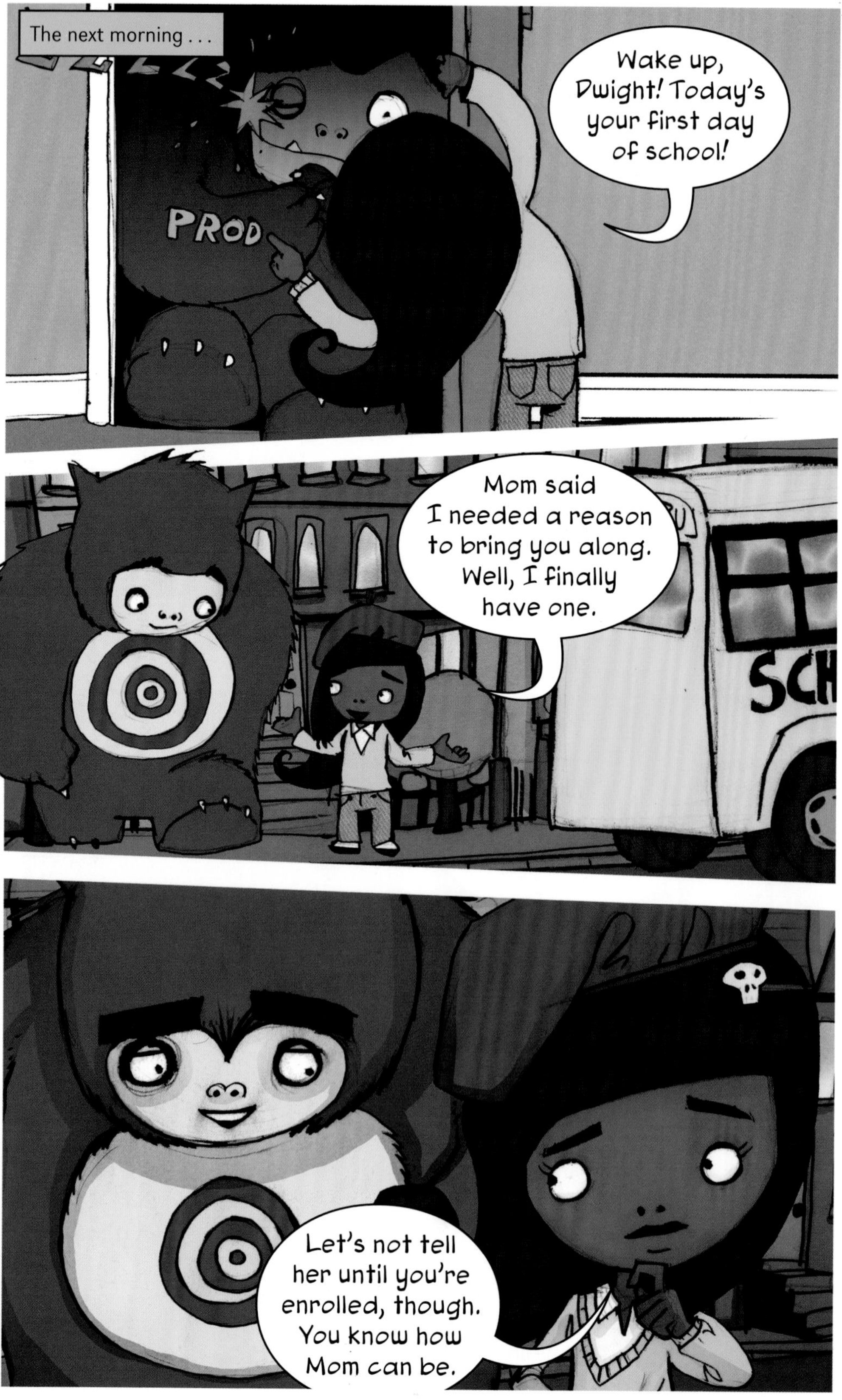
The next morning . . .
PROD
Wake up, Dwight! Today's your first day of school!
Mom said I needed a reason to bring you along. Well, I finally have one.
SCH
Let's not tell her until you're enrolled, though. You know how Mom can be.

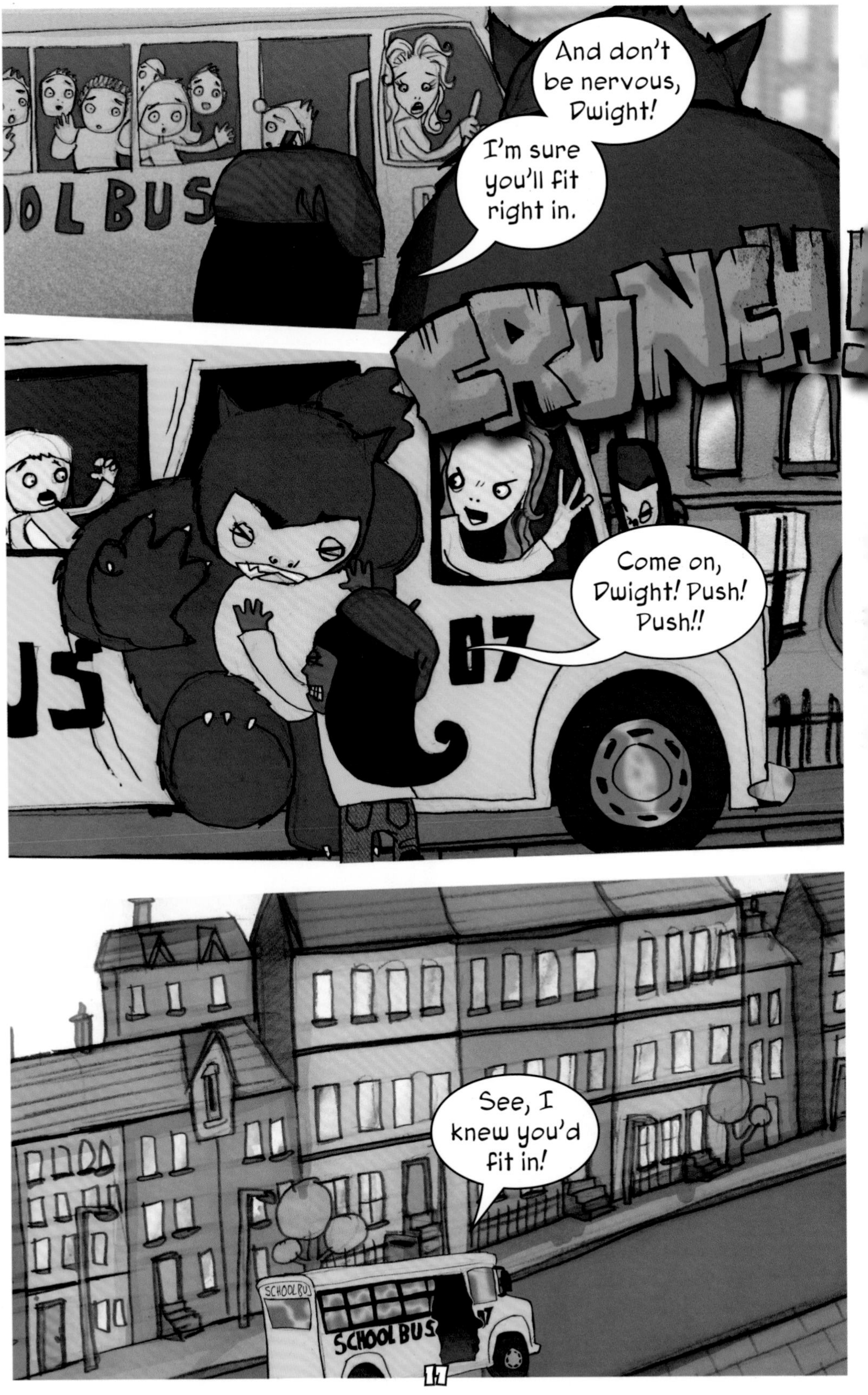
And don't be nervous, Dwight!
I'm sure you'll fit right in.
CRUNCH!
Come on, Dwight! Push! Push!!
See, I knew you'd fit in!
SCHOOL BUS

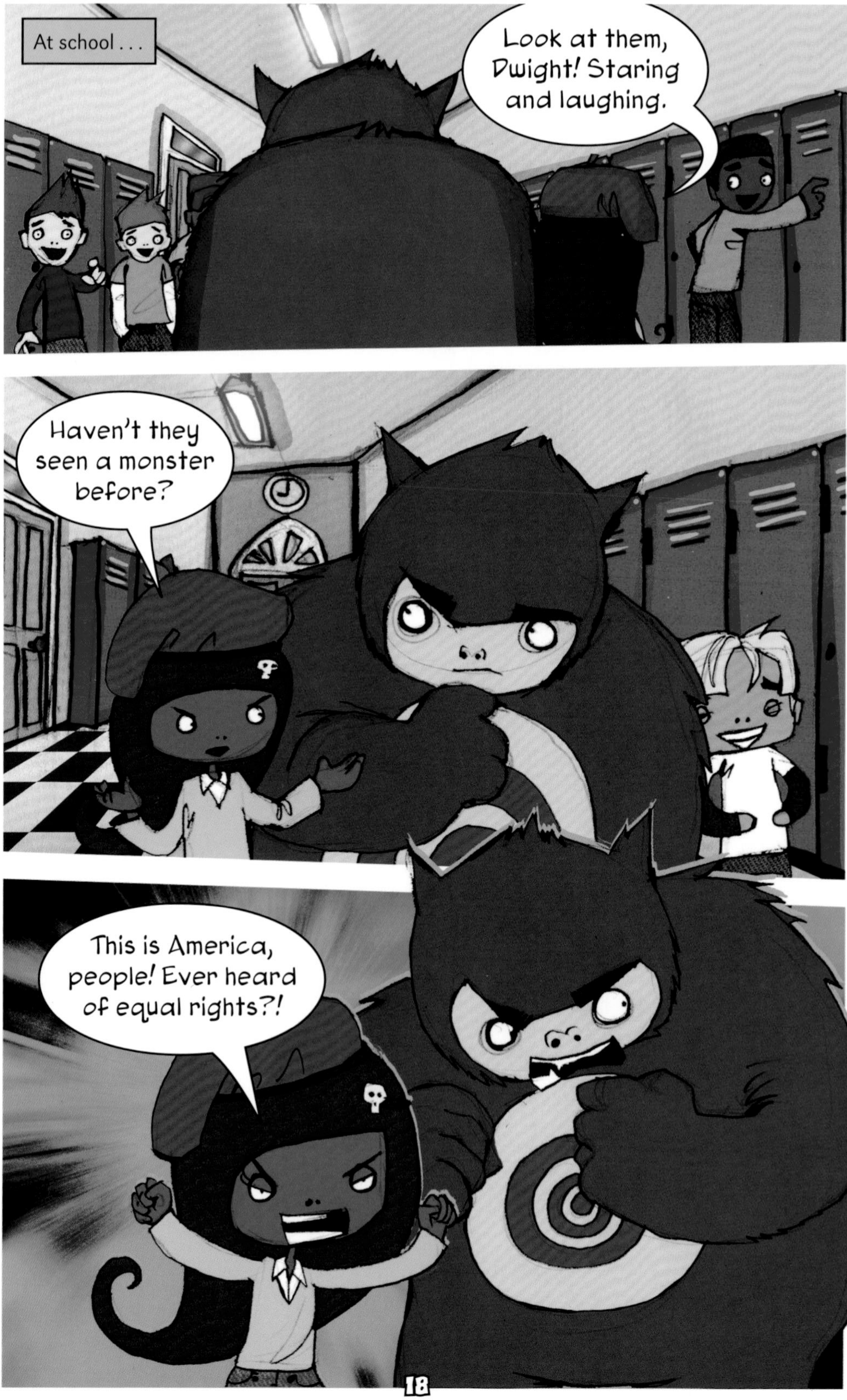
At school . . .
Look at them, Dwight! Staring and laughing.
Haven't they seen a monster before?
This is America, people! Ever heard of equal rights?!

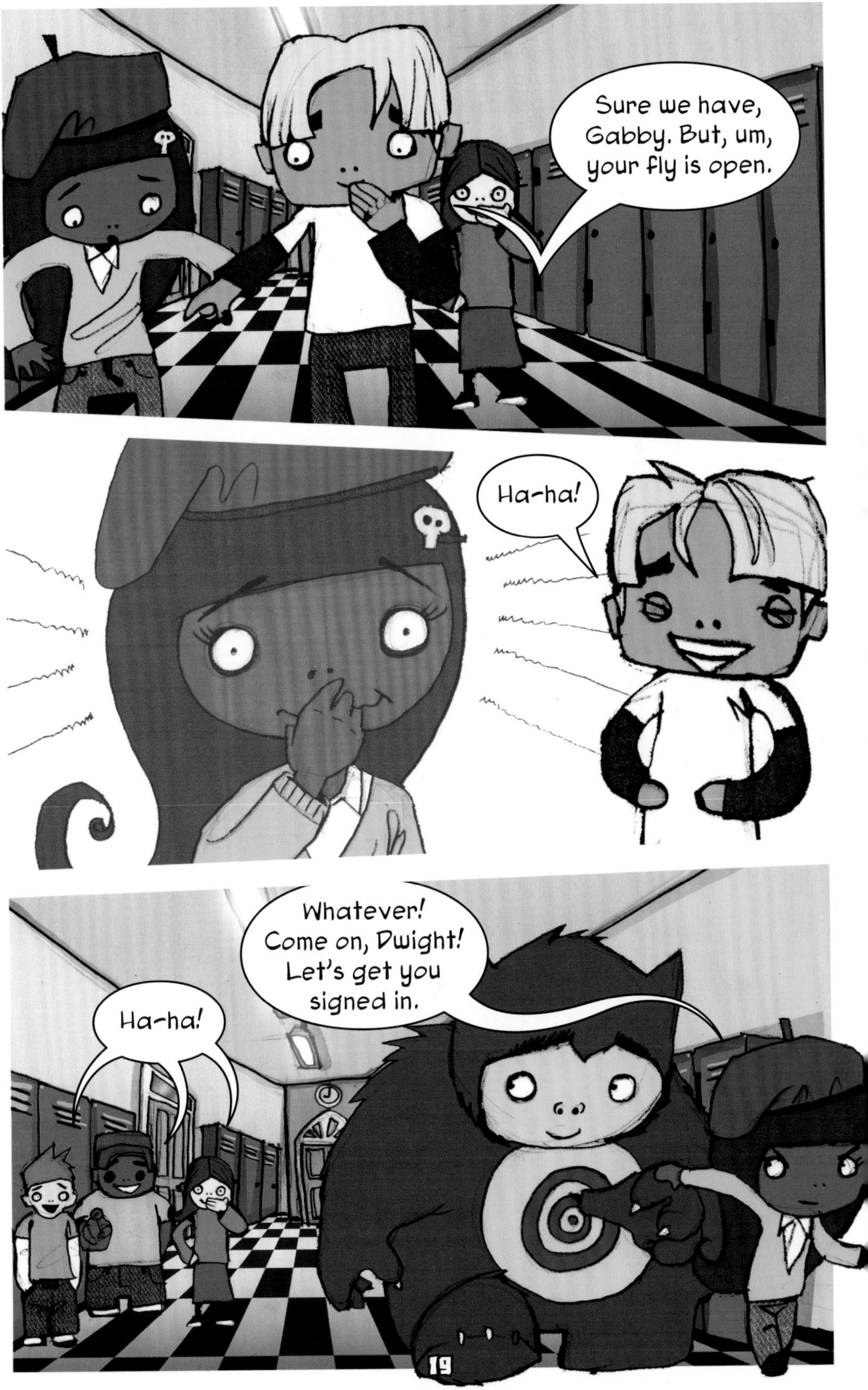
Sure we have, Gabby. But, um, your fly is open.
Ha-ha!
Whatever! Come on, Dwight! Let's get you signed in.
Ha-ha!

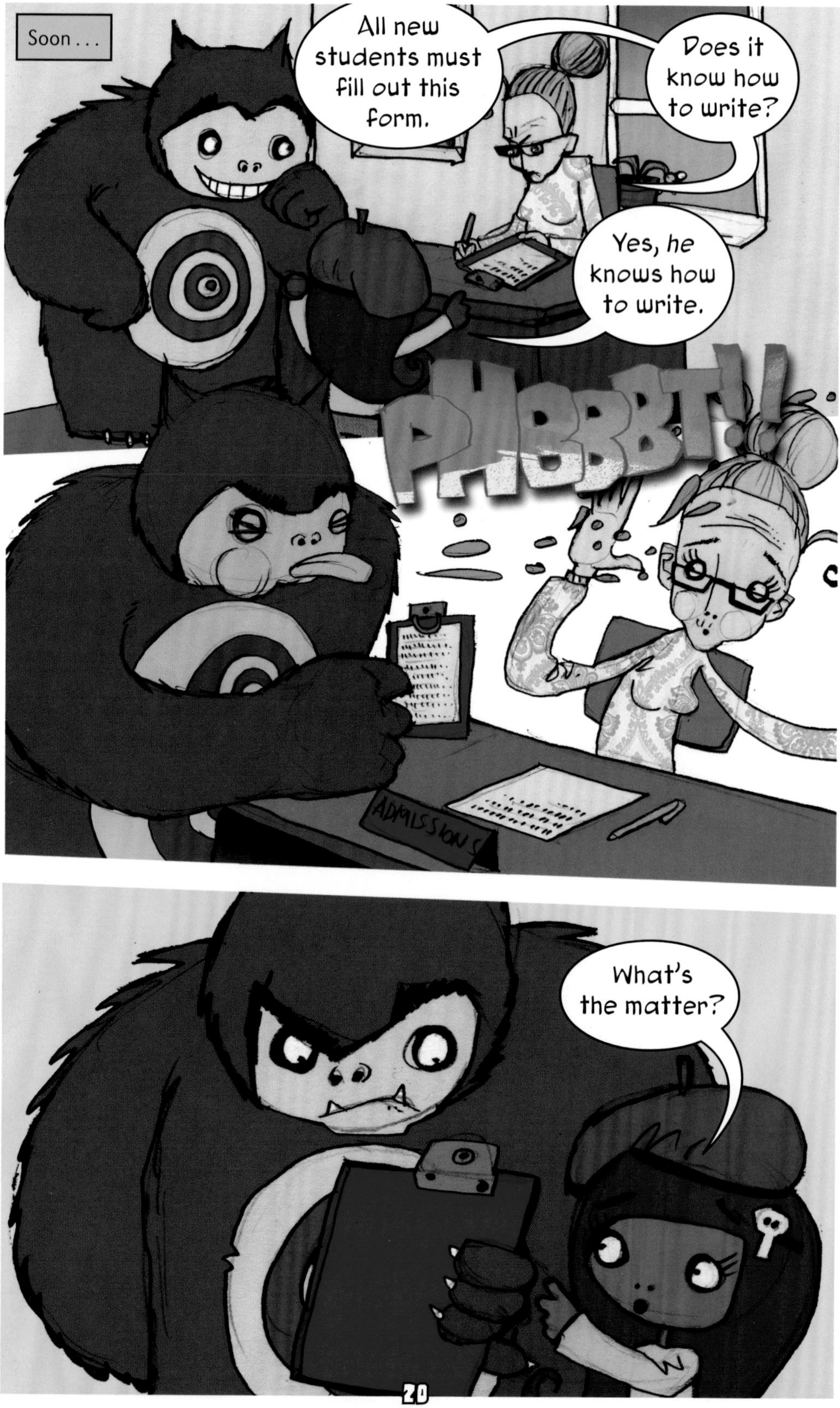
Soon . . .
All new students must fill out this form.
Does it know how to write?
Yes, he knows how to write.
PHBBBT!!
ADMISSIONS
What's the matter?

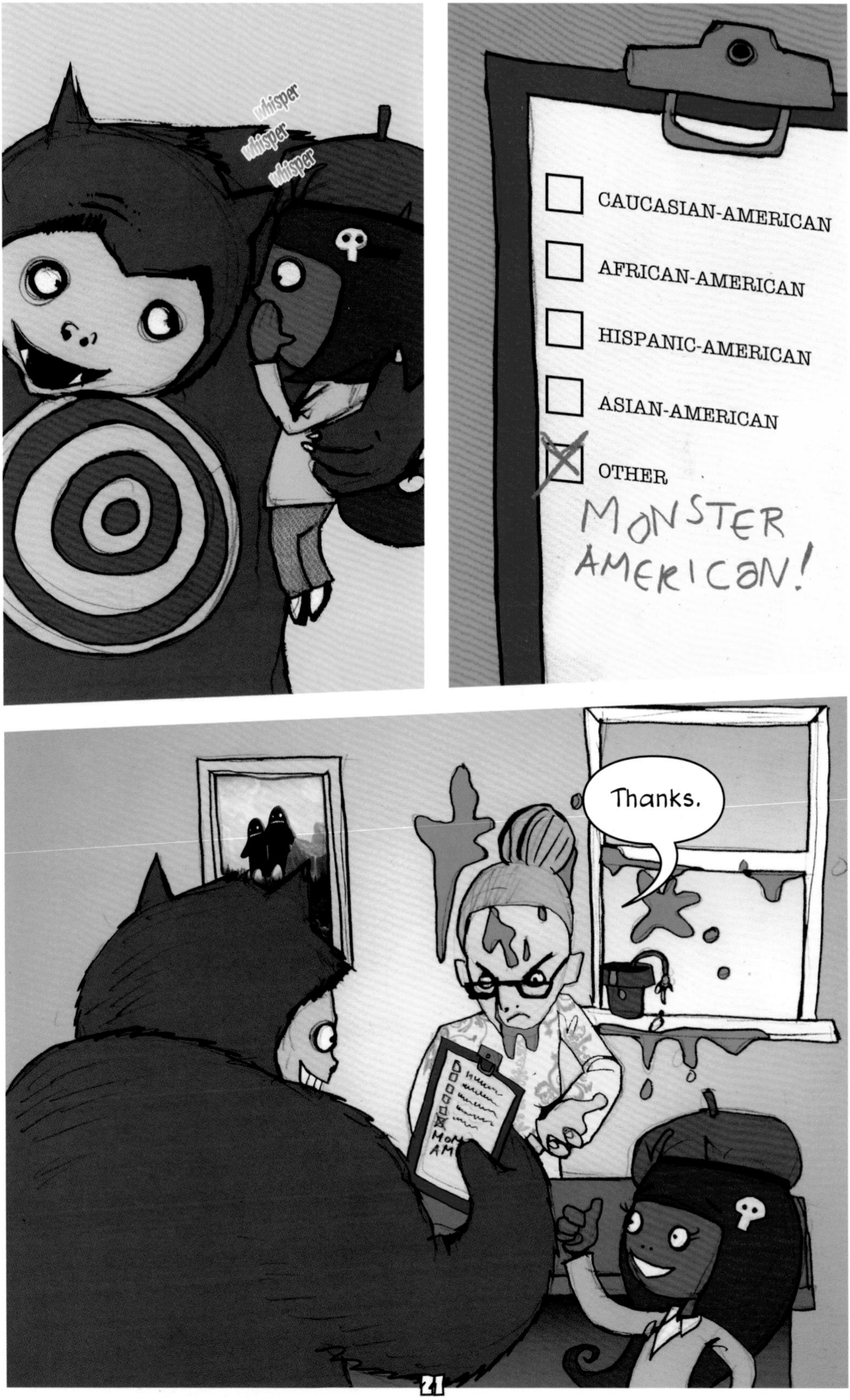
whisper
whisper
whisper
CAUCASIAN-AMERICAN
AFRICAN-AMERICAN
HISPANIC-AMERICAN
ASIAN-AMERICAN
OTHER
MONSTER AMERICAN!
Thanks.

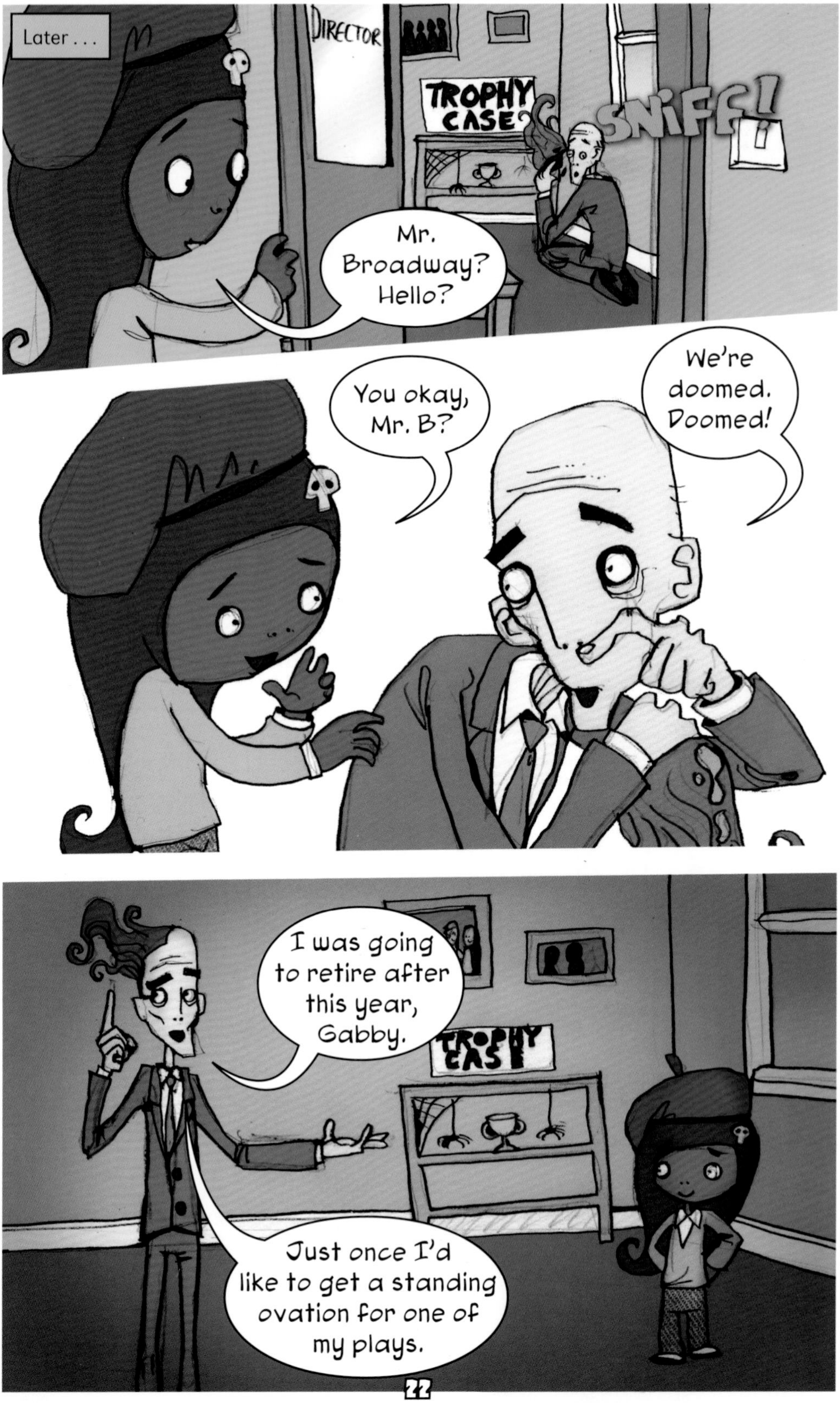
Later . . .
DIRECTOR
TROPHY CASE
SNIFF!
Mr. Broadway? Hello?
You okay, Mr. B?
We're doomed. Doomed!
I was going to retire after this year, Gabby.
TROPHY CASE
Just once I'd like to get a standing ovation for one of my plays.

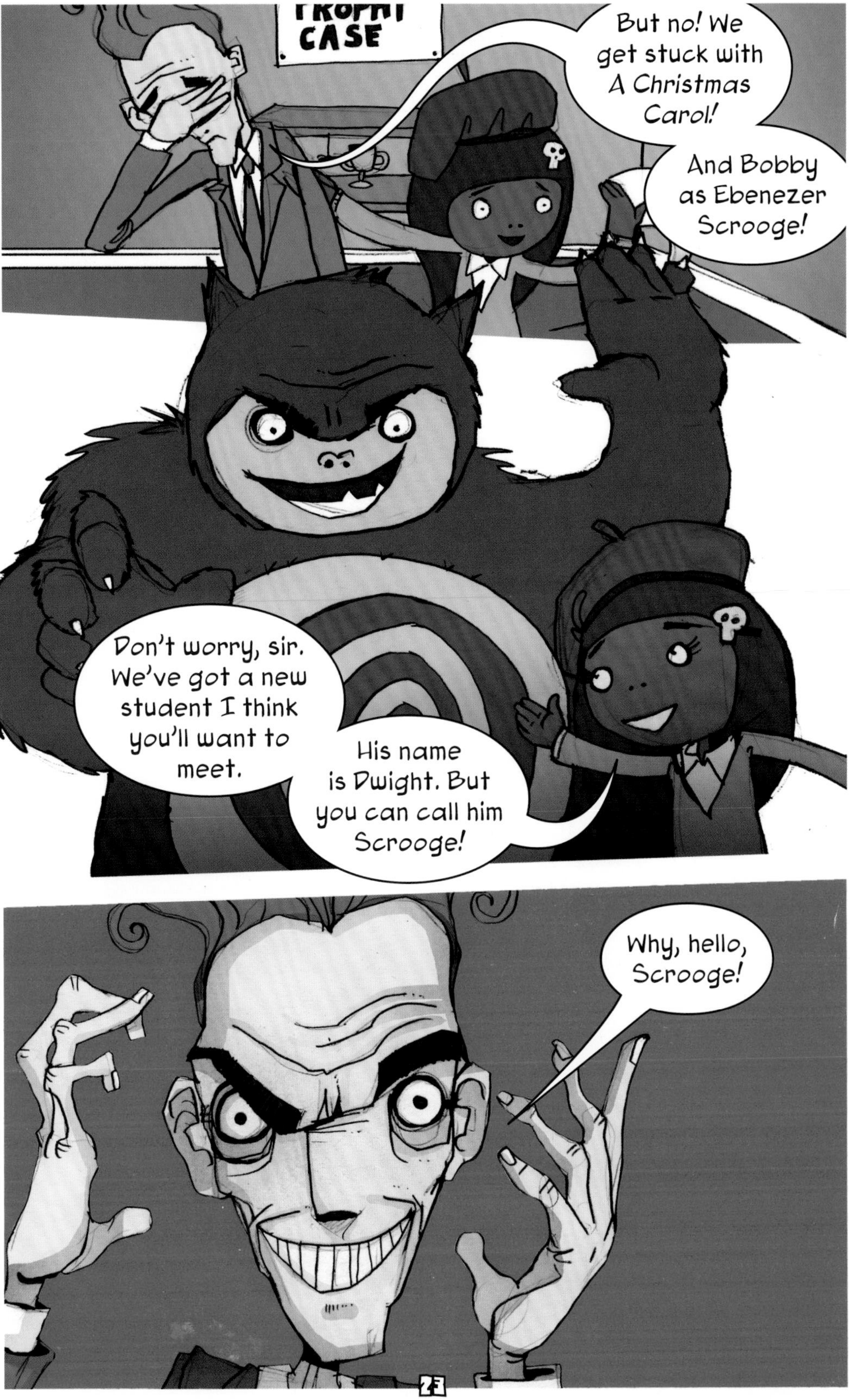
TROPHY CASE
But no! We get stuck with A Christmas Carol!
And Bobby as Ebenezer Scrooge!
Don't worry, sir. We've got a new student I think you'll want to meet.
His name is Dwight. But you can call him Scrooge!
Why, hello, Scrooge!

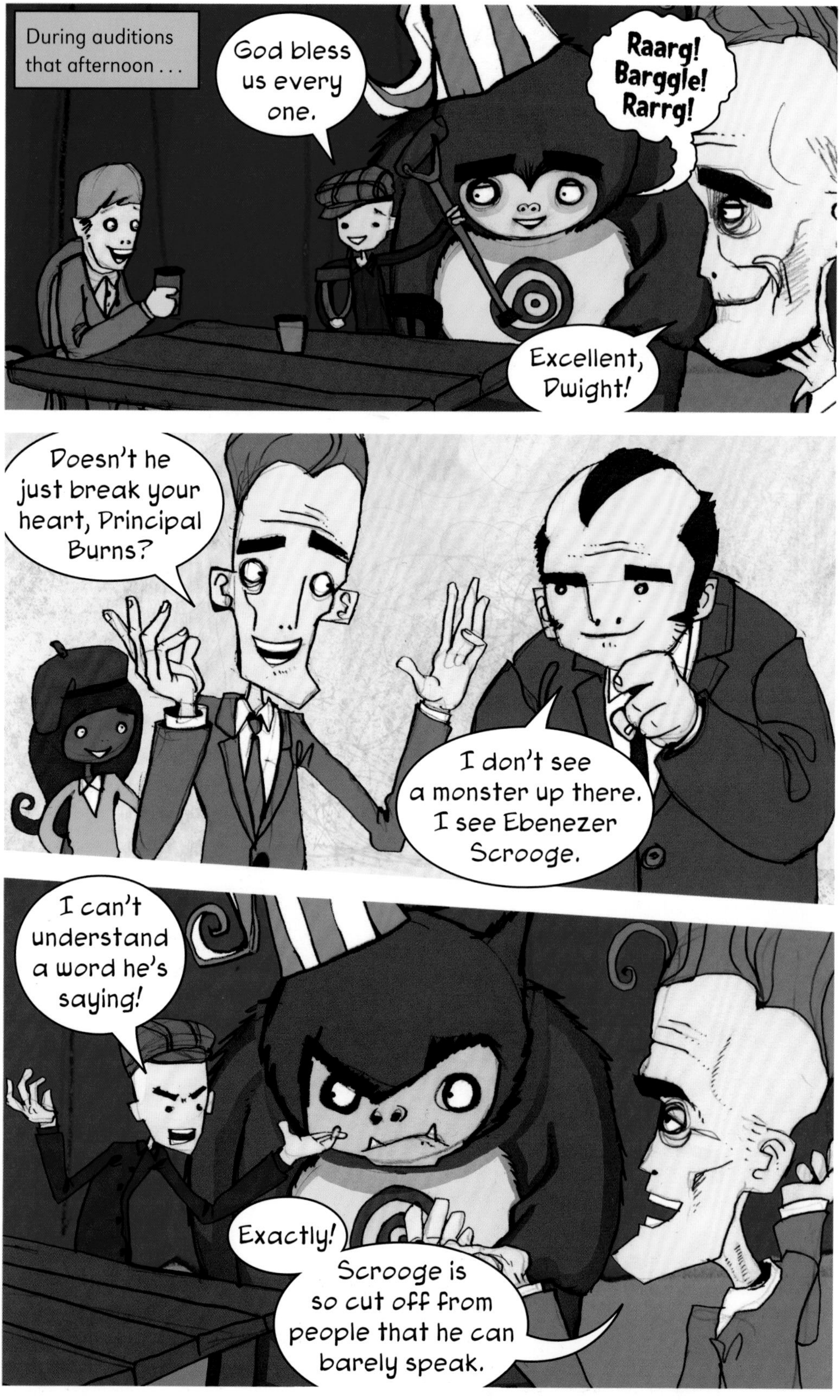
During auditions that afternoon . . .
God bless us every one.
Raarg! Barggle! Rarrg!
Excellent, Dwight!
Doesn't he just break your heart, Principal Burns?
I don't see a monster up there. I see Ebenezer Scrooge.
I can't understand a word he's saying!
Exactly!
Scrooge is so cut off from people that he can barely speak.

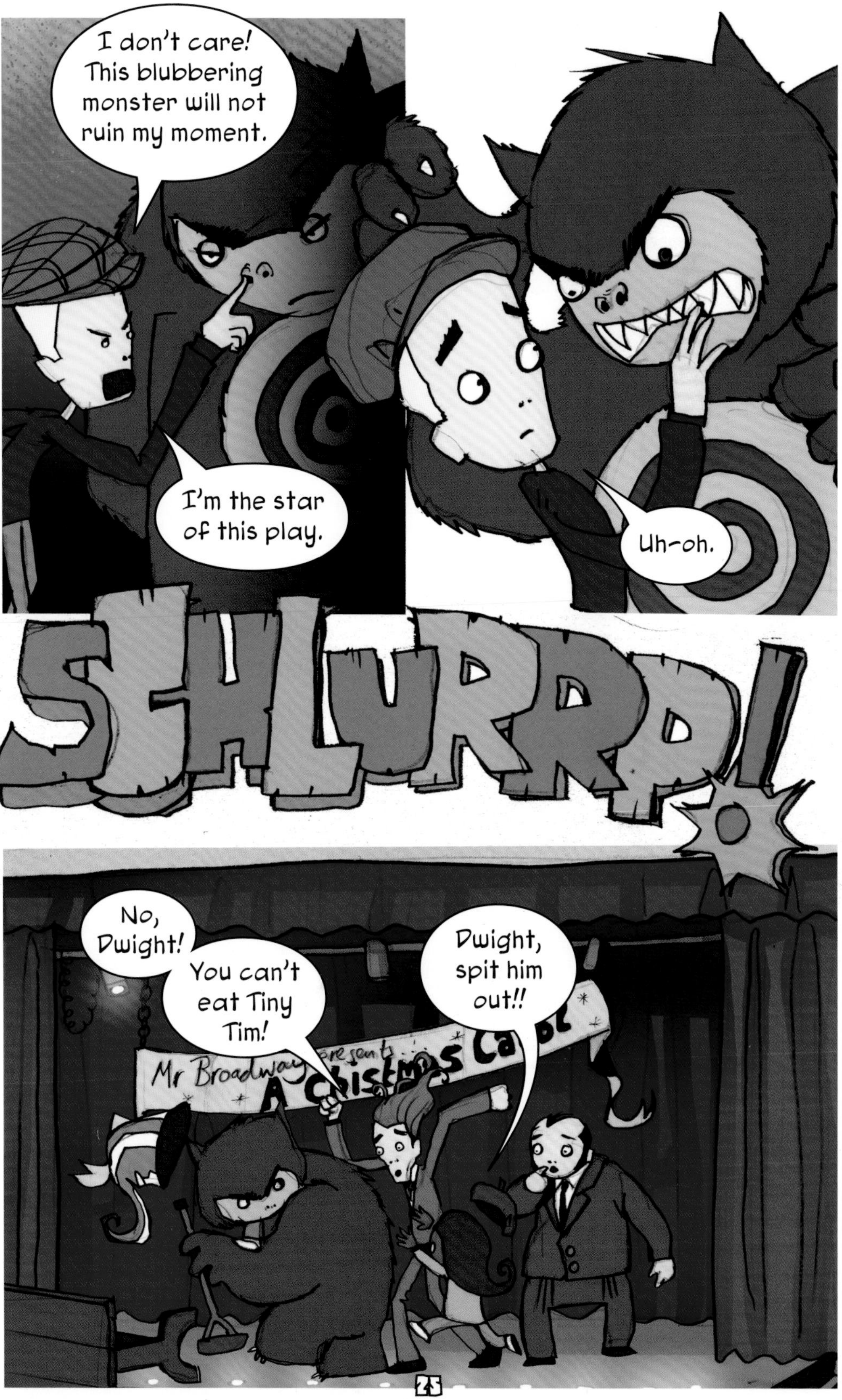

I don't care! This blubbering monster will not ruin my moment.
I'm the star of this play.
Uh-oh.
SCHLURRP!
No, Dwight!
You can't eat Tiny Tim!
Dwight, spit him out!!
Mr Broadway

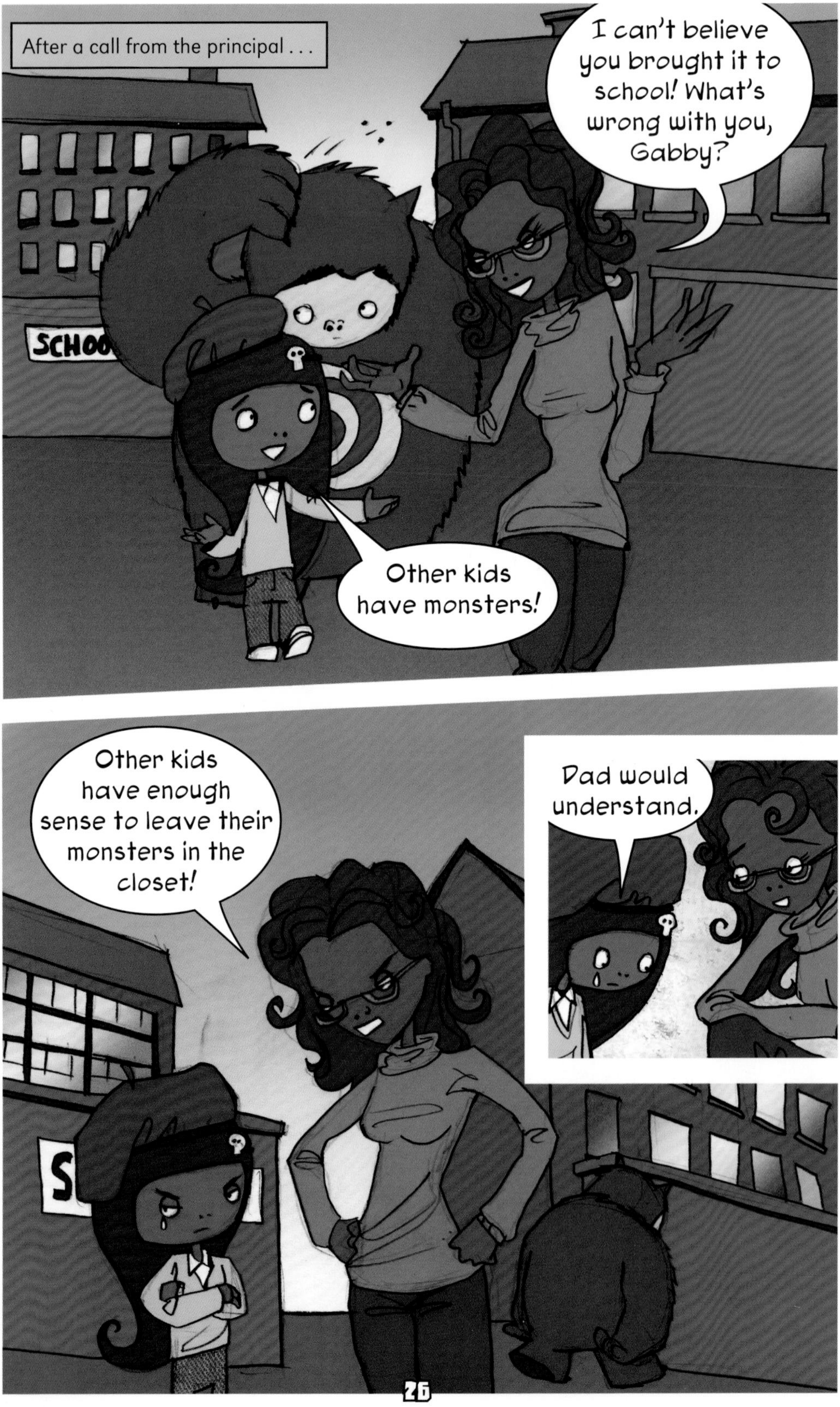
After a call from the principal . . .
I can't believe you brought it to school! What's wrong with you, Gabby?
SCHOO
Other kids have monsters!
Other kids have enough sense to leave their monsters in the closet!
Dad would understand.

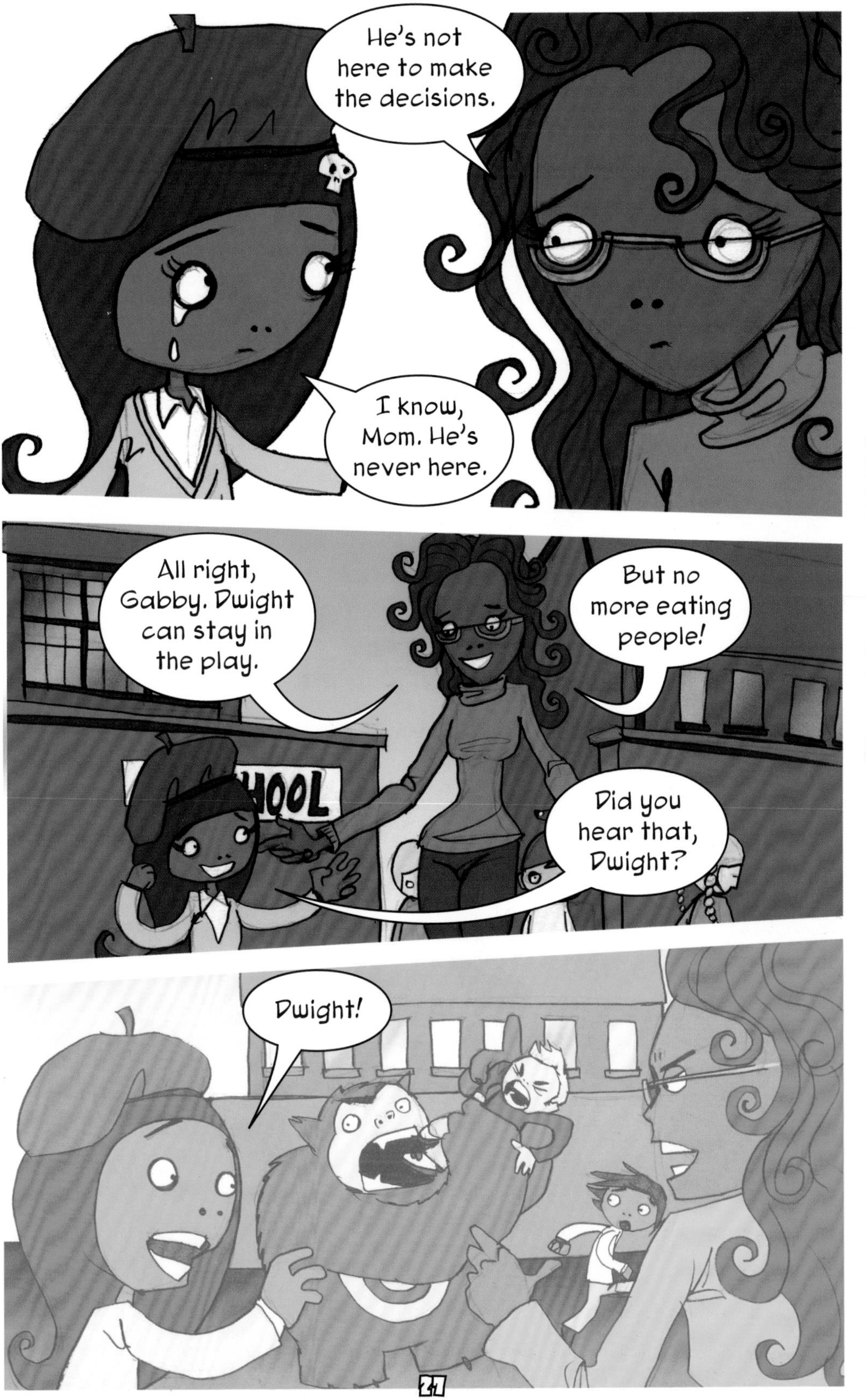

He's not here to make the decisions.
I know, Mom. He's never here.
All right, Gabby. Dwight can stay in the play.
But no more eating people!
HOOL
Did you hear that, Dwight?
Dwight!

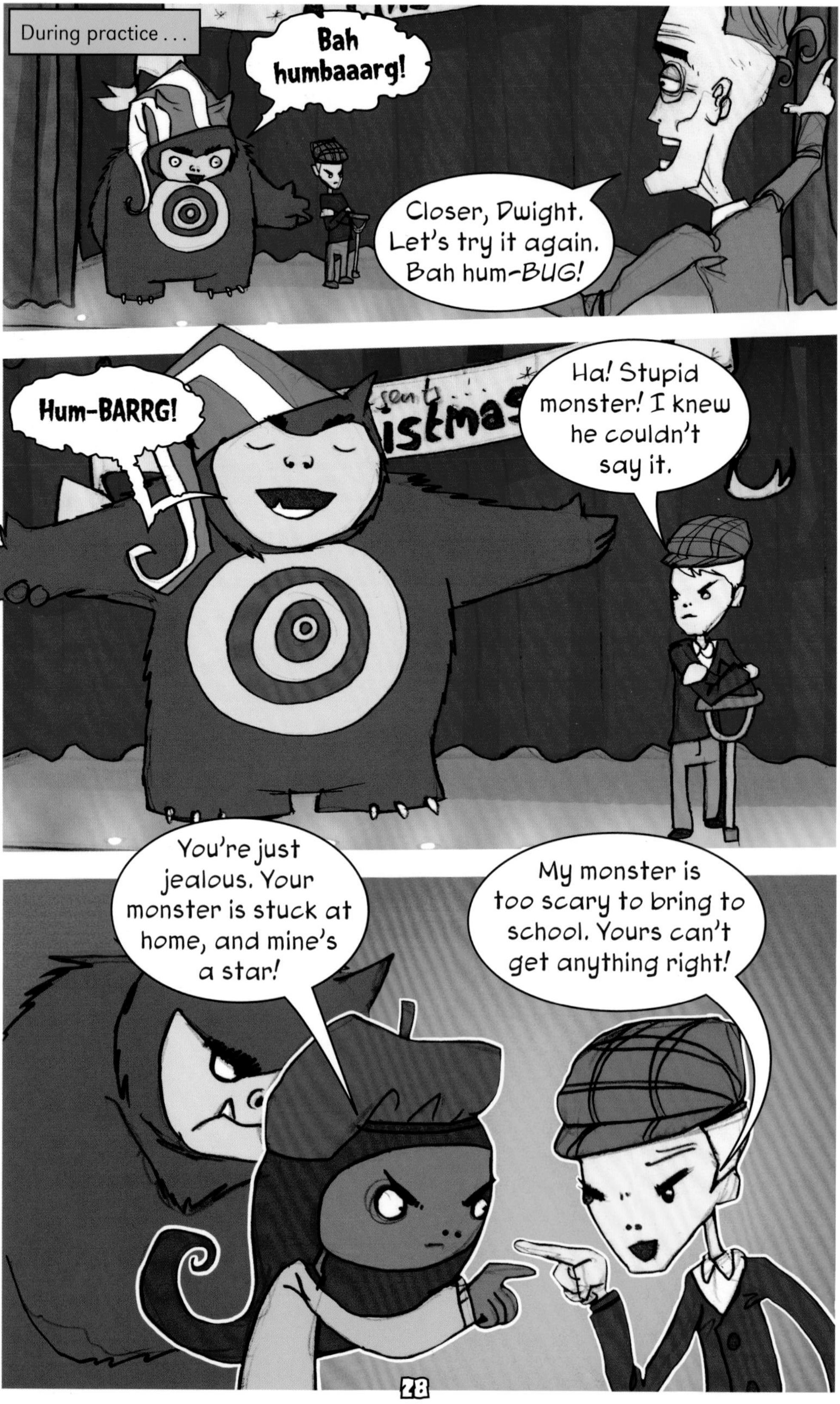
During practice . . .
Bah humbaaarg!
Closer, Dwight. Let's try it again. Bah hum-BUG!
Hum-BARRG!
Ha! Stupid monster! I knew he couldn't say it.
You're just jealous. Your monster is stuck at home, and mine's a star!
My monster is too scary to bring to school. Yours can't get anything right!

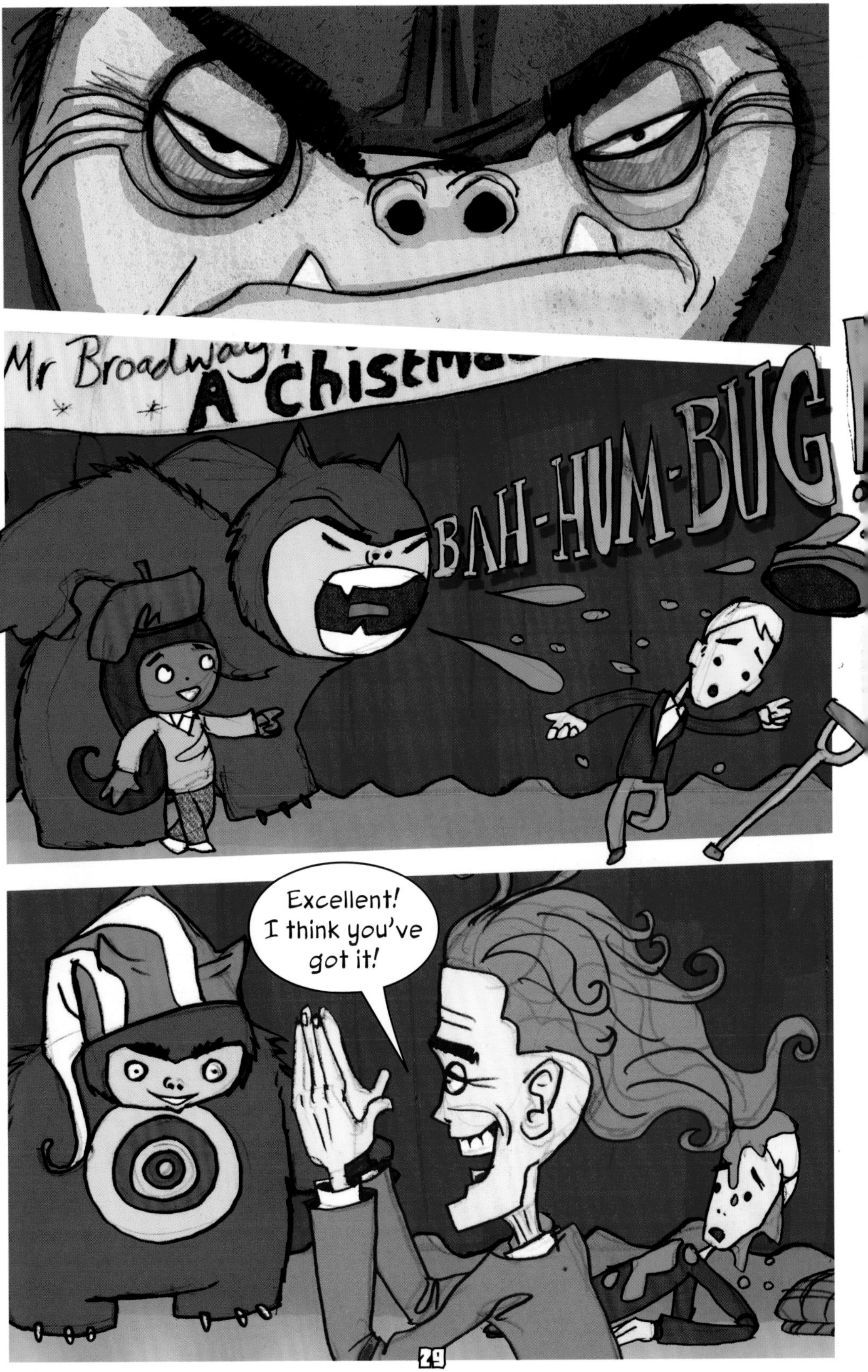
Mr Broadway
A Chistma
BAH-HUM-BUG!
Excellent! I think you've got it!

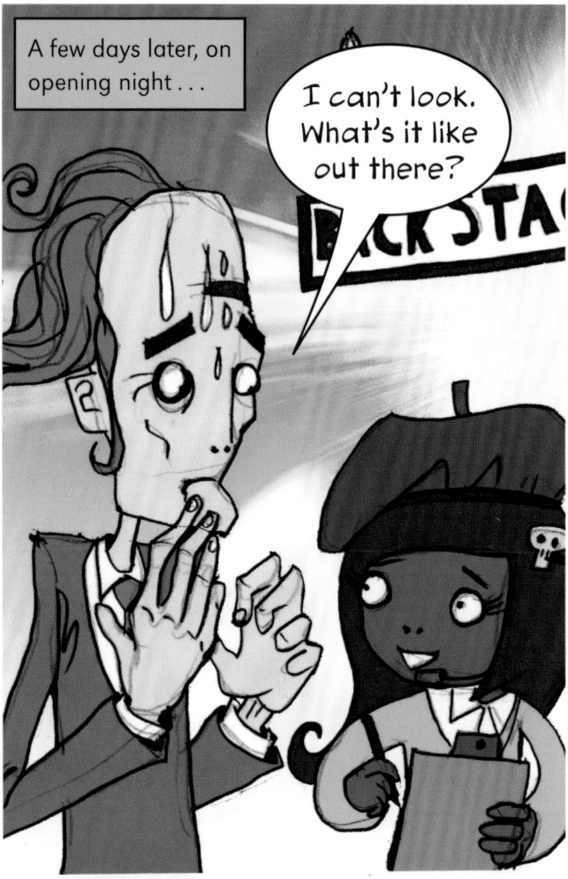
A few days later, on opening night . . .
I can't look. What's it like out there?
BACKSTAG

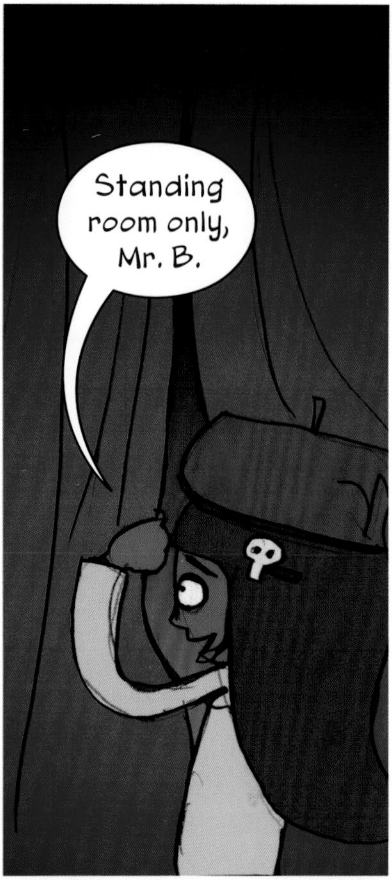
Standing room only, Mr. B.

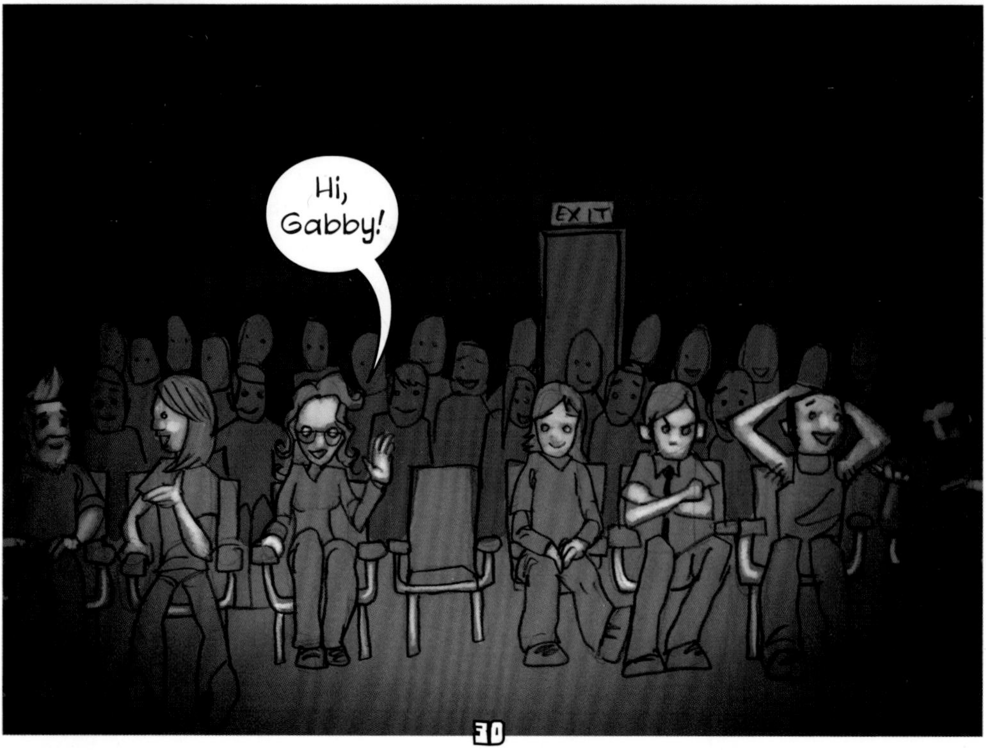
Hi, Gabby!
EXIT

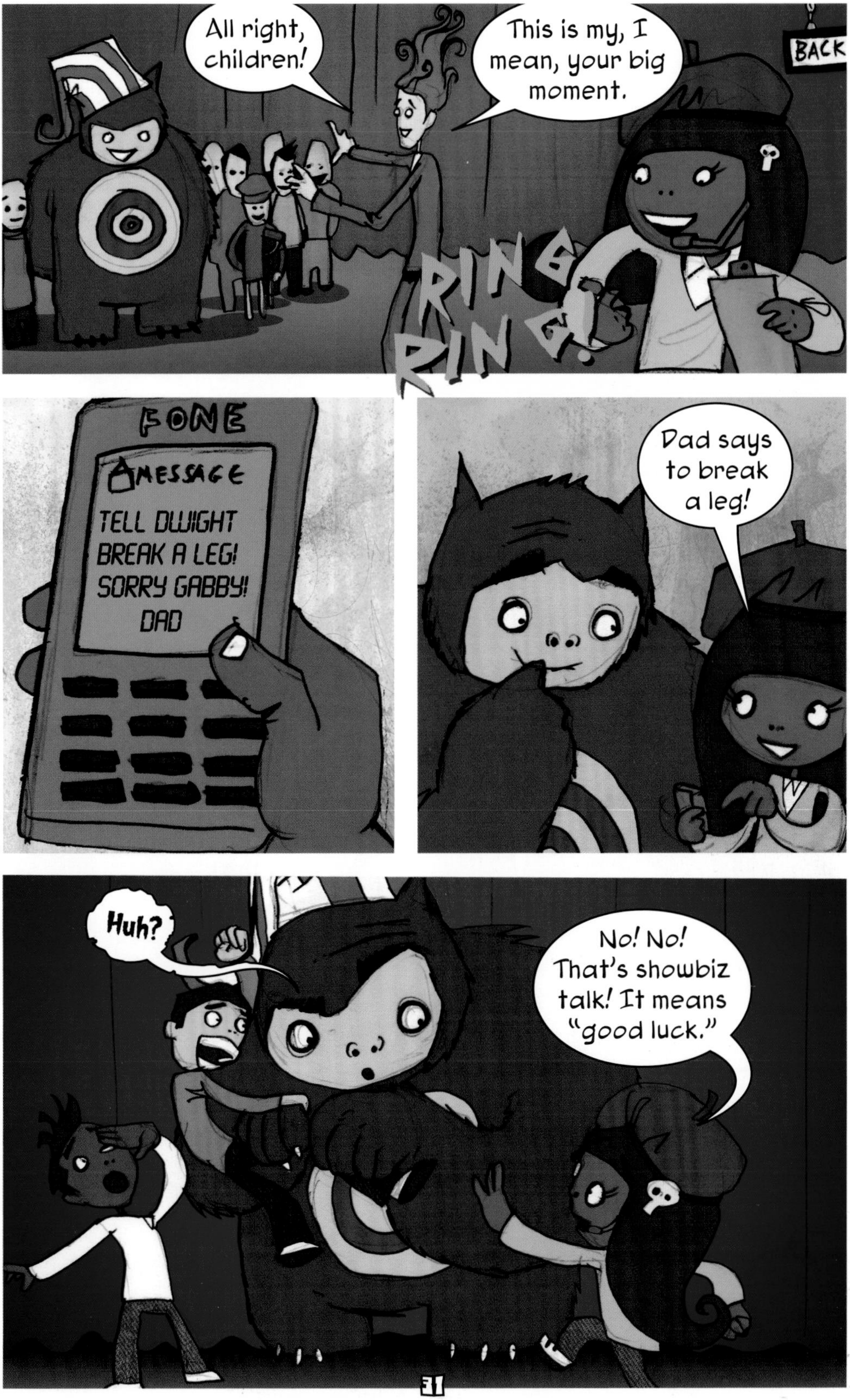
All right, children!
This is my, I mean, your big moment.
BACK
RING RING!
FONE
MESSAGE
TELL DWIGHT BREAK A LEG! SORRY GABBY! DAD
Dad says to break a leg!
Huh?
No! No! That's showbiz talk! It means "good luck."

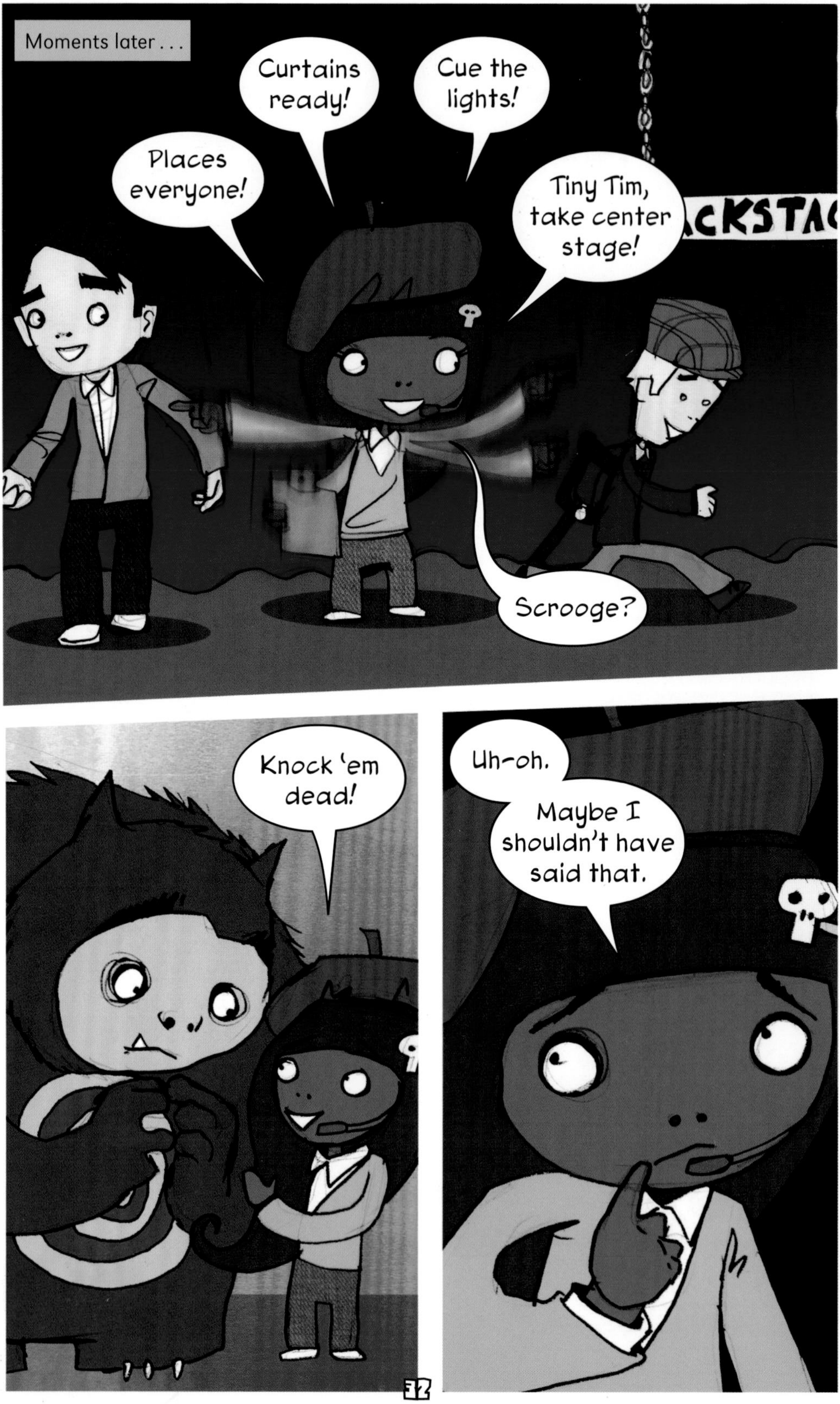
Moments later . . .
Places everyone!
Curtains ready!
Cue the lights!
Tiny Tim, take center stage!
Scrooge?
Knock 'em dead!
Uh-oh.
Maybe I shouldn't have said that.

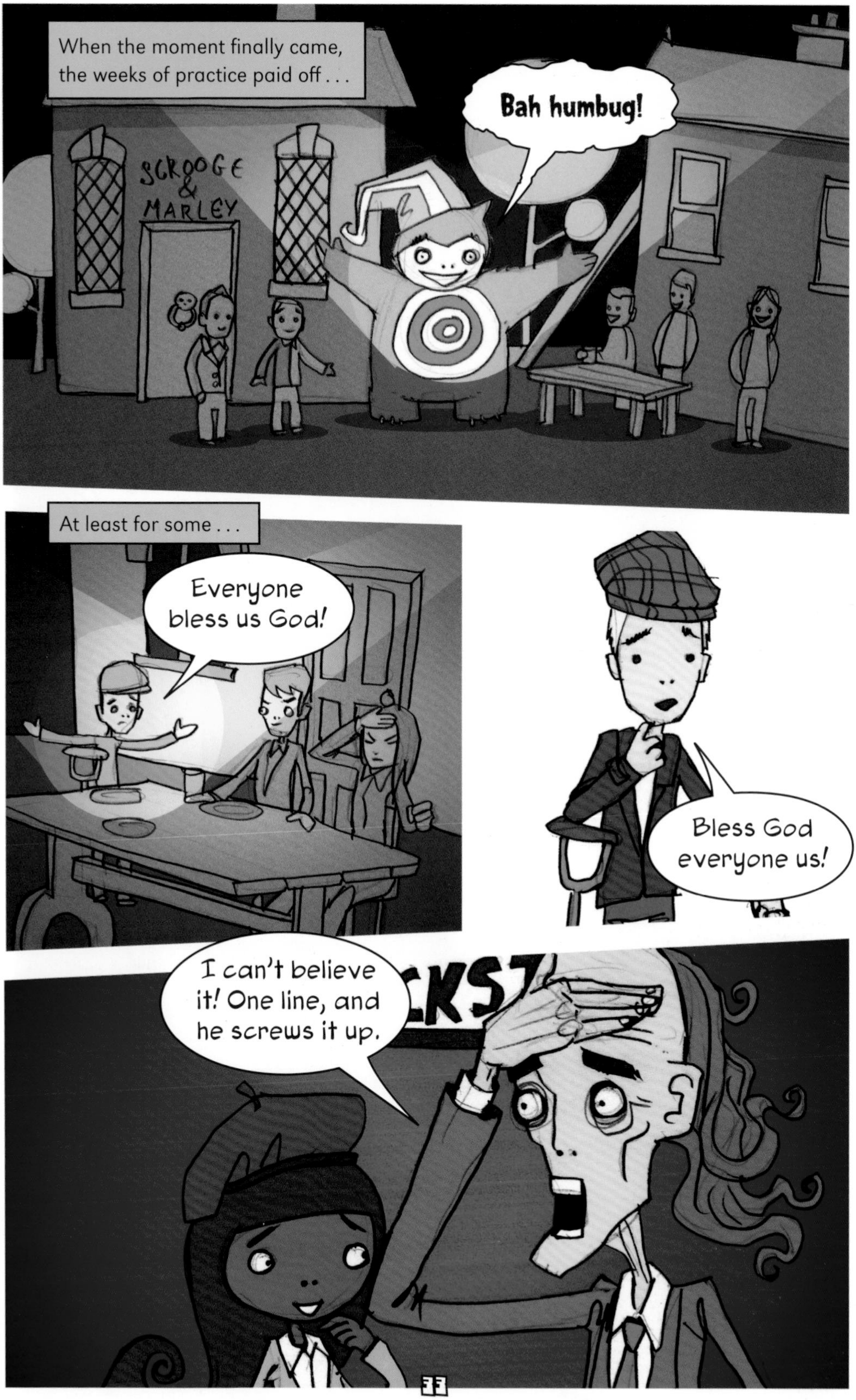
When the moment finally came, the weeks of practice paid off . . .
SCROOGE & MARLEY
Bah humbug!
At least for some . . .
Everyone bless us God!
Bless God everyone us!
I can't believe it! One line, and he screws it up.

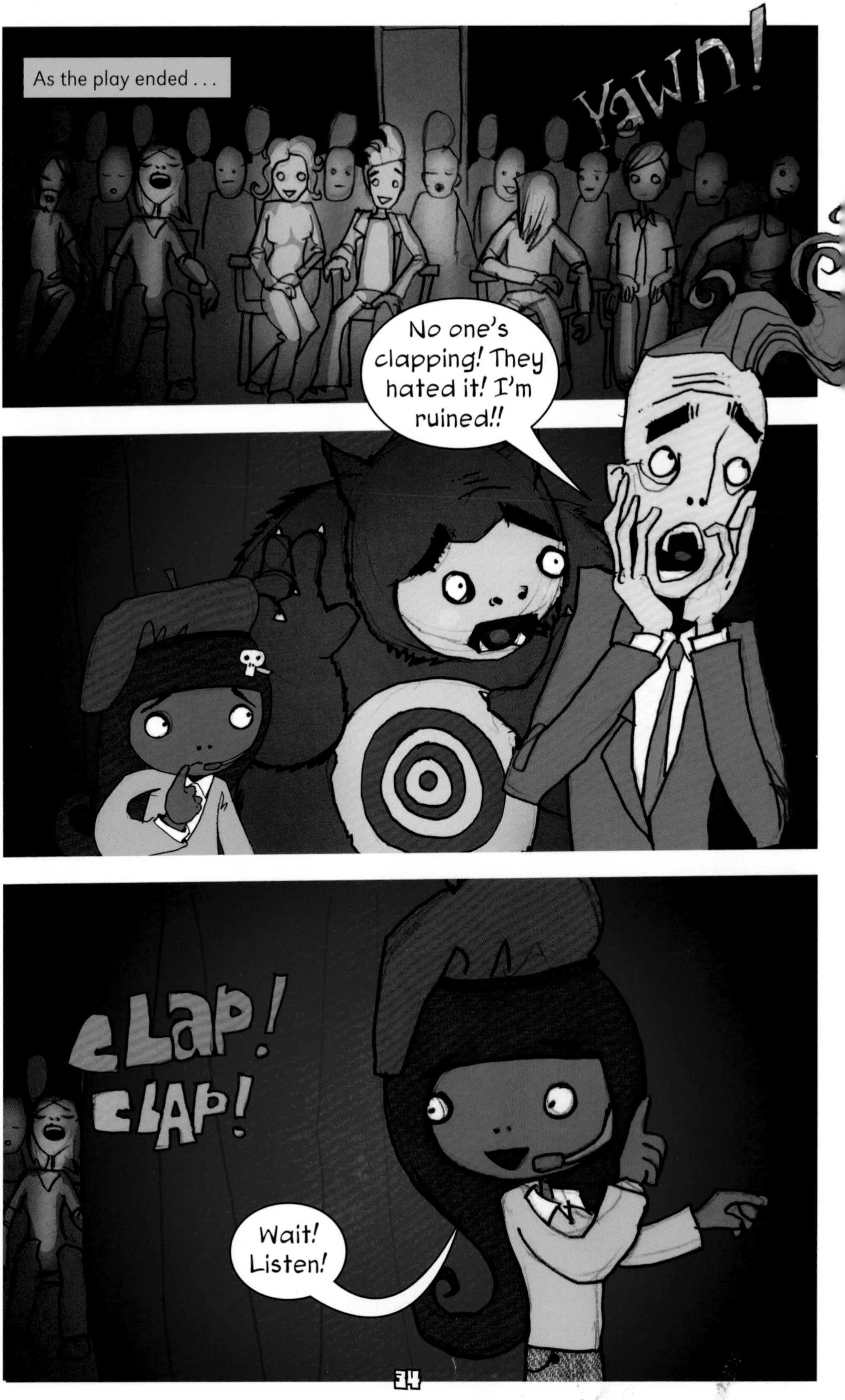
As the play ended . . .
Yawn!
No one's clapping! They hated it! I'm ruined!!
CLAP!
CLAP!
Wait! Listen!

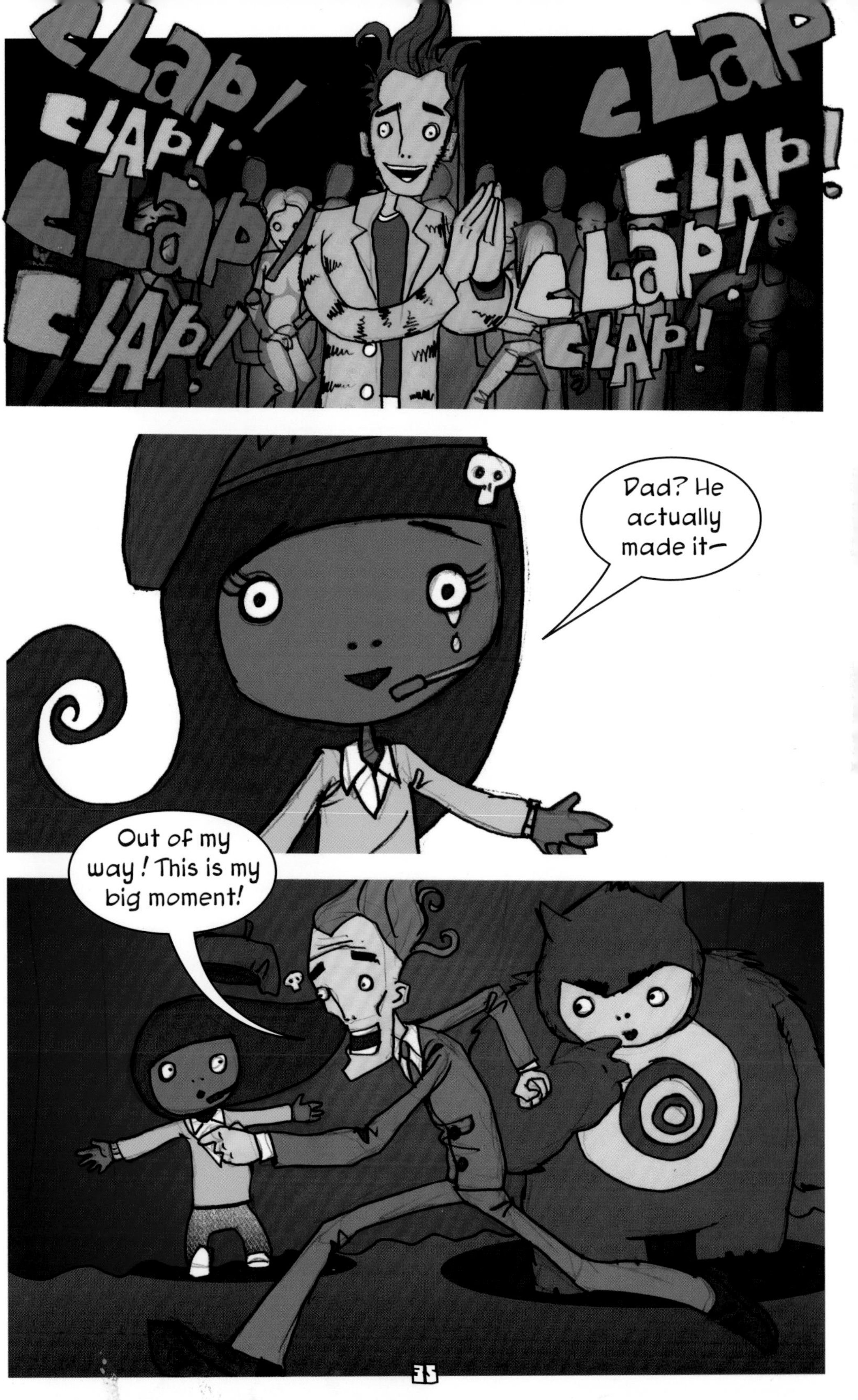
CLAP! CLAP! CLAP! CLAP!
CLAP! CLAP! CLAP! CLAP!
Dad? He actually made it—
Out of my way! This is my big moment!

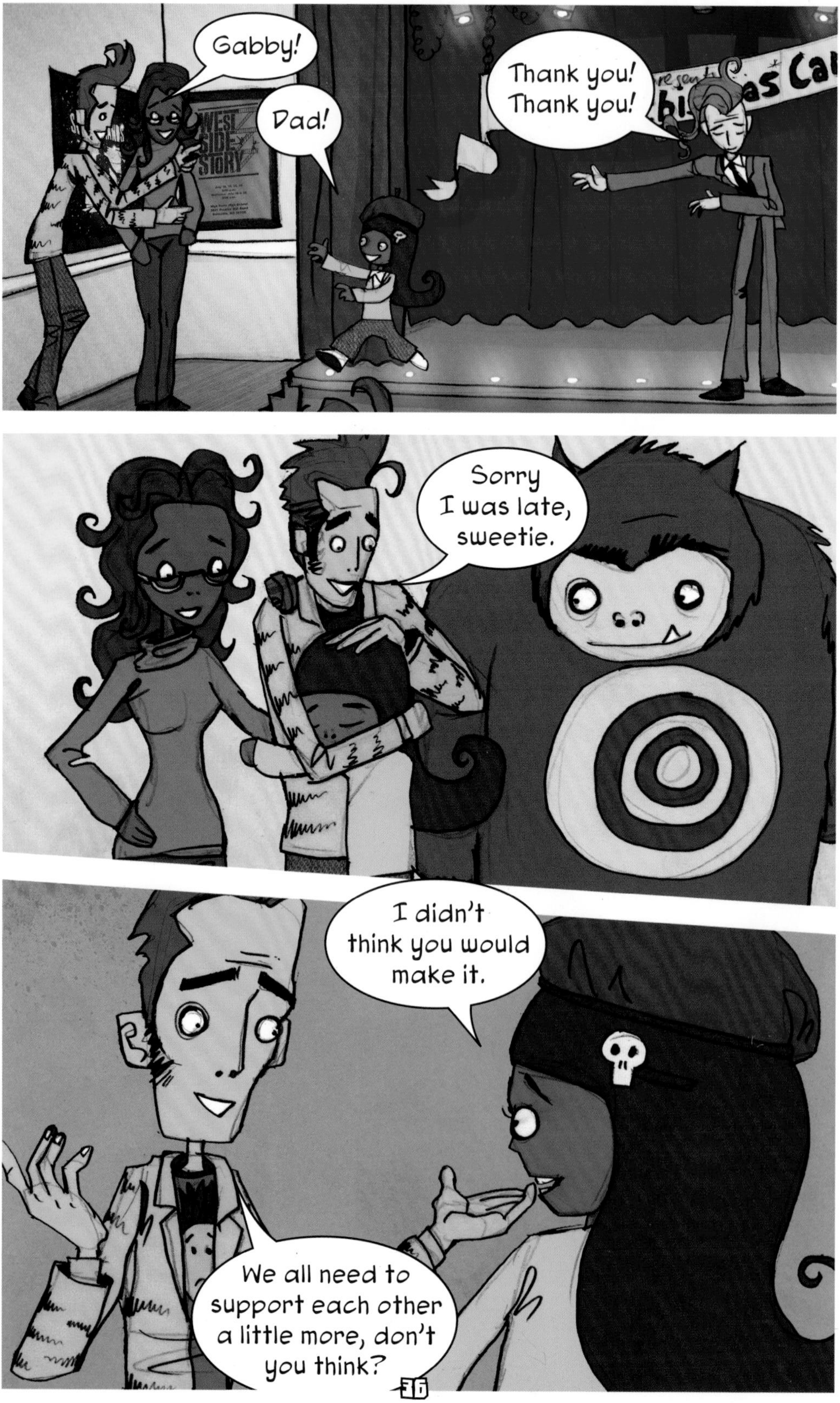

Gabby!
Dad!
Thank you! Thank you!
Sorry I was late, sweetie.
I didn't think you would make it.
We all need to support each other a little more, don't you think?

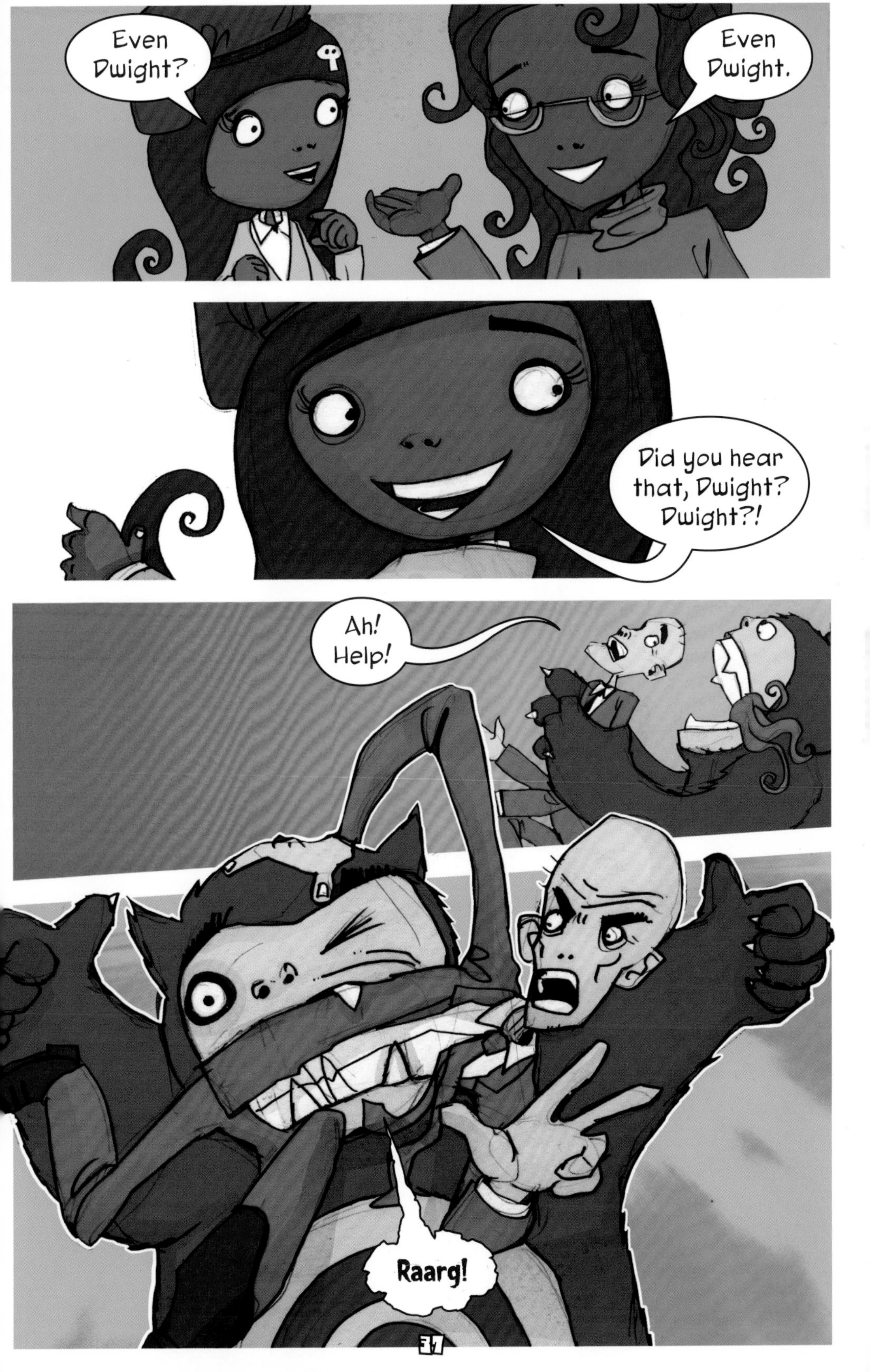
Even Dwight?
Even Dwight.
Did you hear that, Dwight? Dwight?!
Ah! Help!
Raarg!

MONSTER SPELLER

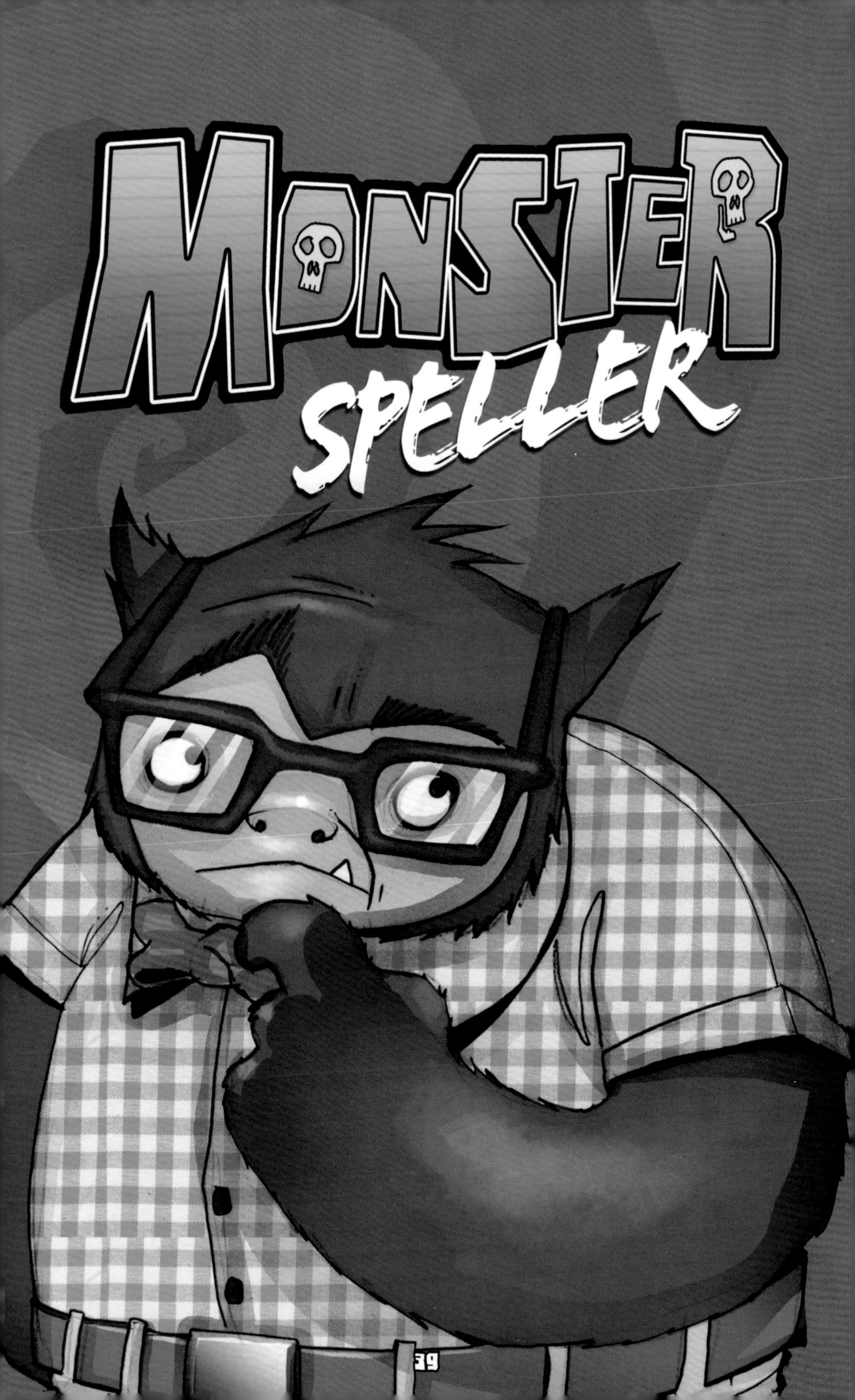

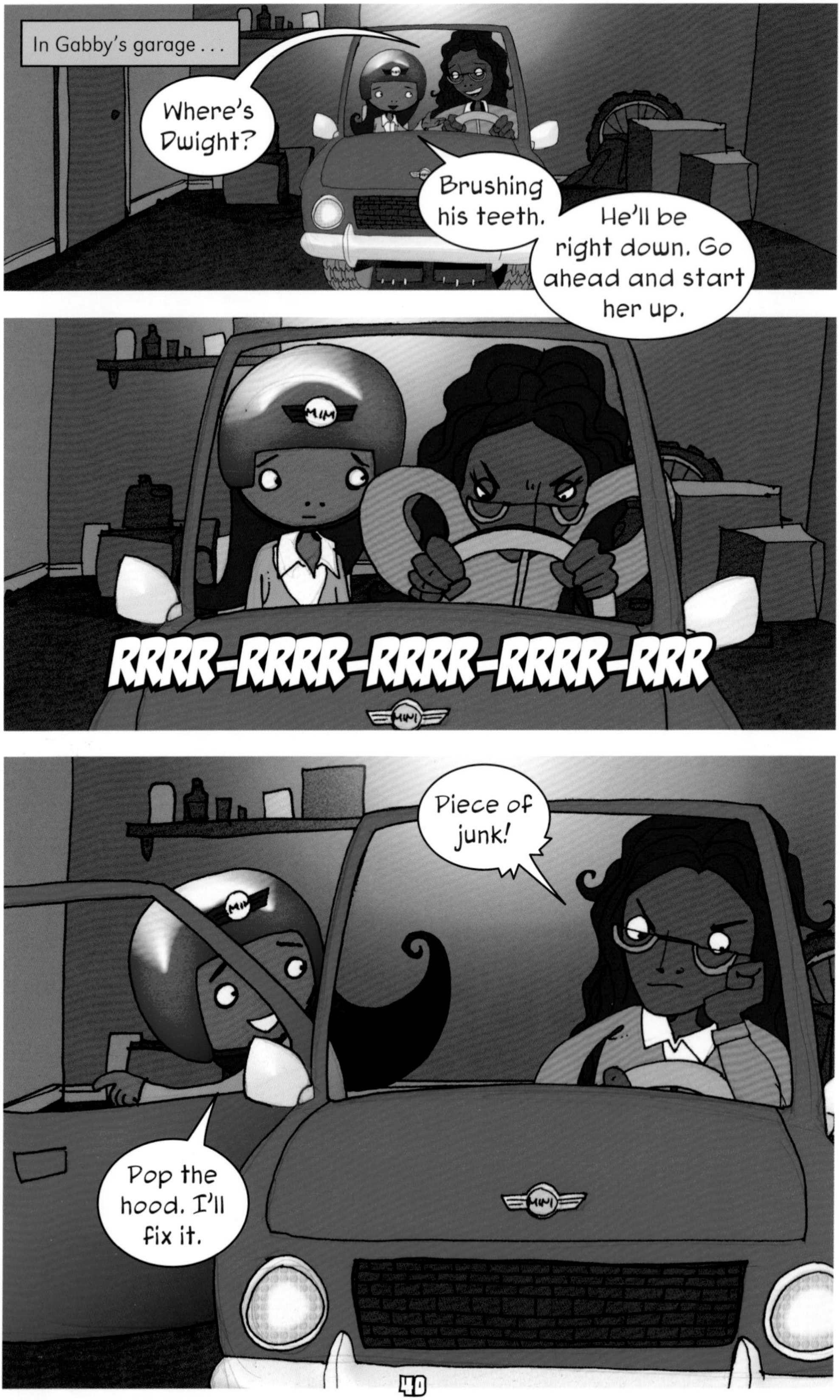
In Gabby's garage . . .
Where's Dwight?
Brushing his teeth.
He'll be right down. Go ahead and start her up.
RRRR-RRRR-RRRR-RRRR-RRR
Piece of junk!
Pop the hood. I'll fix it.

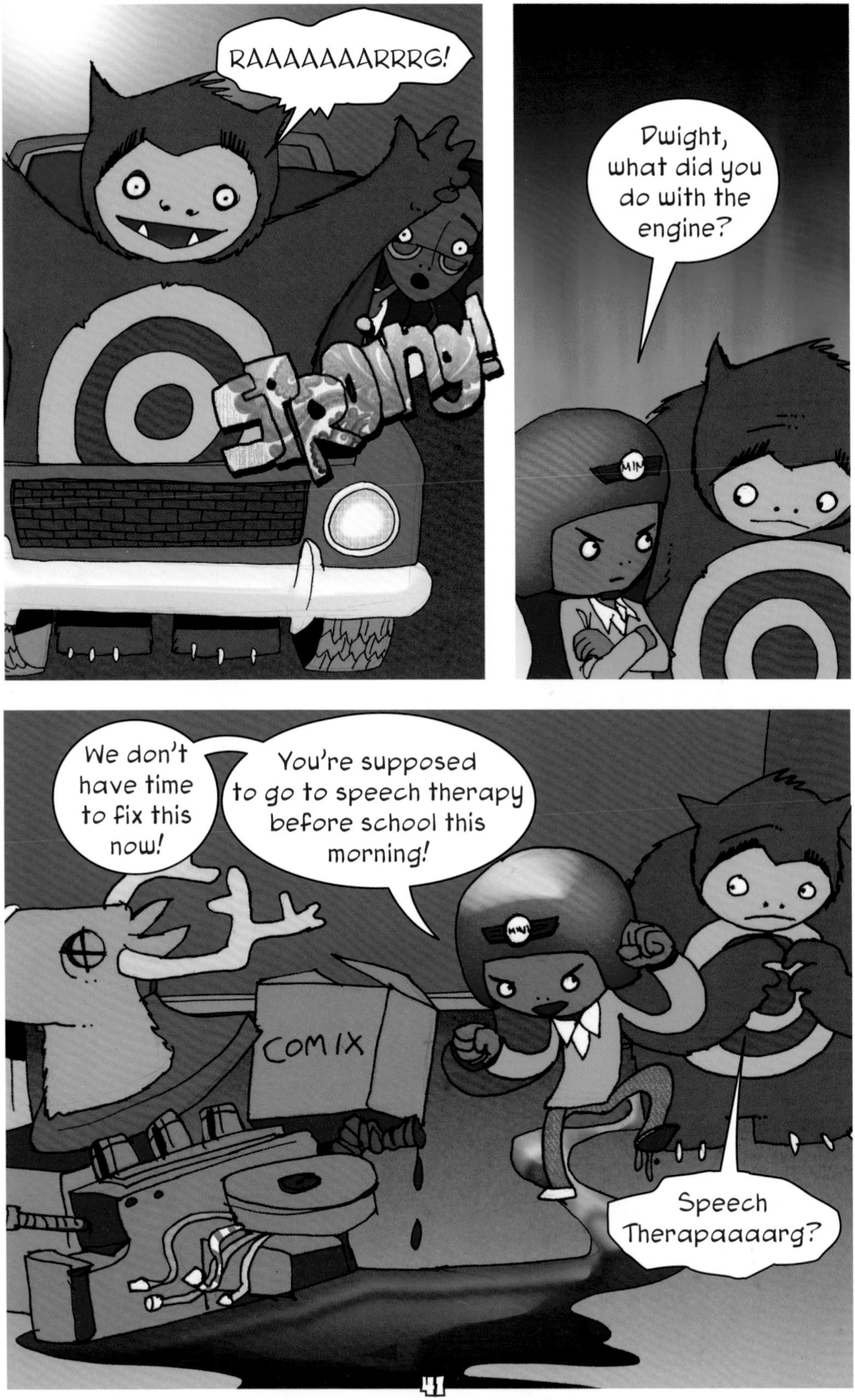
RAAAAAAARRRG!
SPROING!
Dwight, what did you do with the engine?
We don't have time to fix this now!
You're supposed to go to speech therapy before school this morning!
COMIX
Speech Therapaaaarg?

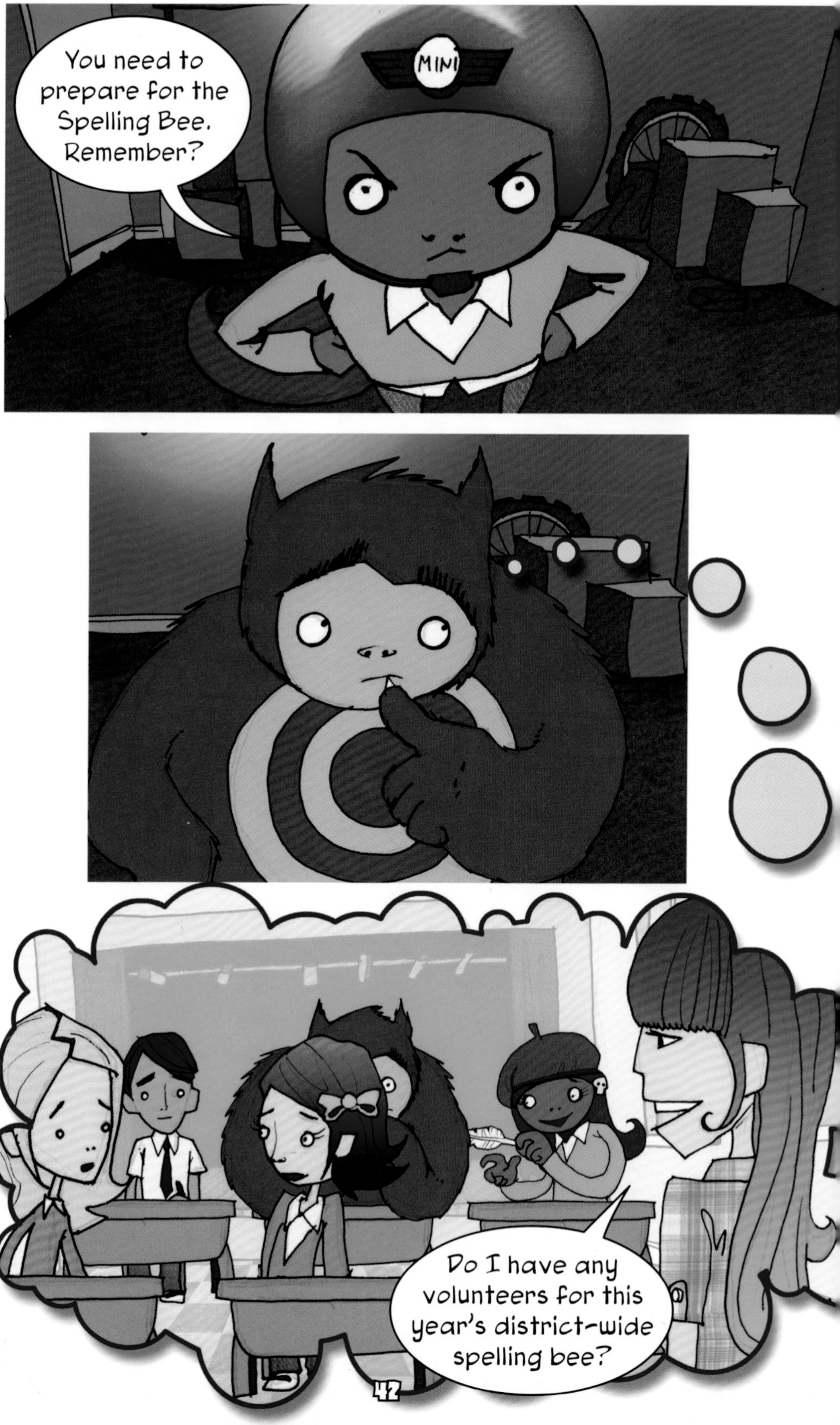
MINI
You need to prepare for the Spelling Bee. Remember?
Do I have any volunteers for this year's district-wide spelling bee?

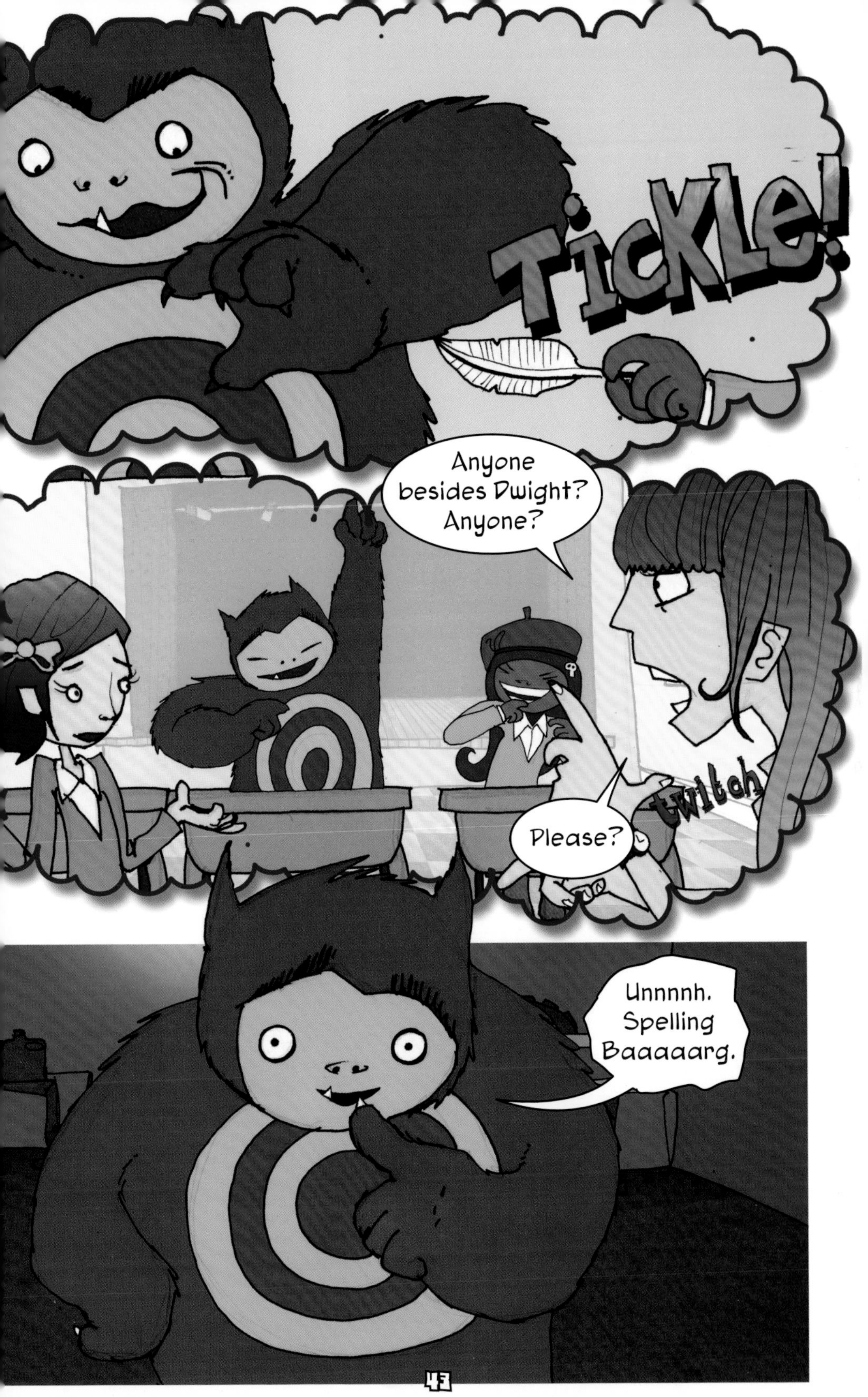
TICKLE!
Anyone besides Dwight? Anyone?
twitch
Please?
Unnnnh. Spelling Baaaaarg.

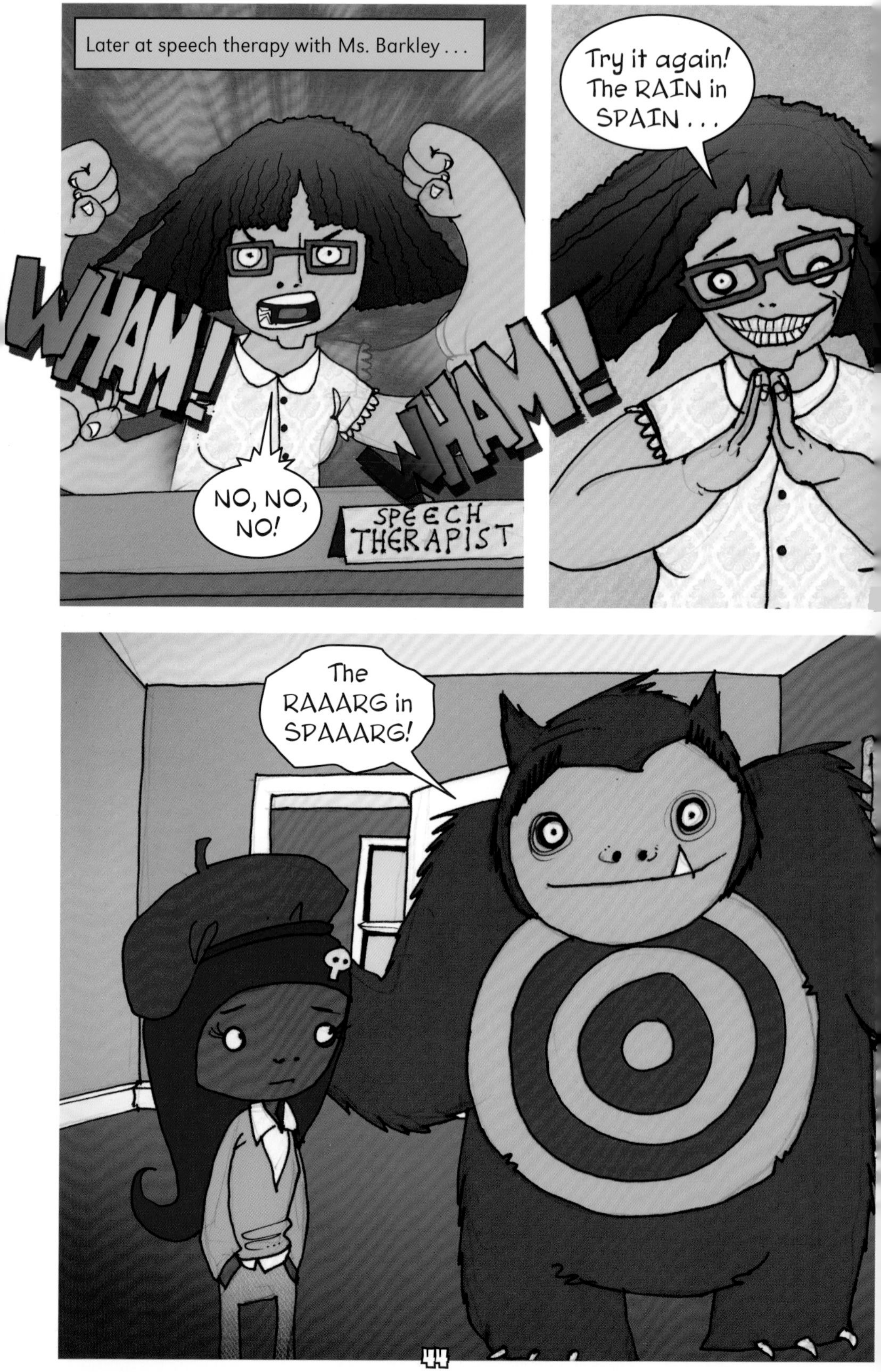
Later at speech therapy with Ms. Barkley . . .
WHAM!
NO, NO, NO!
SPEECH THERAPIST
WHAM!
Try it again! The RAIN in SPAIN . . .
The RAAARG in SPAAARG!

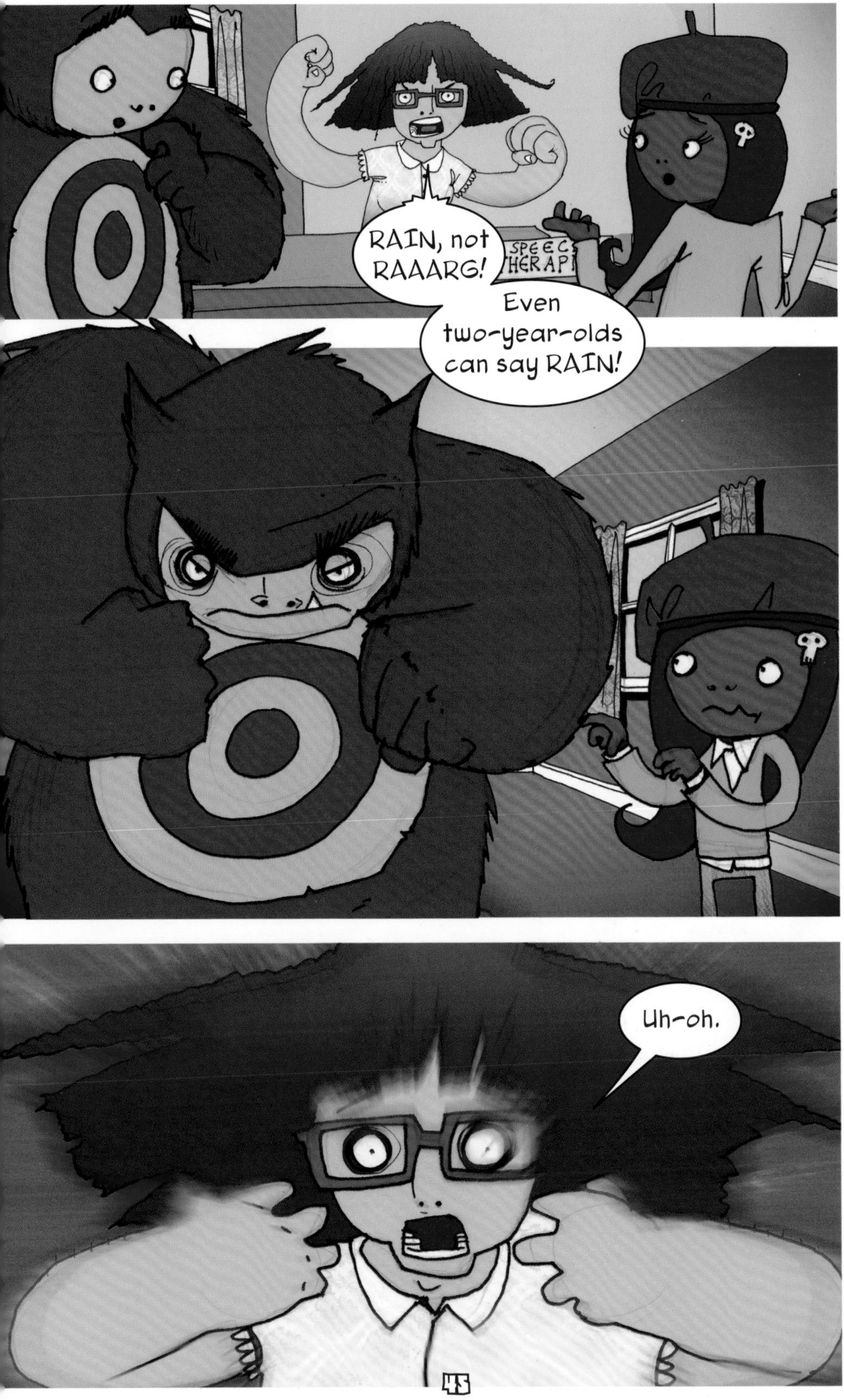
SPEECH THERAPY
RAIN, not RAAARG!
Even two-year-olds can say RAIN!
Uh-oh.

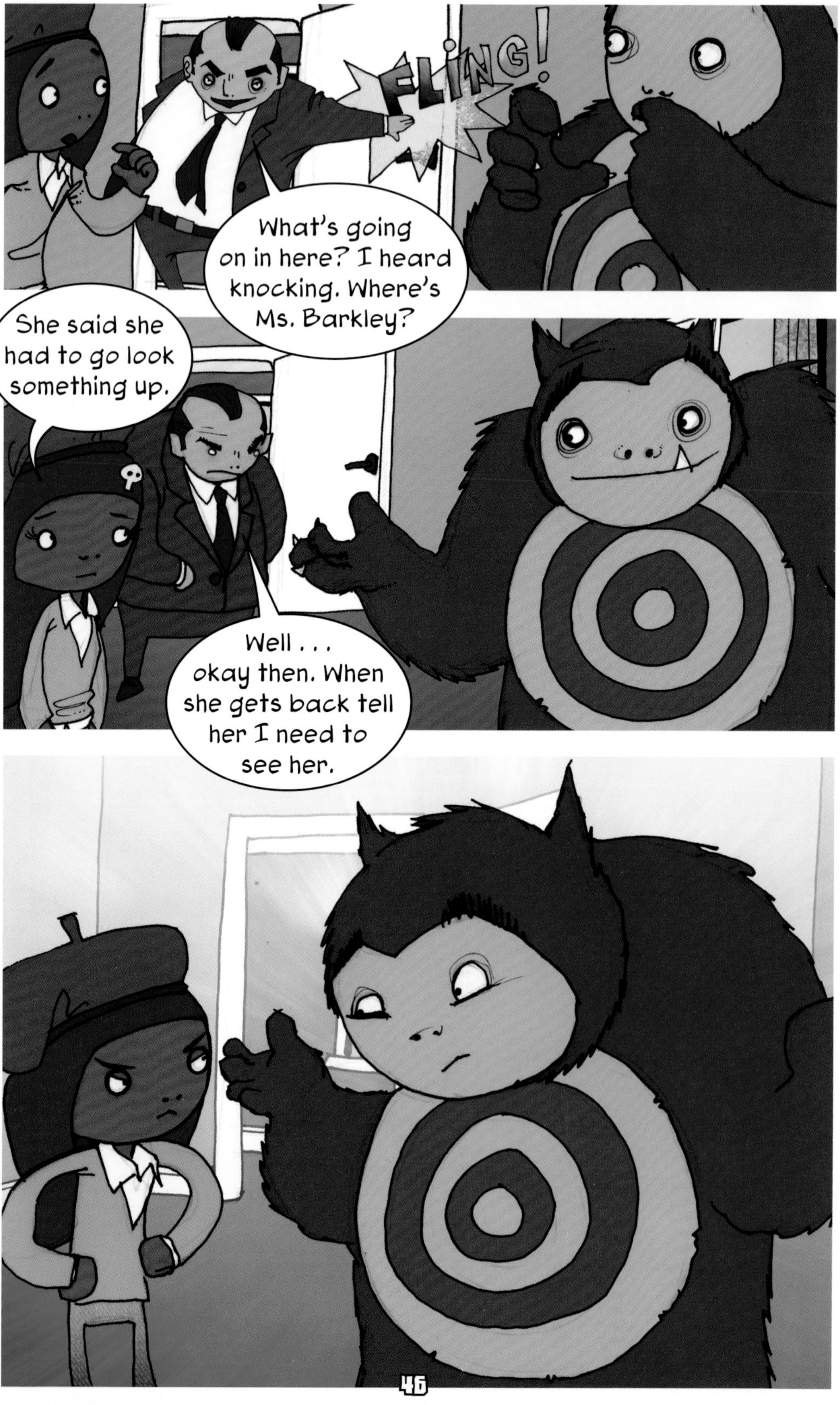
FLING!
What's going on in here? I heard knocking. Where's Ms. Barkley?
She said she had to go look something up.
Well . . . okay then. When she gets back tell her I need to see her.

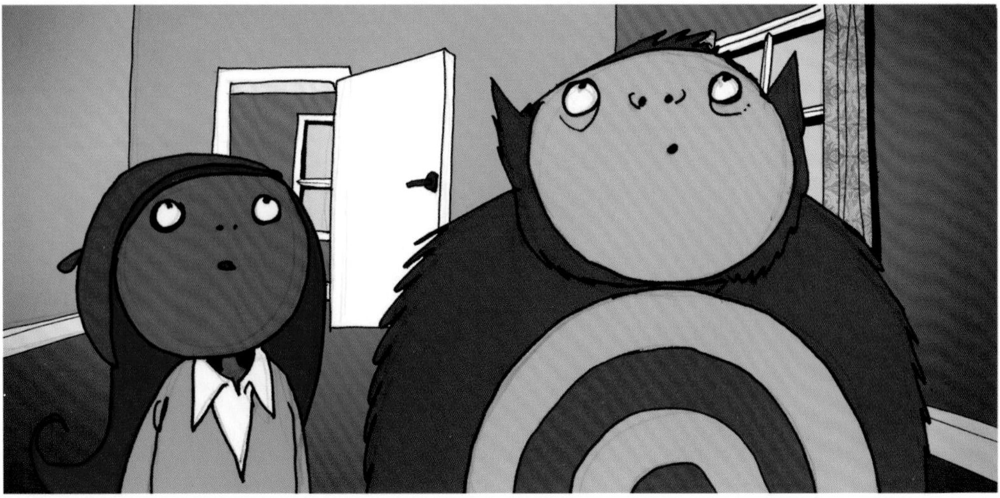

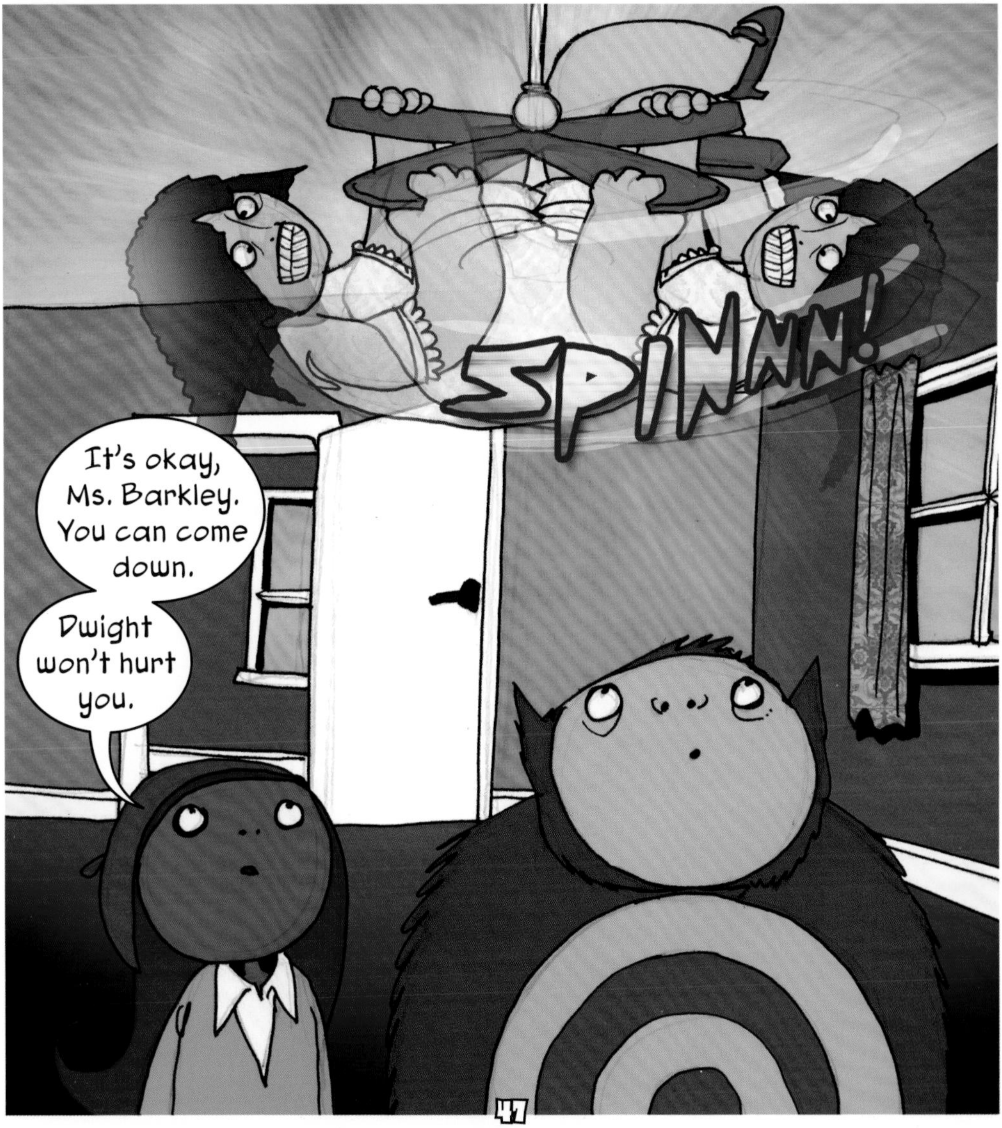
SPINNN!
It's okay, Ms. Barkley. You can come down.
Dwight won't hurt you.

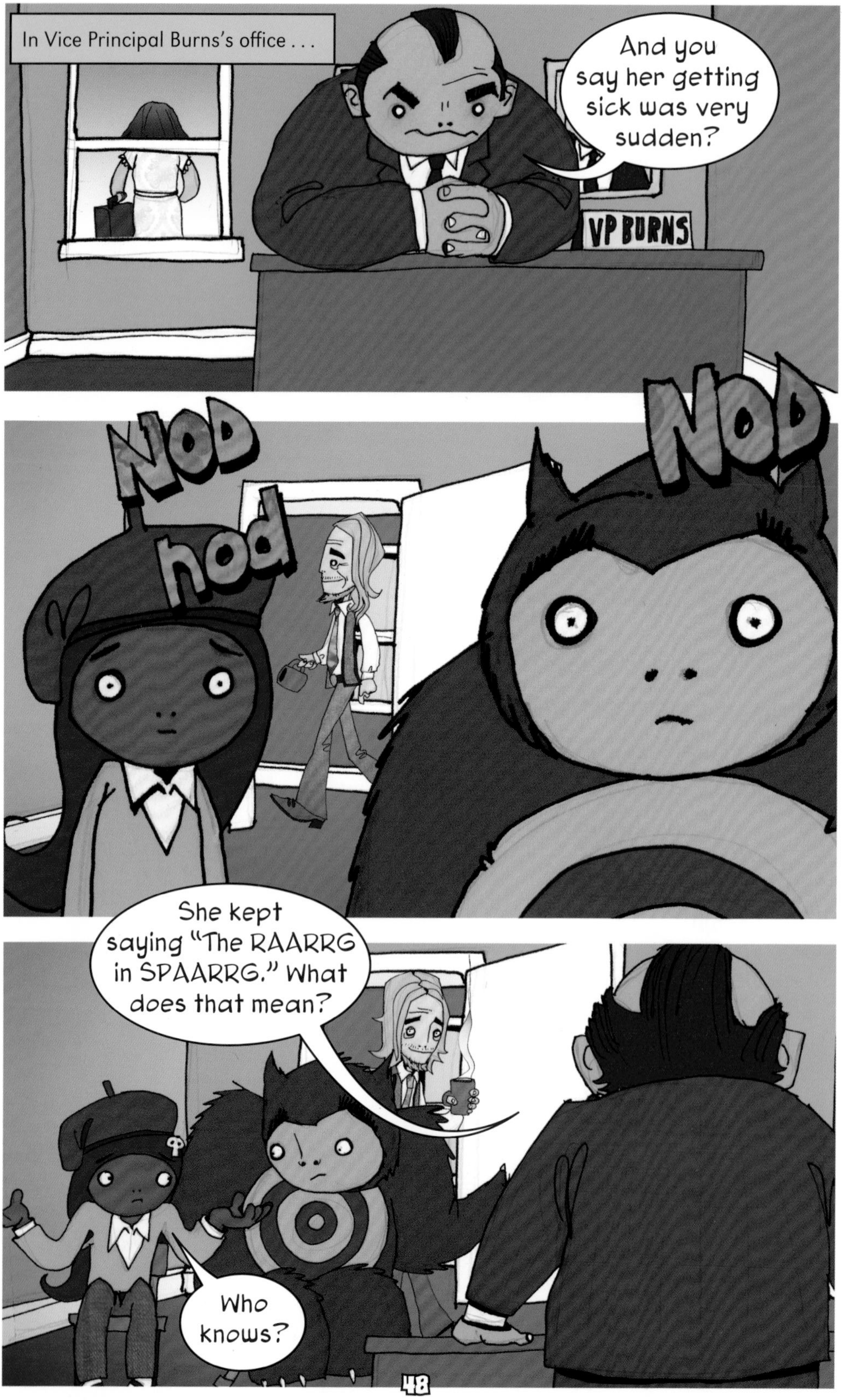

In Vice Principal Burns's office . . .
And you say her getting sick was very sudden?
VP BURNS
NOD
nod
NOD
She kept saying "The RAARRG in SPAARRG." What does that mean?
Who knows?

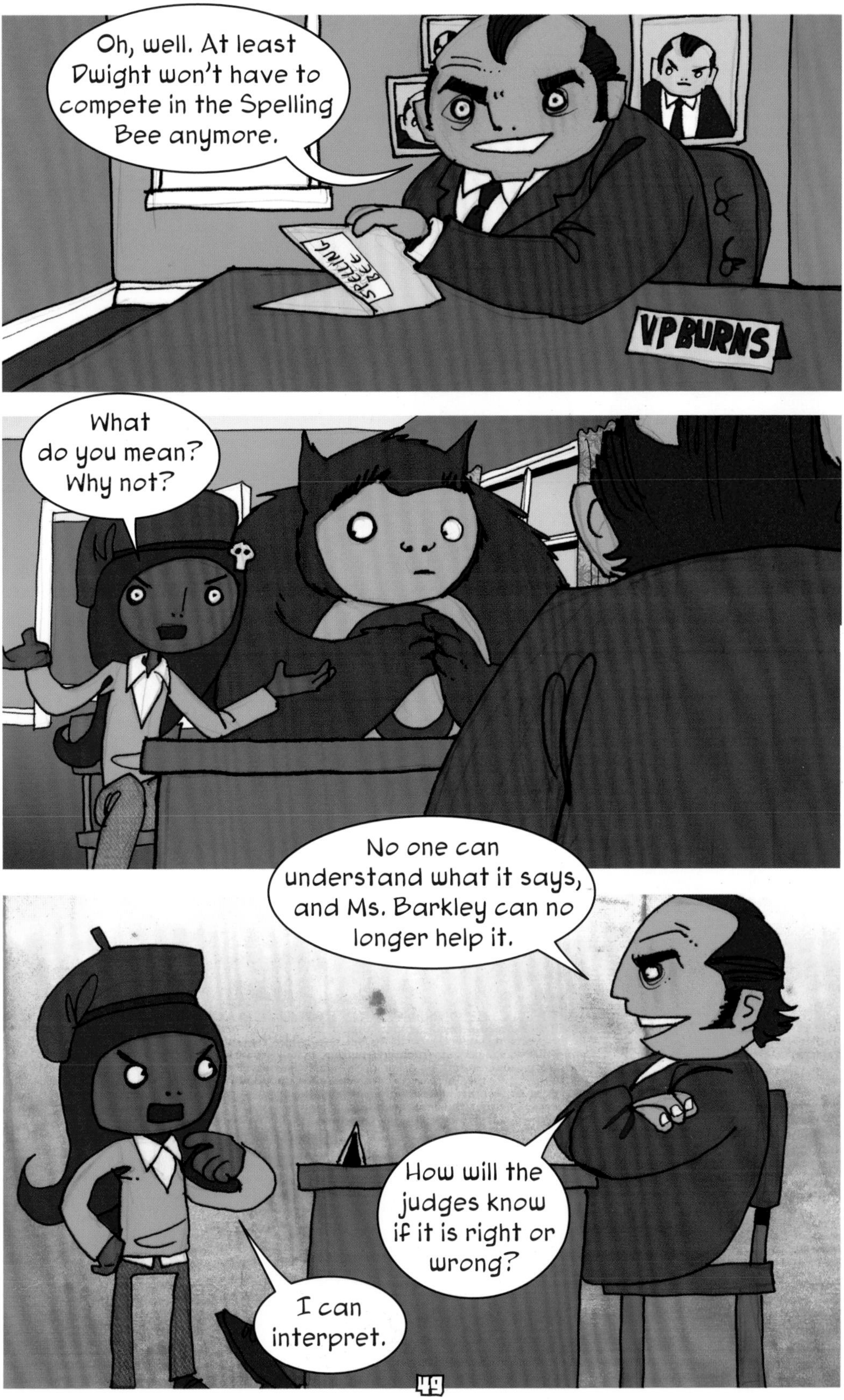
Oh, well. At least Dwight won't have to compete in the Spelling Bee anymore.
SPELLING BEE
VP BURNS
What do you mean? Why not?
No one can understand what it says, and Ms. Barkley can no longer help it.
How will the judges know if it is right or wrong?
I can interpret.

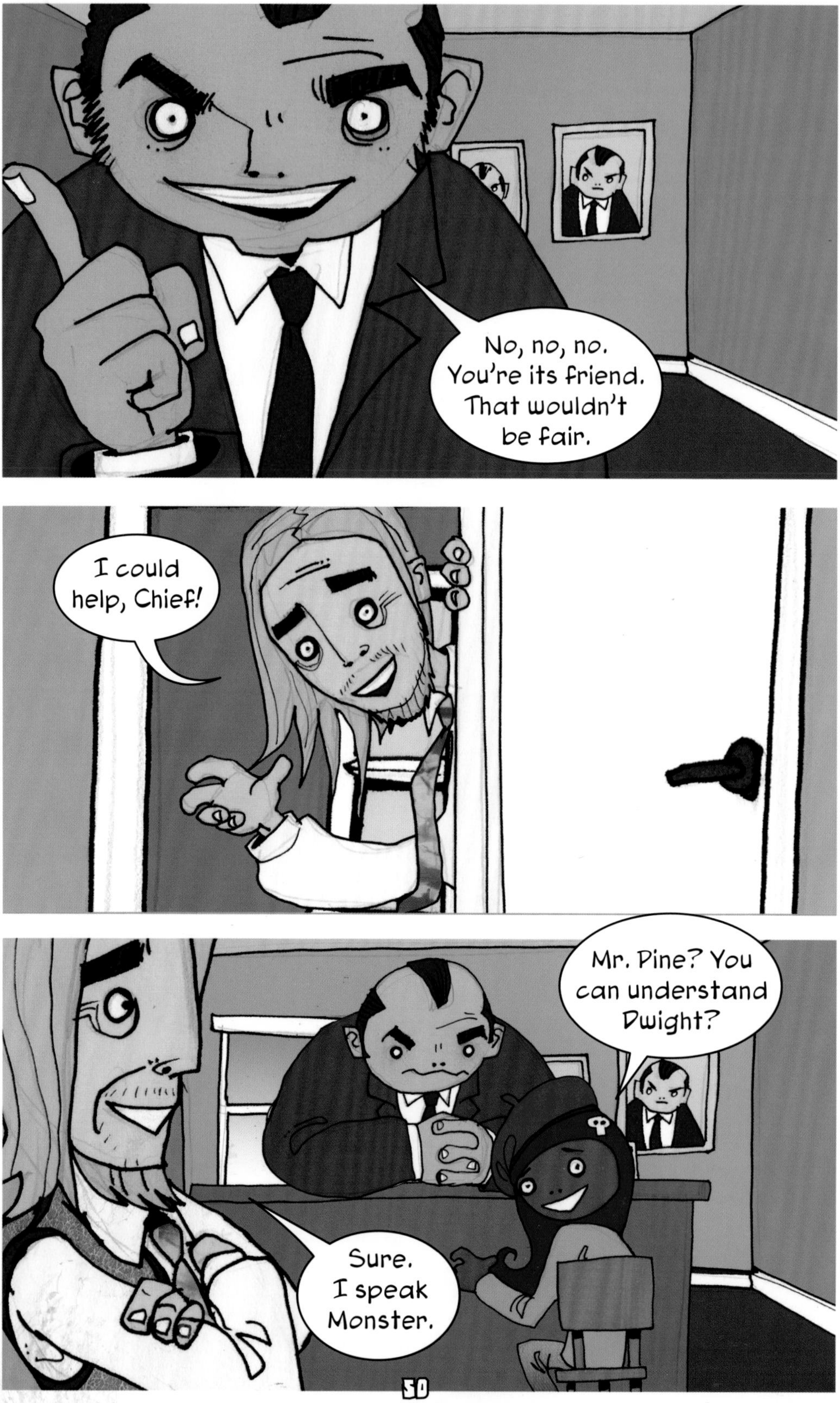
No, no, no.
You're its friend.
That wouldn't
be fair.
I could
help, Chief!
Mr. Pine? You
can understand
Dwight?
Sure.
I speak
Monster.

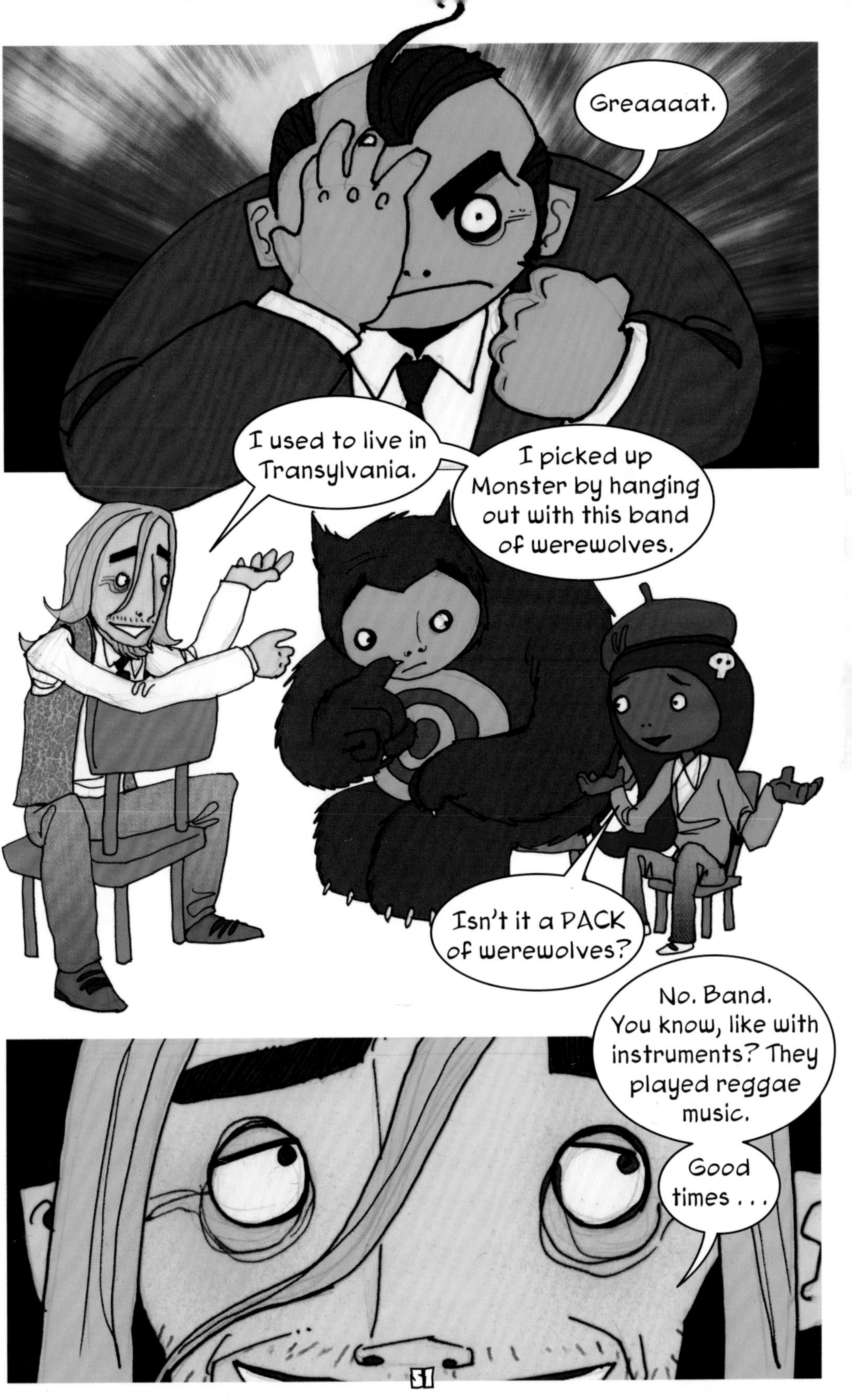
Greaaaat.
I used to live in Transylvania.
I picked up Monster by hanging out with this band of werewolves.
Isn't it a PACK of werewolves?
No. Band. You know, like with instruments? They played reggae music.
Good times . . .

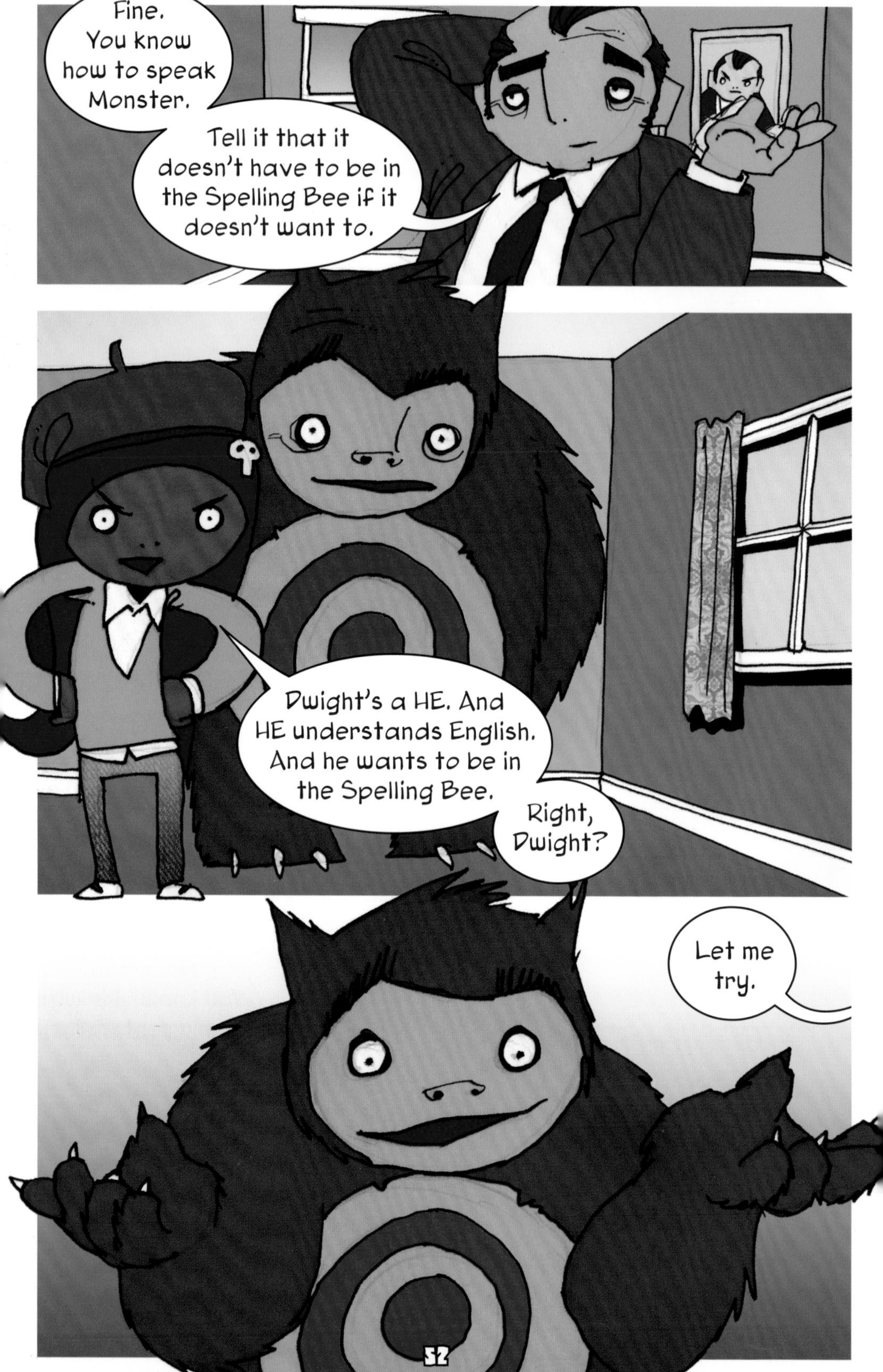
Fine. You know how to speak Monster.
Tell it that it doesn't have to be in the Spelling Bee if it doesn't want to.
Dwight's a HE. And HE understands English. And he wants to be in the Spelling Bee.
Right, Dwight?
Let me try.

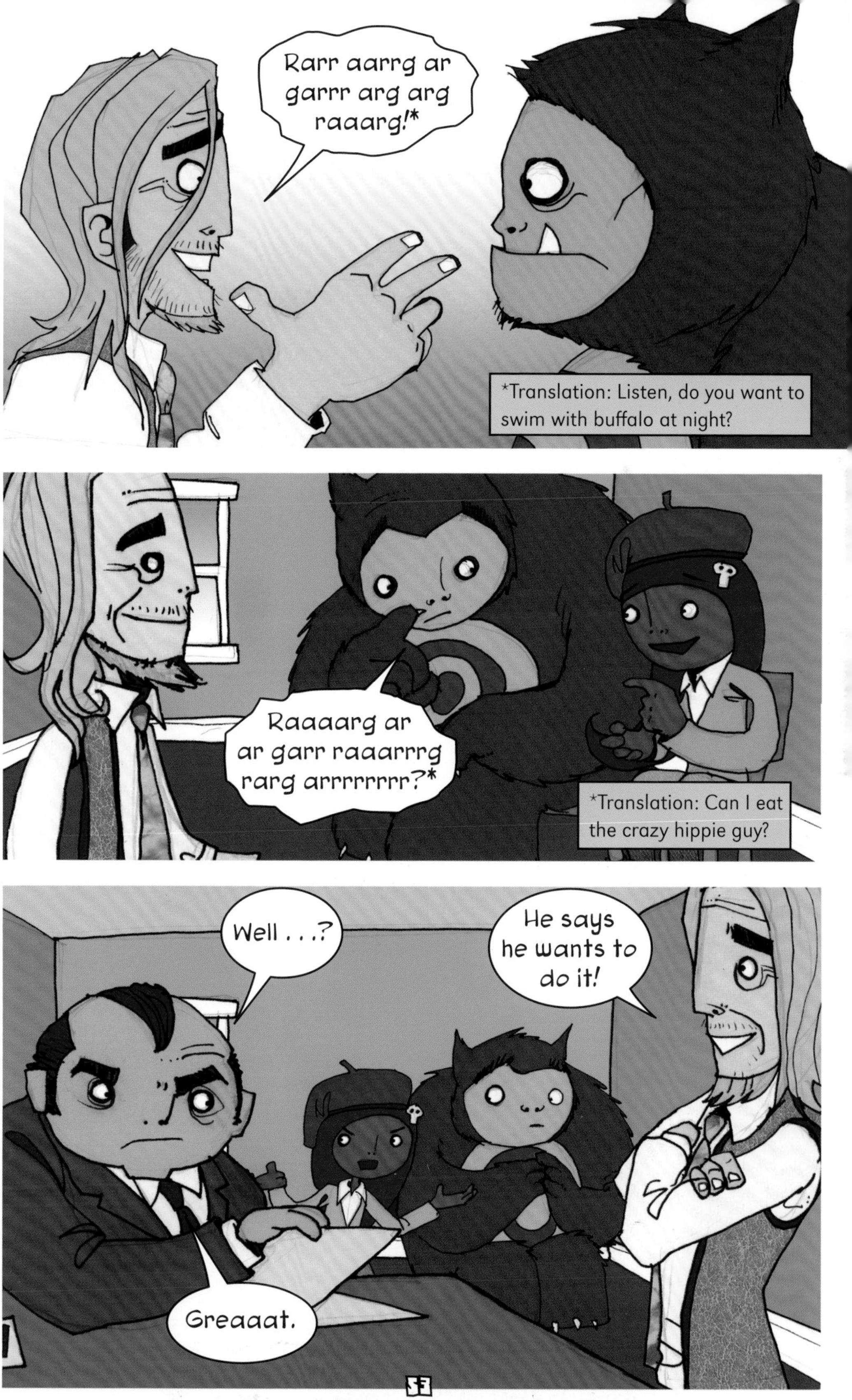
Rarr aarrg ar garrr arg arg raaarg!*
*Translation: Listen, do you want to swim with buffalo at night?
Raaaarg ar ar garr raaarrrg rarg arrrrrrrr?*
*Translation: Can I eat the crazy hippie guy?
Well . . .?
He says he wants to do it!
Greaaat.

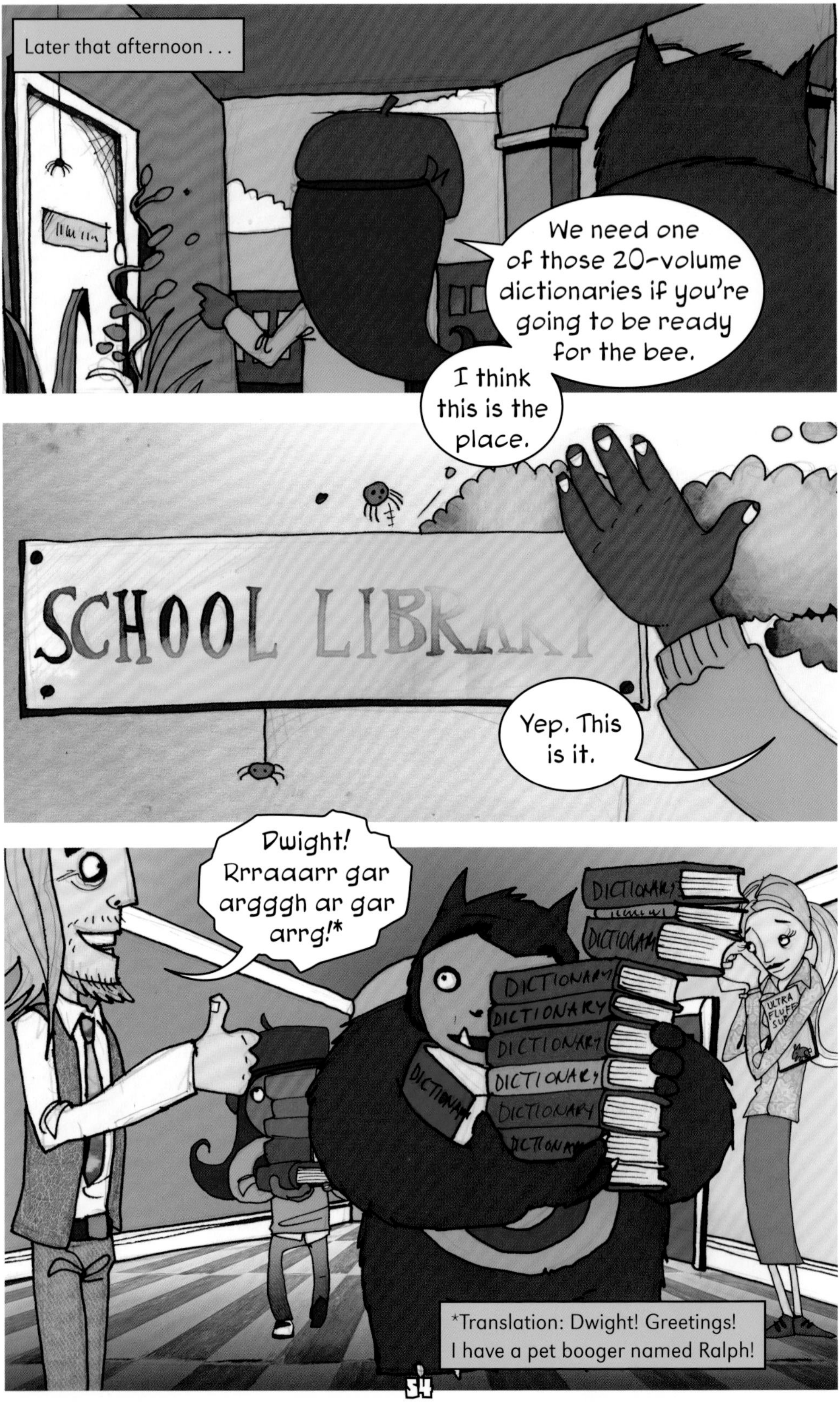

Later that afternoon . . .
We need one of those 20-volume dictionaries if you're going to be ready for the bee.
I think this is the place.
SCHOOL LIBRARY
Yep. This is it.
Dwight! Rrraaarr gar argggh ar gar arrg!*
DICTIONARY
DICTIONARY
DICTIONARY
DICTIONARY
DICTIONARY
ULTRA FLUFF
*Translation: Dwight! Greetings! I have a pet booger named Ralph!

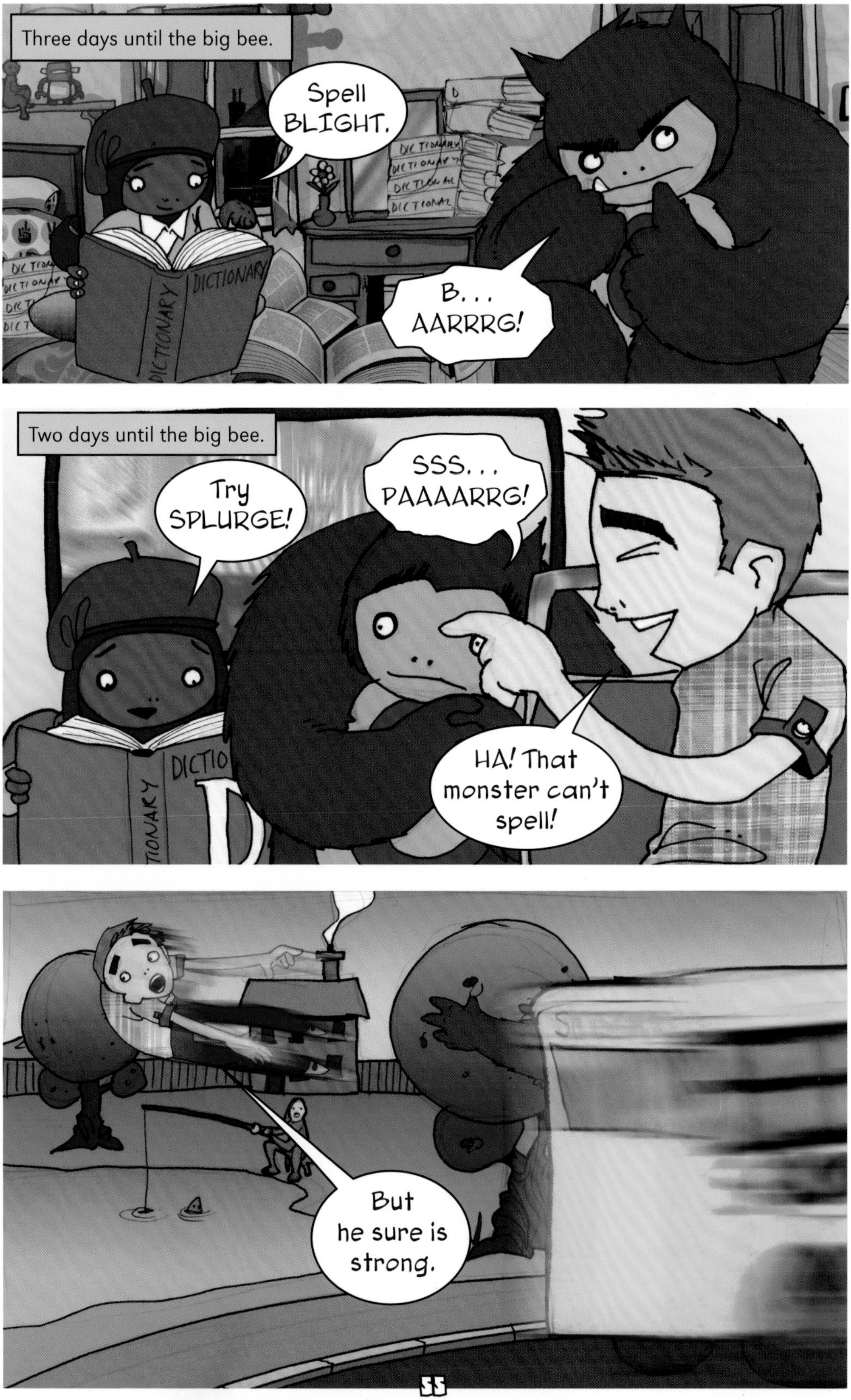
Three days until the big bee.
Spell BLIGHT.
B. . . AARRRG!
Two days until the big bee.
Try SPLURGE!
SSS. . . PAAAARRG!
HA! That monster can't spell!
But he sure is strong.

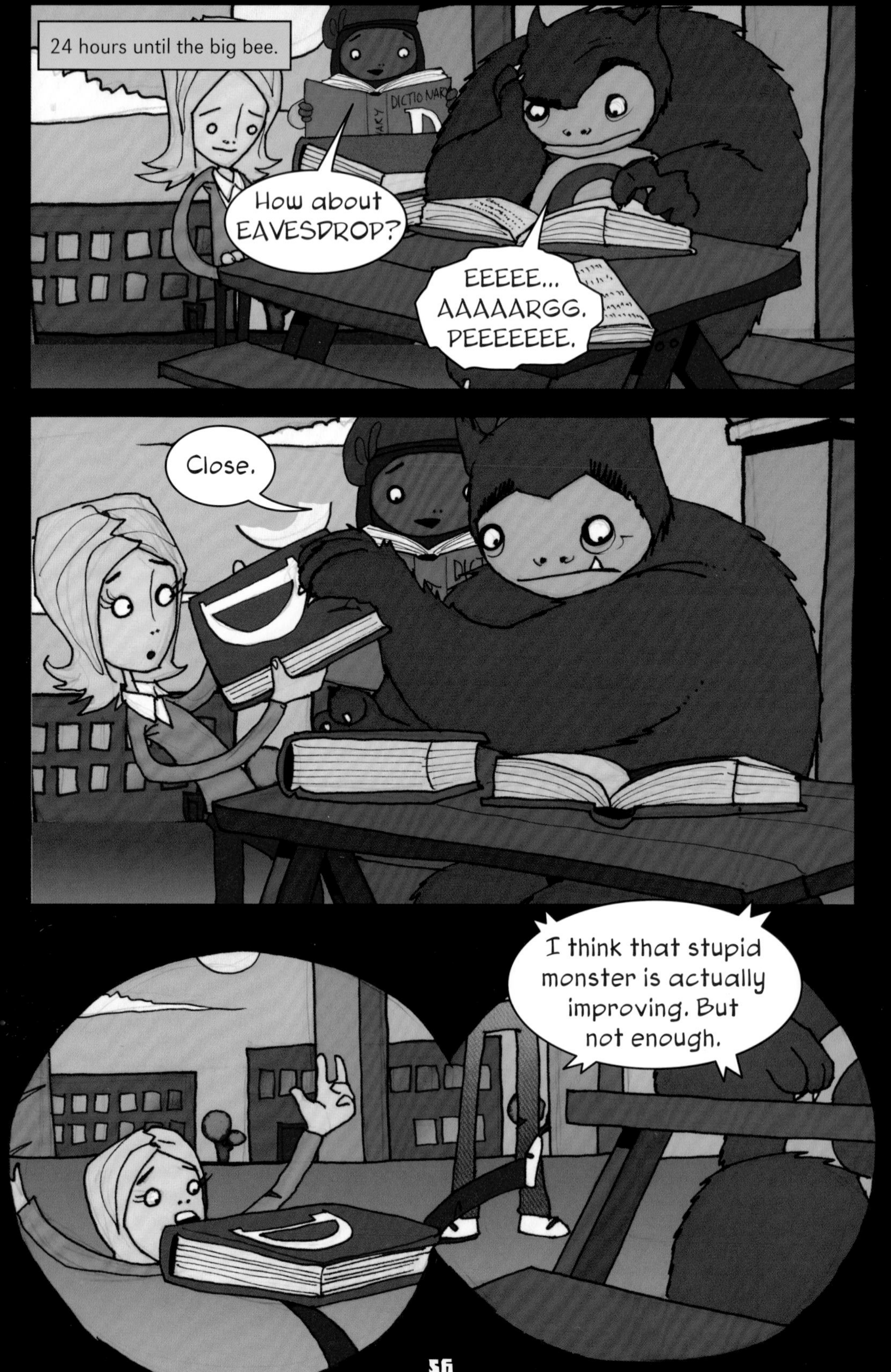
24 hours until the big bee.
How about EAVESDROP?
EEEEE... AAAAARGG. PEEEEEEE.
Close.
I think that stupid monster is actually improving. But not enough.

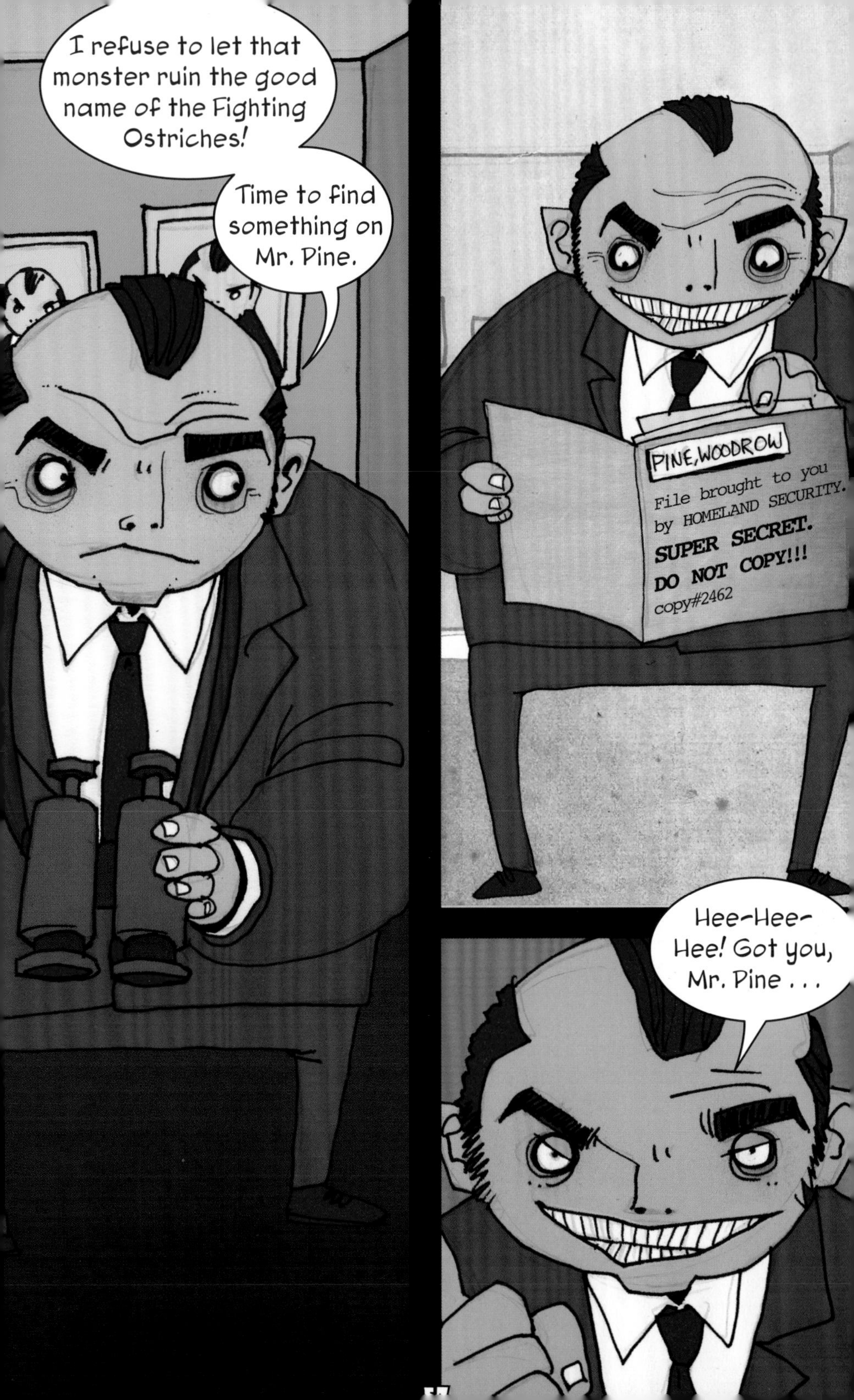
I refuse to let that monster ruin the good name of the Fighting Ostriches!
Time to find something on Mr. Pine.
PINE, WOODROW
File brought to you by HOMELAND SECURITY.
SUPER SECRET.
DO NOT COPY!!!
copy#2462
Hee-Hee-Hee! Got you, Mr. Pine . . .

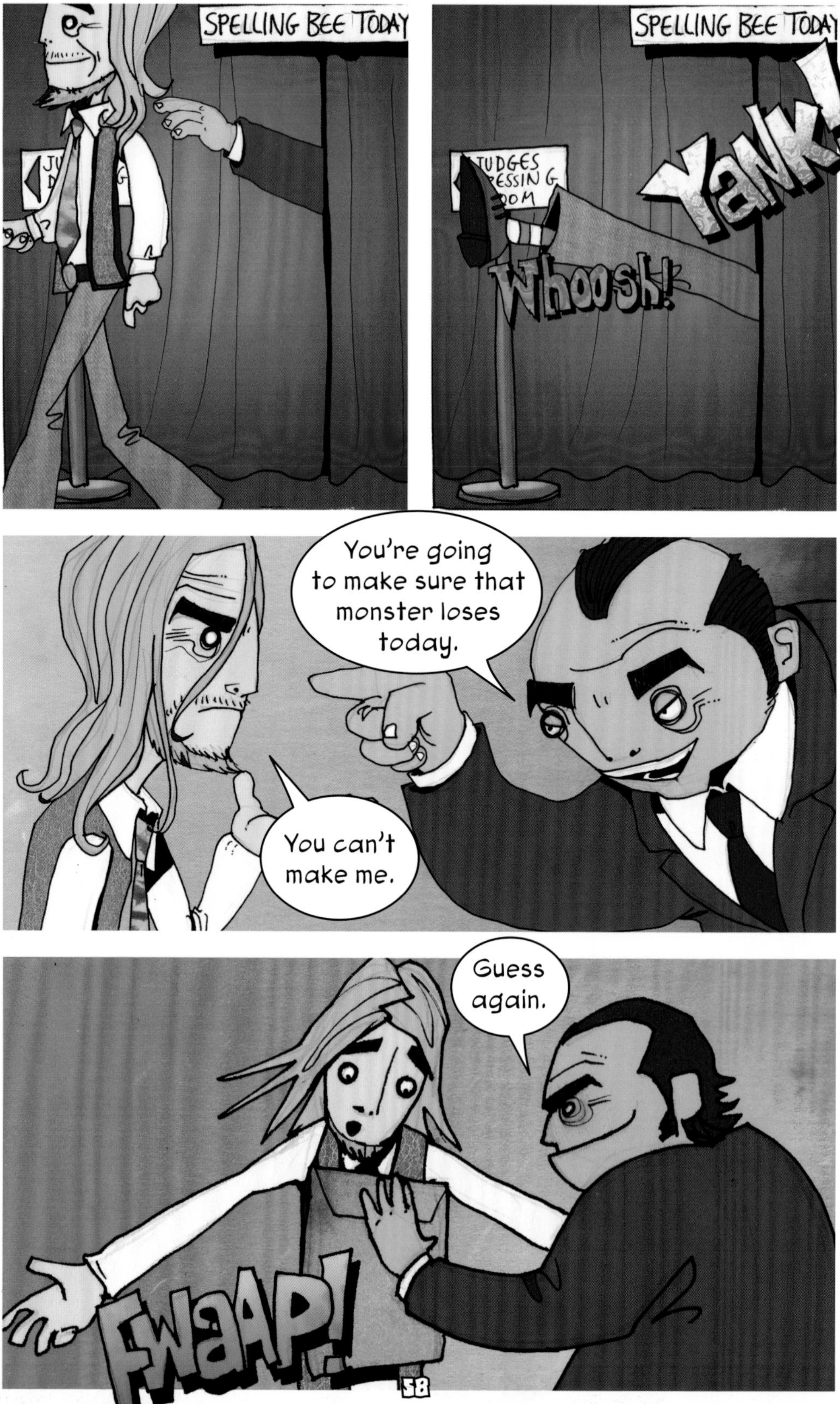
SPELLING BEE TODAY
SPELLING BEE TODAY
YANK!
Whoosh!
You're going to make sure that monster loses today.
You can't make me.
Guess again.
FWAAP!

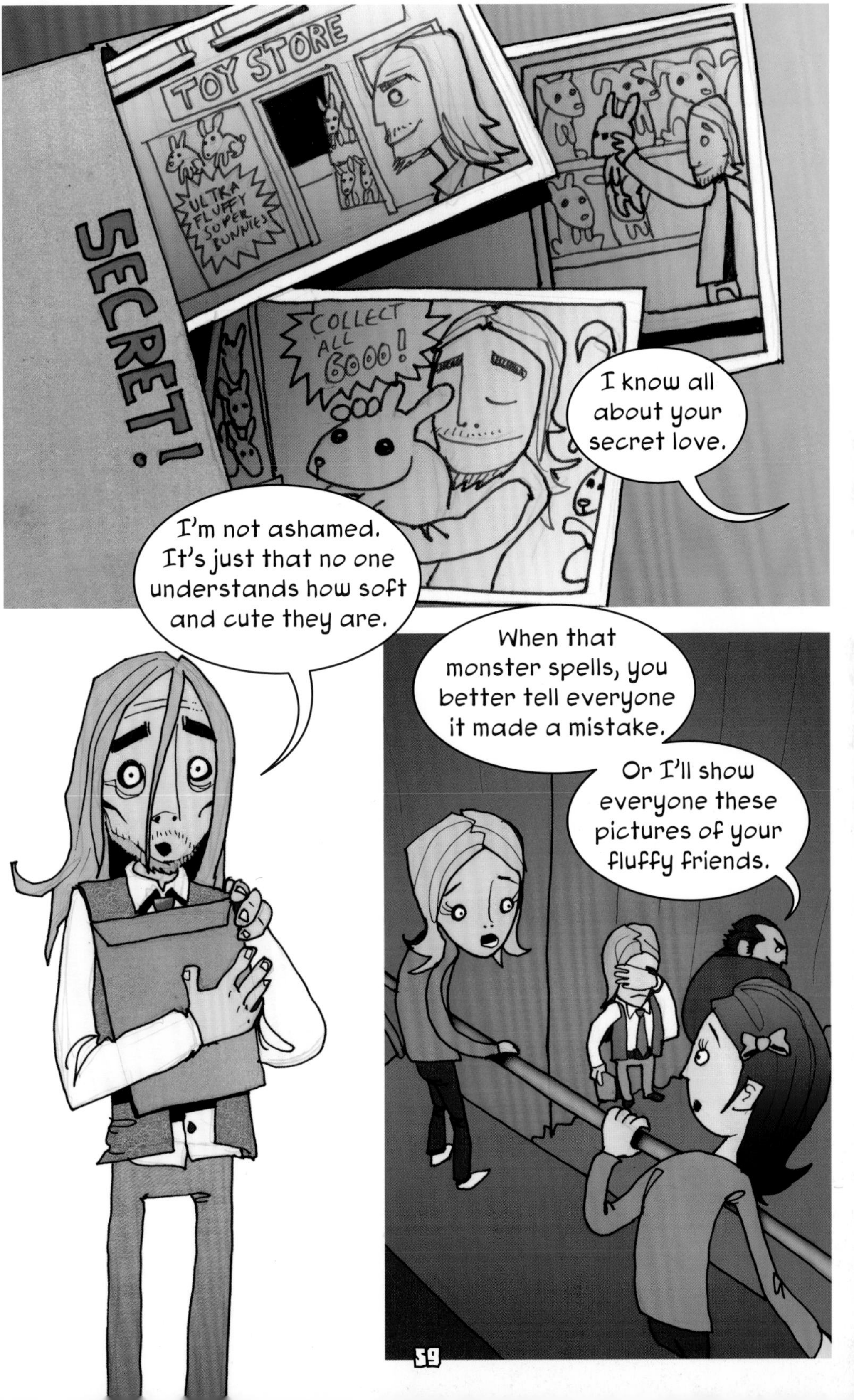
TOY STORE
ULTRA FLUFFY SUPER BUNNIES
COLLECT ALL 6000!
SECRET!
I know all about your secret love.
I'm not ashamed. It's just that no one understands how soft and cute they are.
When that monster spells, you better tell everyone it made a mistake.
Or I'll show everyone these pictures of your fluffy friends.

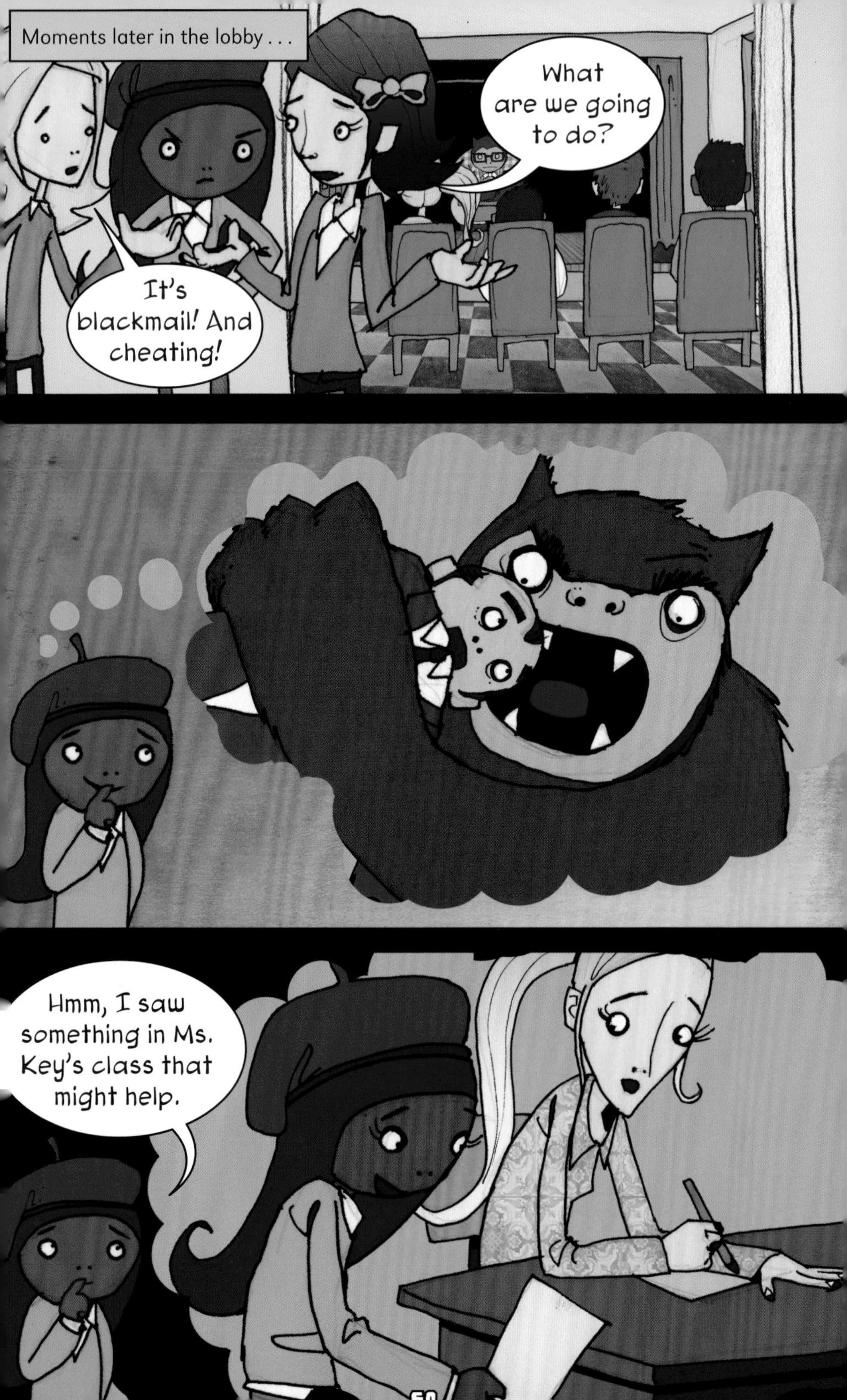
Moments later in the lobby . . .
It's blackmail! And cheating!
What are we going to do?
Hmm, I saw something in Ms. Key's class that might help.

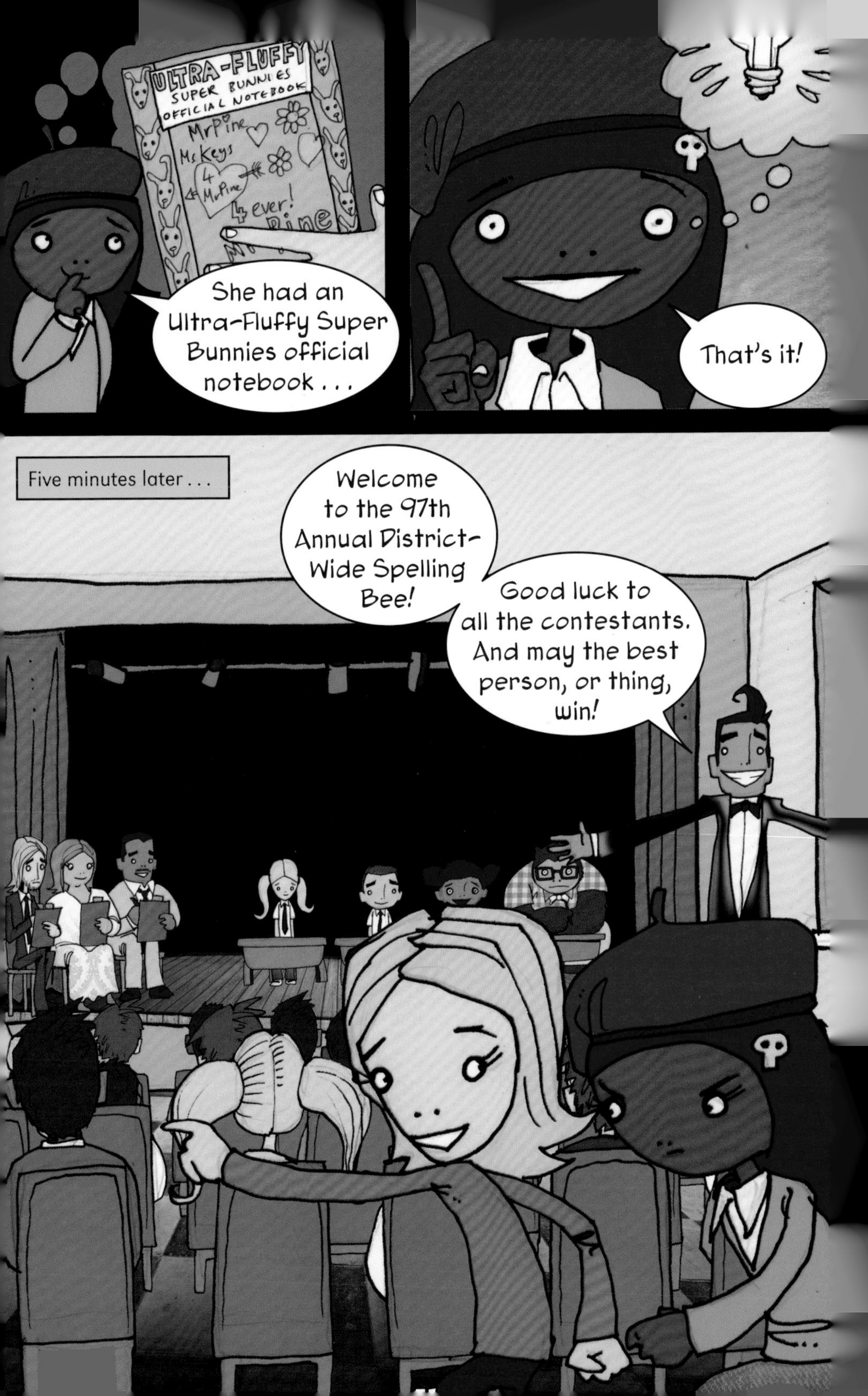
ULTRA-FLUFFY SUPER BUNNIES OFFICIAL NOTEBOOK
She had an Ultra-Fluffy Super Bunnies official notebook . . .
That's it!
Five minutes later . . .
Welcome to the 97th Annual District-Wide Spelling Bee!
Good luck to all the contestants. And may the best person, or thing, win!

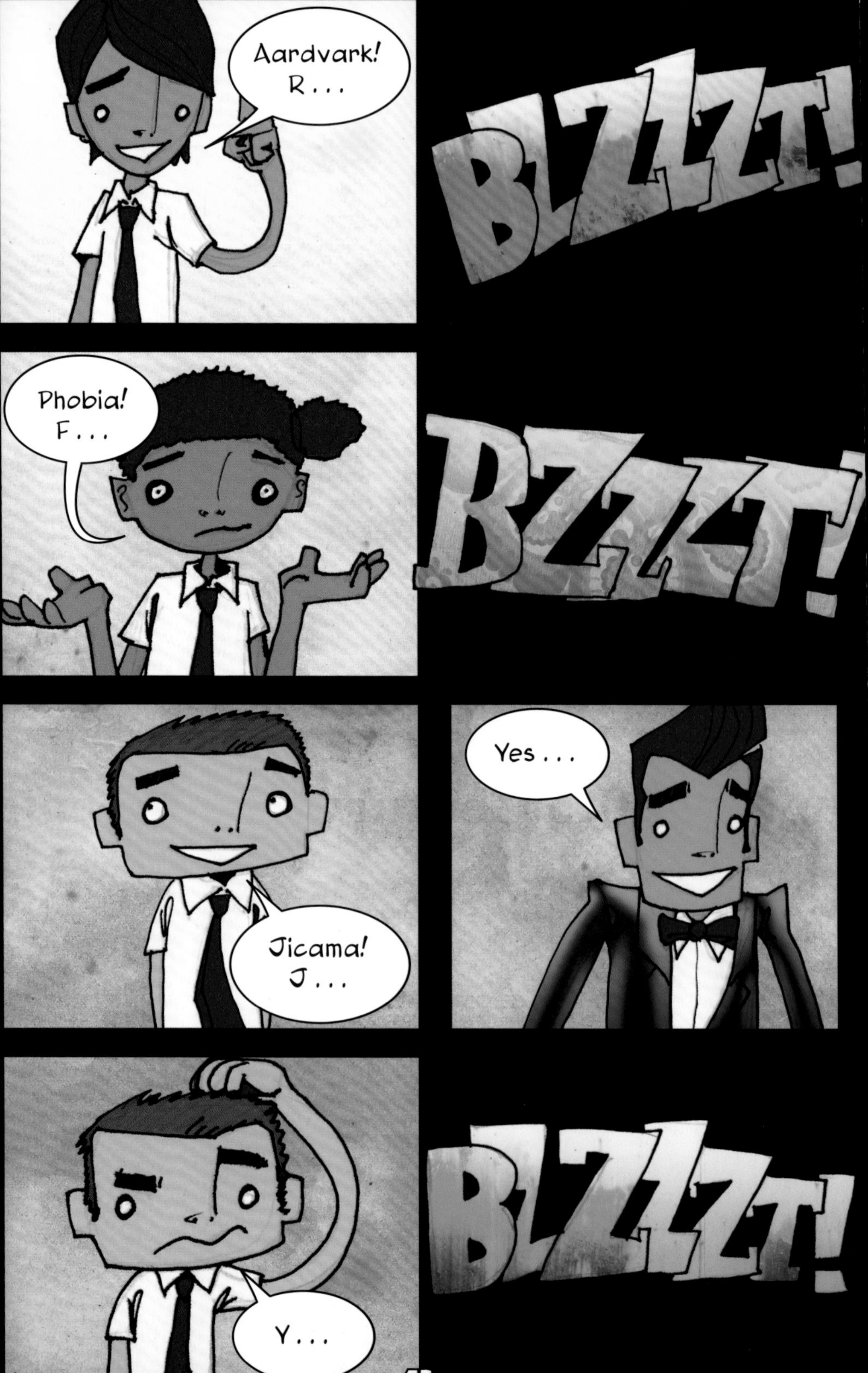
Aardvark! R . . .
BZZZZT!
Phobia! F . . .
BZZZT!
Jicama! J . . .
Yes . . .
Y . . .
BZZZZT!

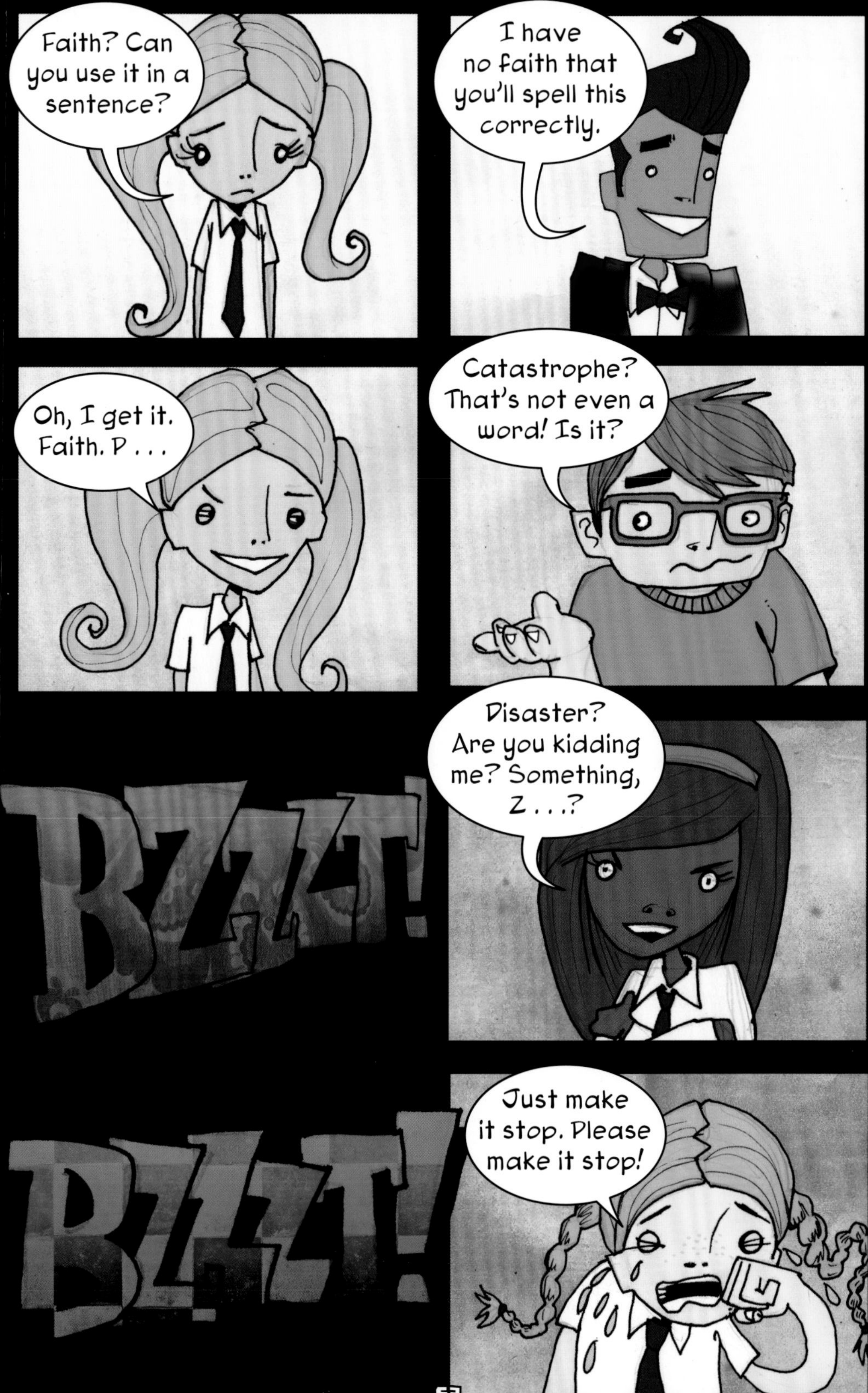
Faith? Can you use it in a sentence?
I have no faith that you'll spell this correctly.
Oh, I get it. Faith. P . . .
Catastrophe? That's not even a word! Is it?
BZZT!
Disaster? Are you kidding me? Something, Z . . .?
BZZT!
Just make it stop. Please make it stop!

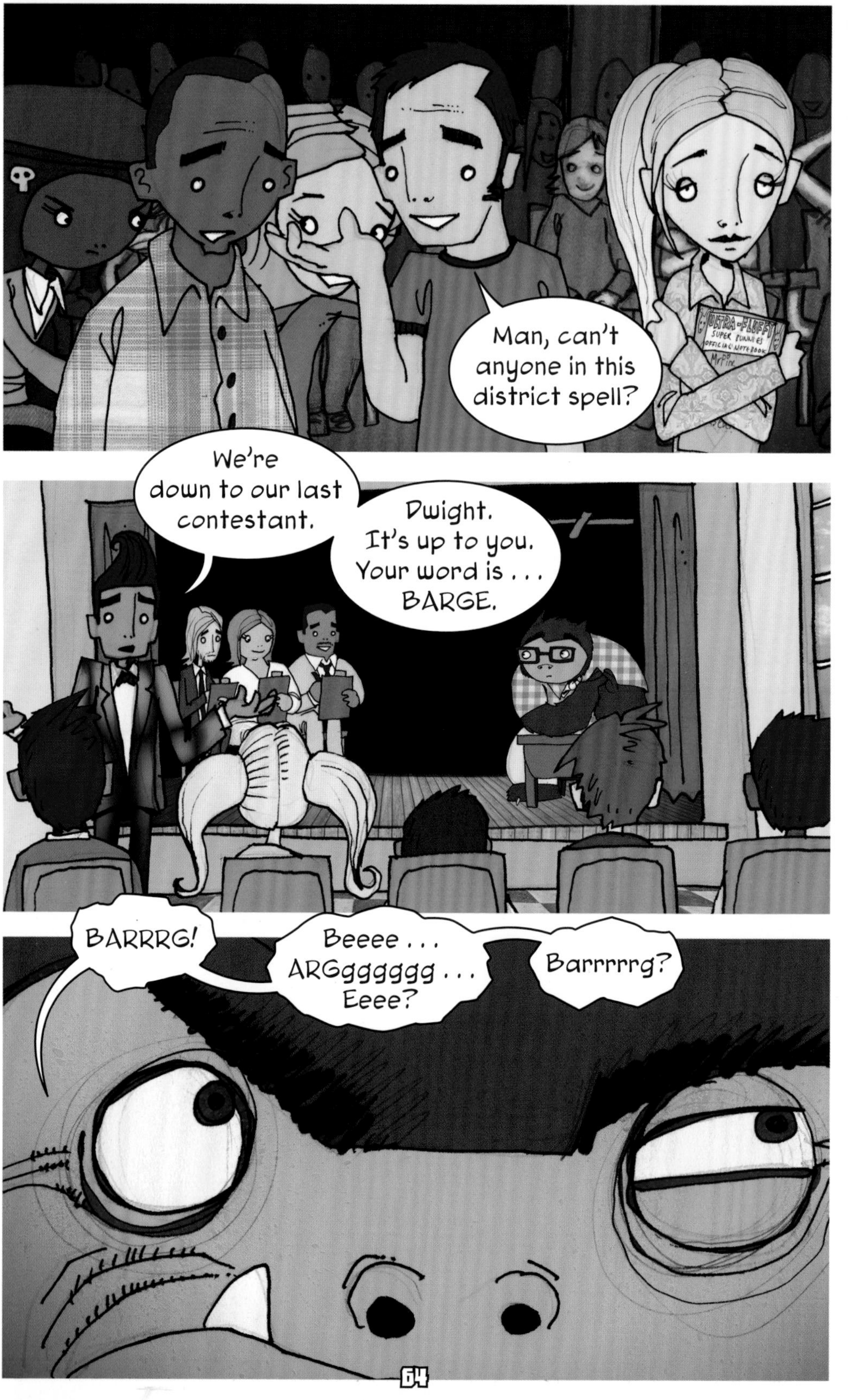
ULTRA-FLUFFY
SUPER BUNNIES
OFFICIAL NOTEBOOK
Man, can't anyone in this district spell?
We're down to our last contestant.
Dwight. It's up to you. Your word is . . . BARGE.
BARRRG!
Beeee . . . ARGgggggg . . . Eeee?
Barrrrrg?

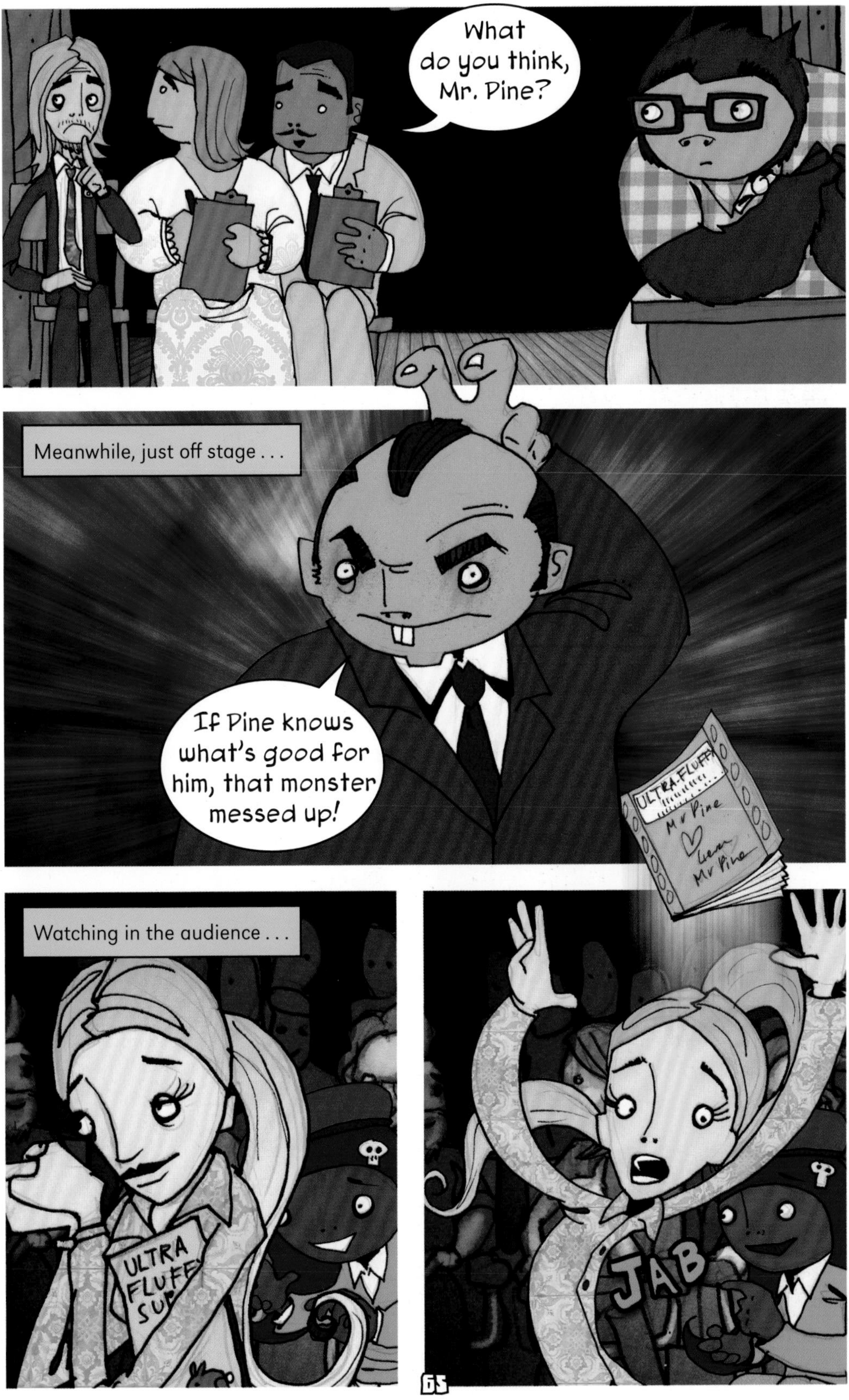
What do you think, Mr. Pine?
Meanwhile, just off stage . . .
If Pine knows what's good for him, that monster messed up!
ULTRA FLUFF
Mr Pine
Love Mr Pine
Watching in the audience . . .
ULTRA FLUFF SUP
JAB

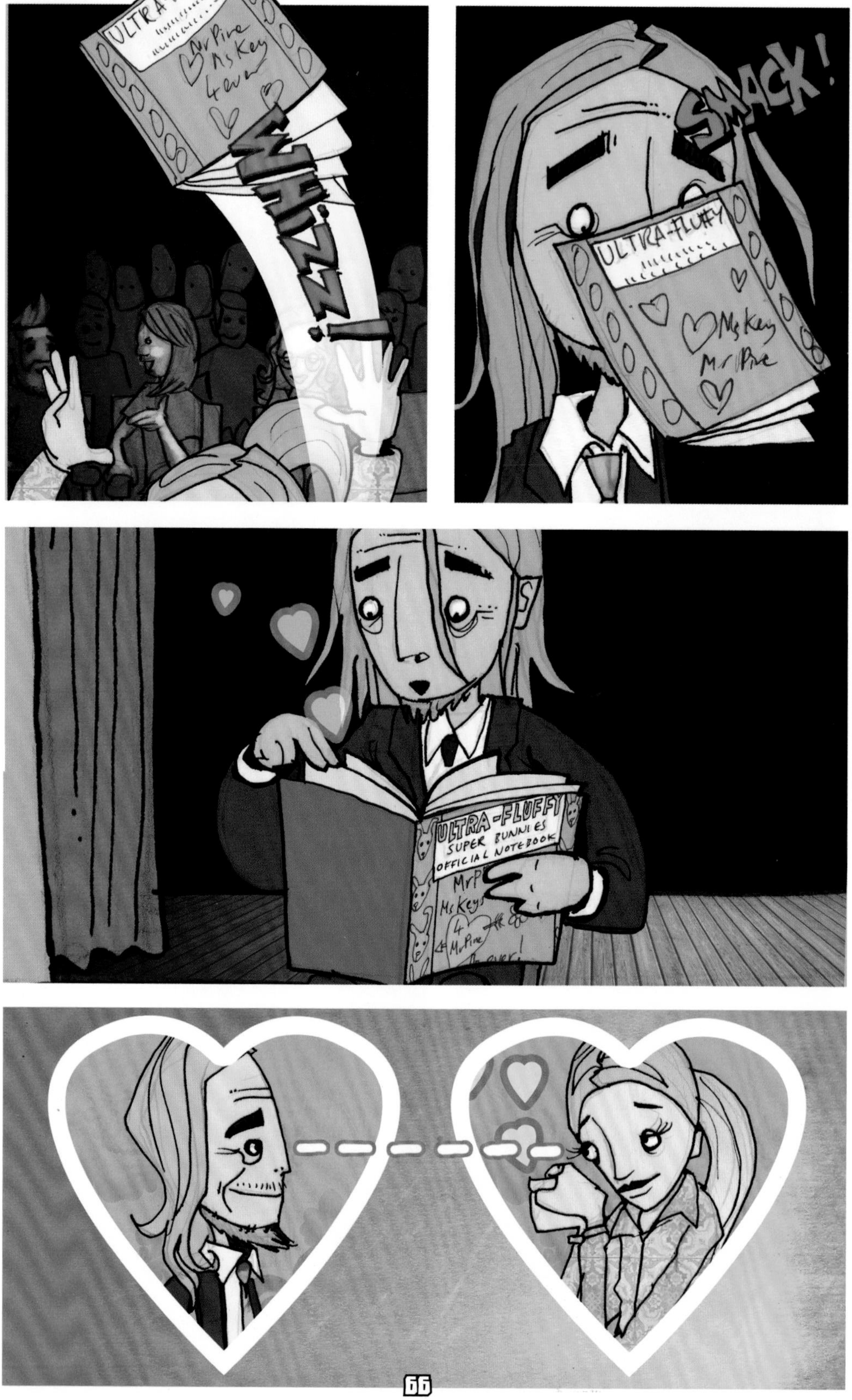
WHIZZ!
SMACK!
ULTRA-FLUFFY
Ms Key
Mr Pire
ULTRA-FLUFFY
SUPER BUNNIES
OFFICIAL NOTEBOOK

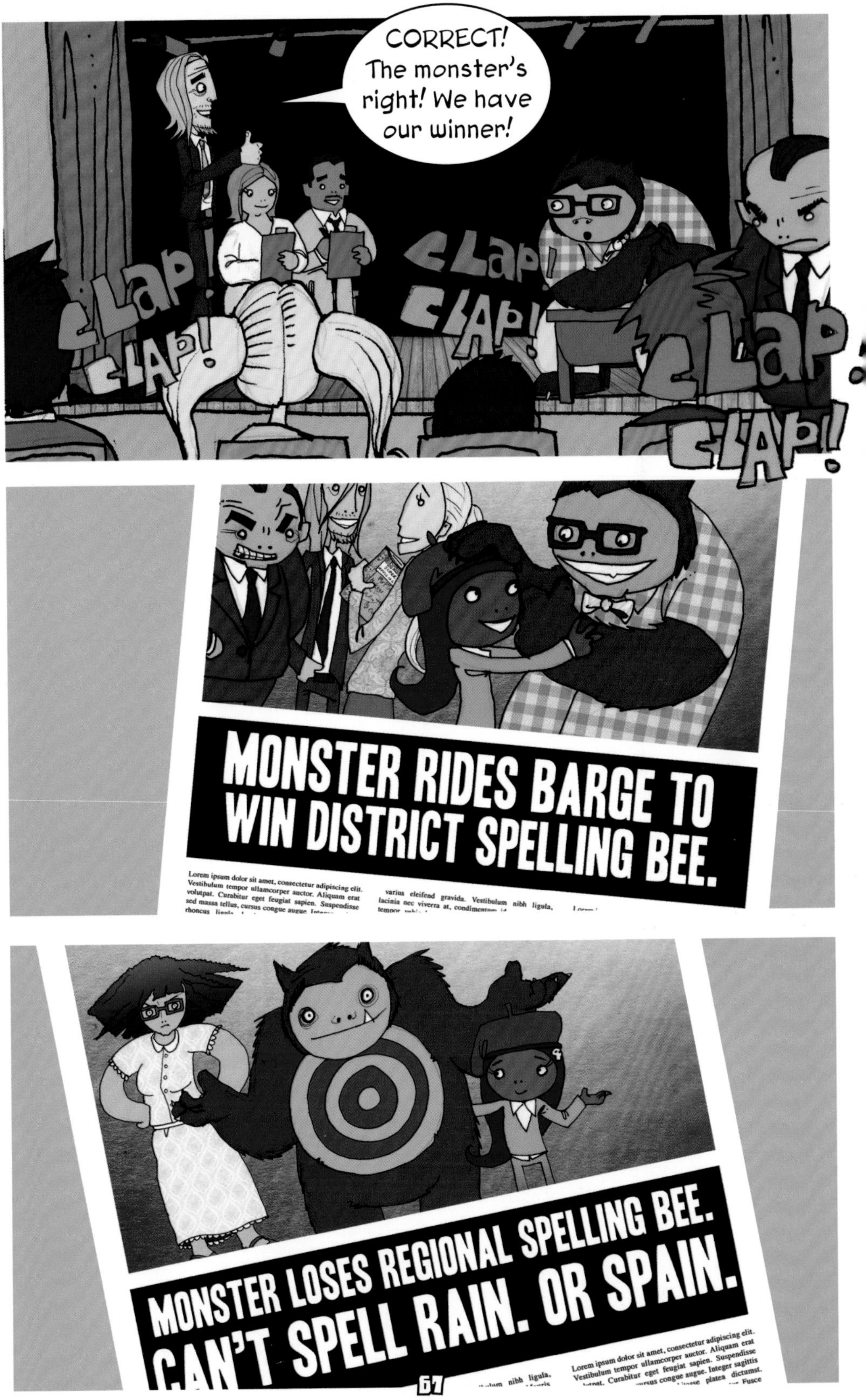

CORRECT! The monster's right! We have our winner!
CLAP! CLAP!
CLAP! CLAP!
CLAP! CLAP!
MONSTER RIDES BARGE TO WIN DISTRICT SPELLING BEE.
Lorem ipsum dolor sit amet, consectetur adipiscing elit.
Vestibulum tempor ullamcorper auctor. Aliquam erat
volutpat. Curabitur eget feugiat sapien. Suspendisse
MONSTER LOSES REGIONAL SPELLING BEE.
CAN'T SPELL RAIN. OR SPAIN.
Lorem ipsum dolor sit amet, consectetur adipiscing elit.
Vestibulum tempor ullamcorper auctor. Aliquam erat

MONSTER MONEYMAKER

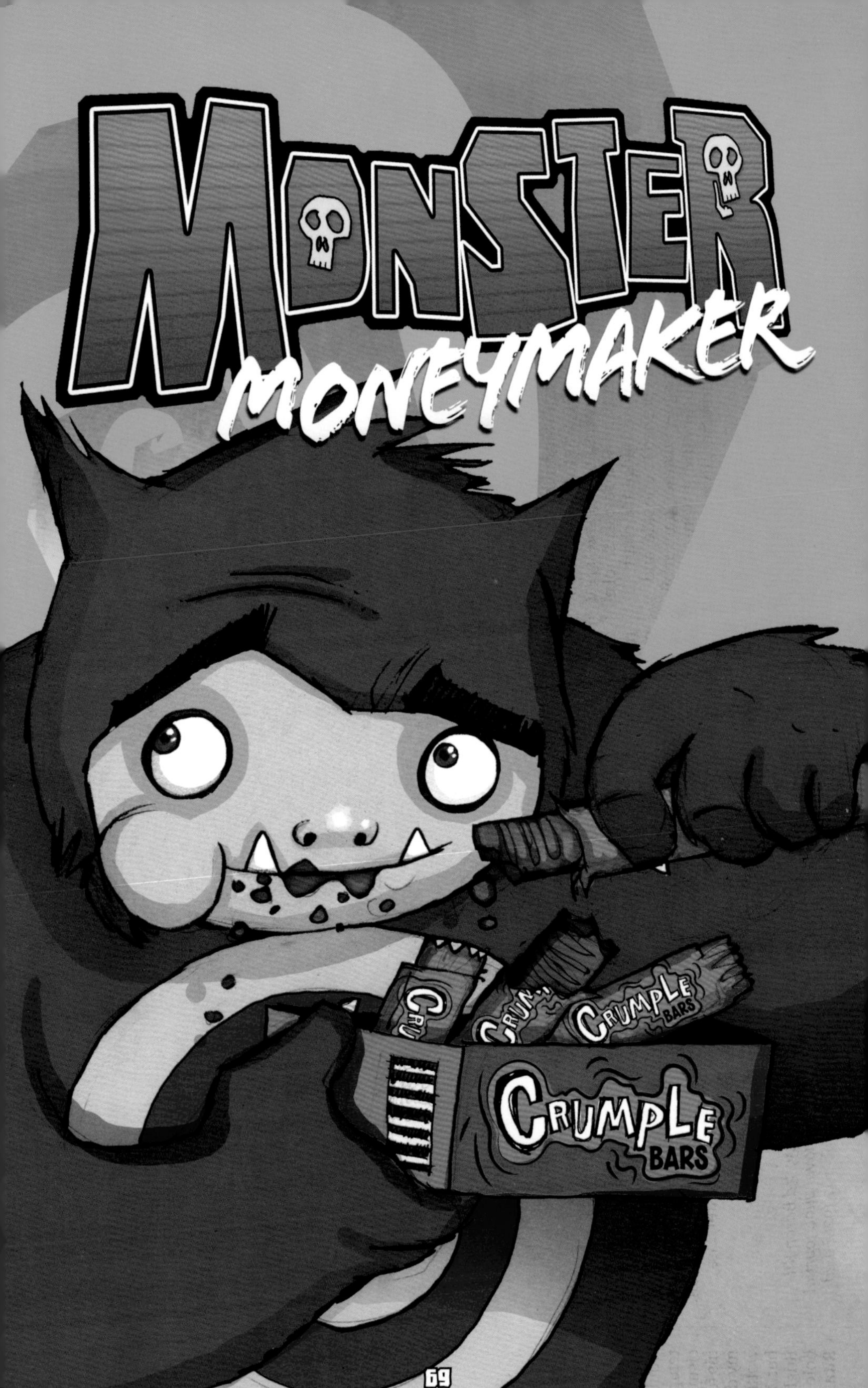
CRUMPLE BARS
CRUMPLE BARS

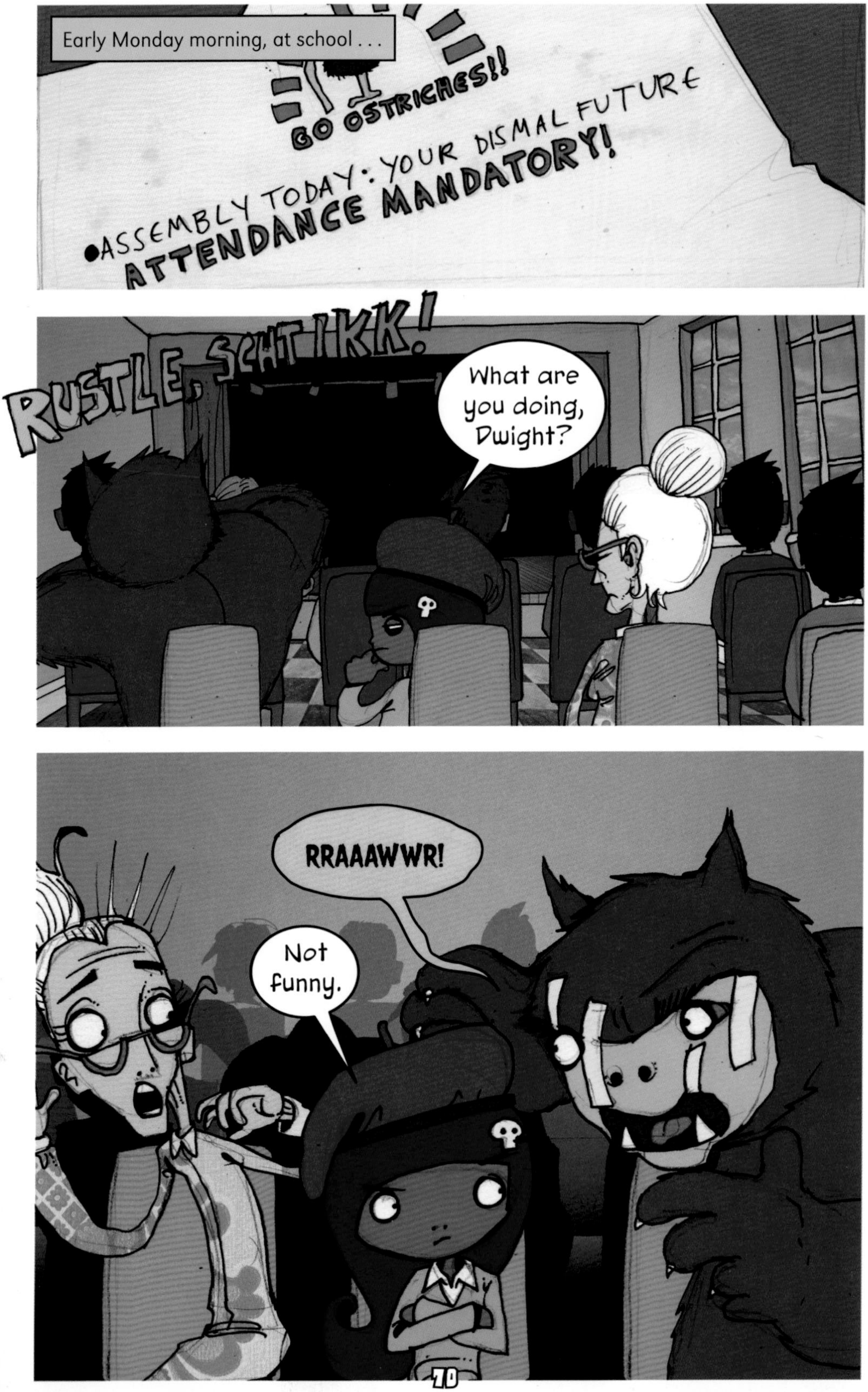
Early Monday morning, at school . . .
GO OSTRICHES!!
•ASSEMBLY TODAY: YOUR DISMAL FUTURE
ATTENDANCE MANDATORY!
RUSTLE, SCHTIKK!
What are you doing, Dwight?
RRAAAWWR!
Not funny.

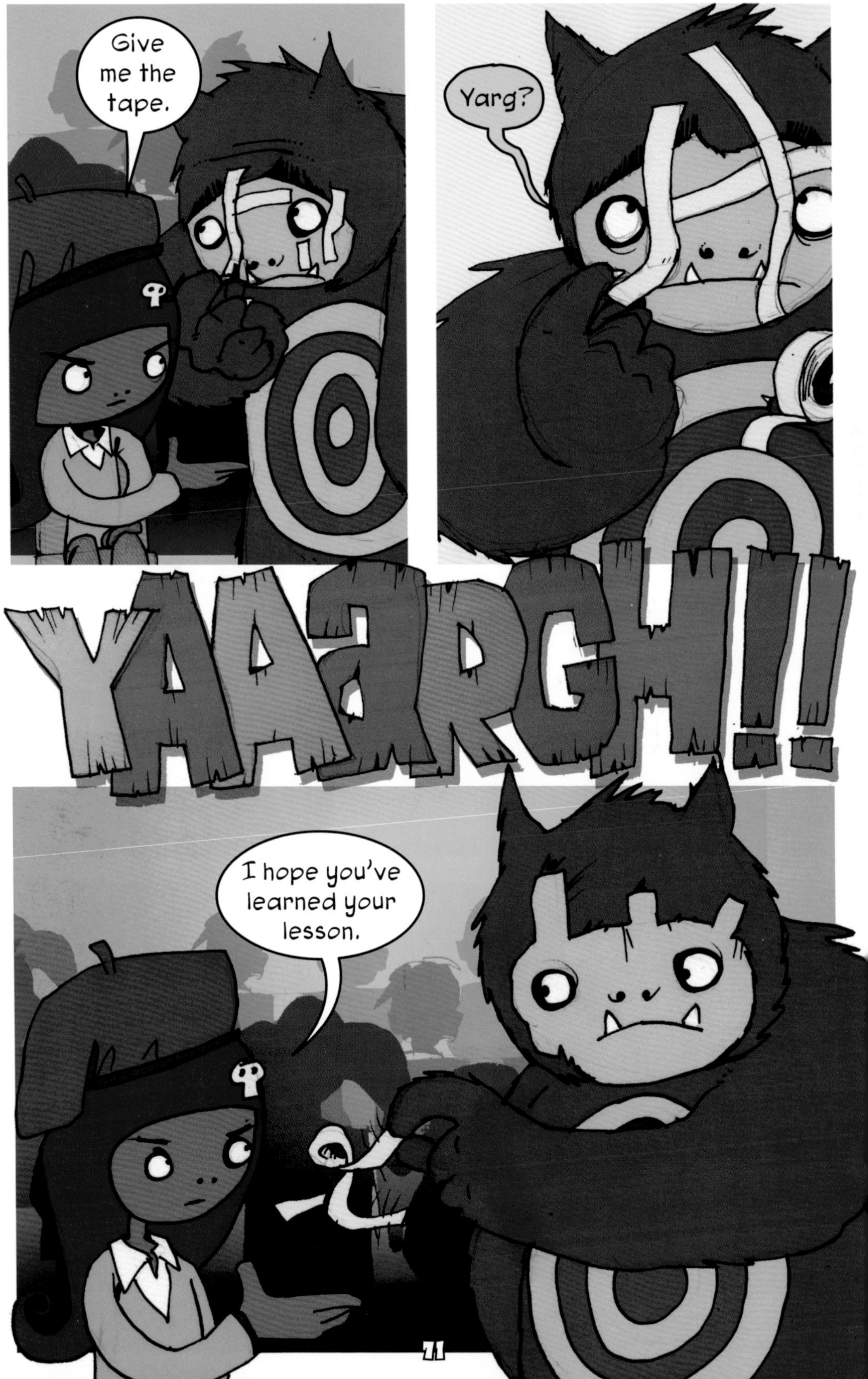
Give me the tape.
Yarg?
YAARGH!!
I hope you've learned your lesson.

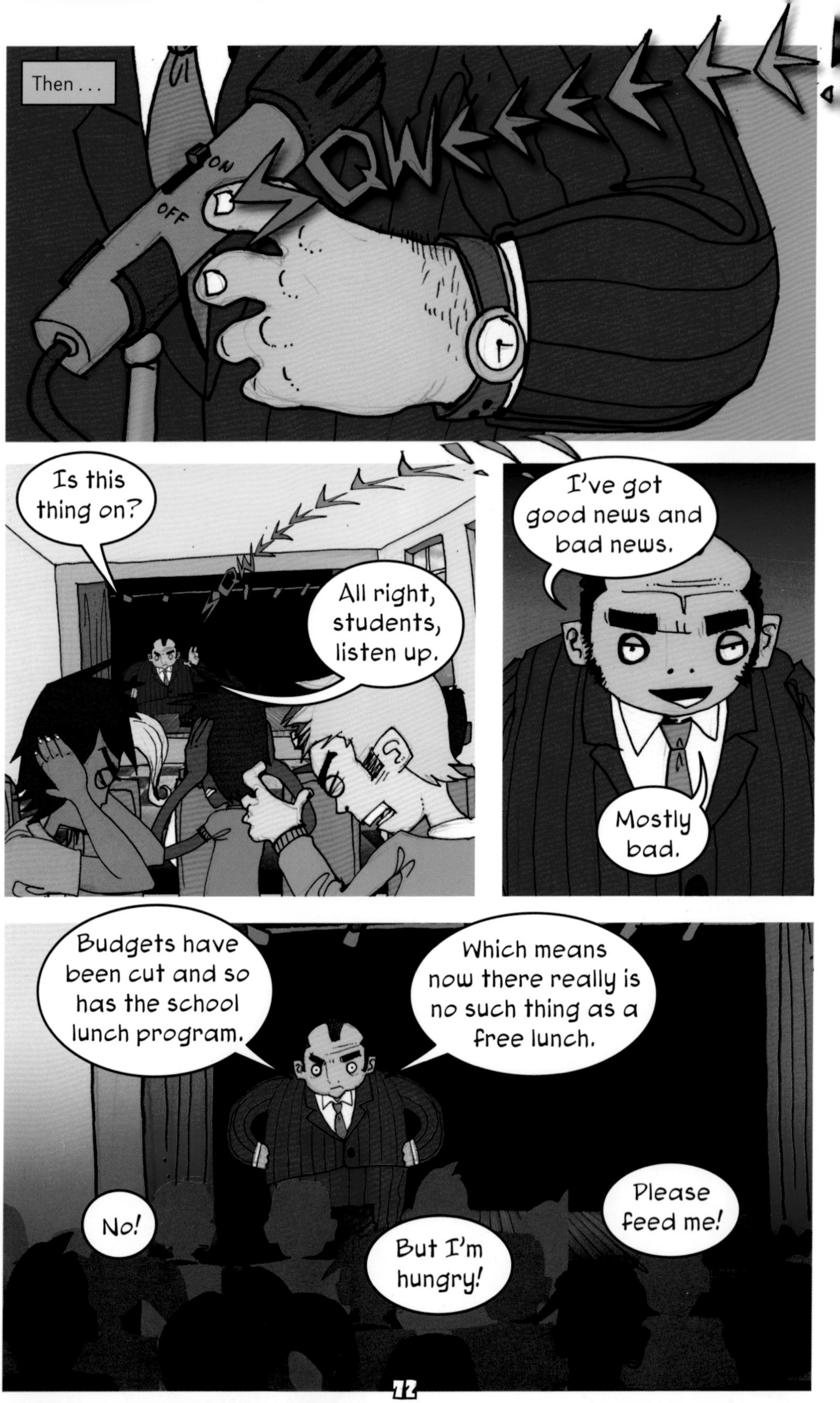
Then . . .
ON
OFF
Is this thing on?
All right, students, listen up.
I've got good news and bad news.
Mostly bad.
Budgets have been cut and so has the school lunch program.
Which means now there really is no such thing as a free lunch.
No!
But I'm hungry!
Please feed me!

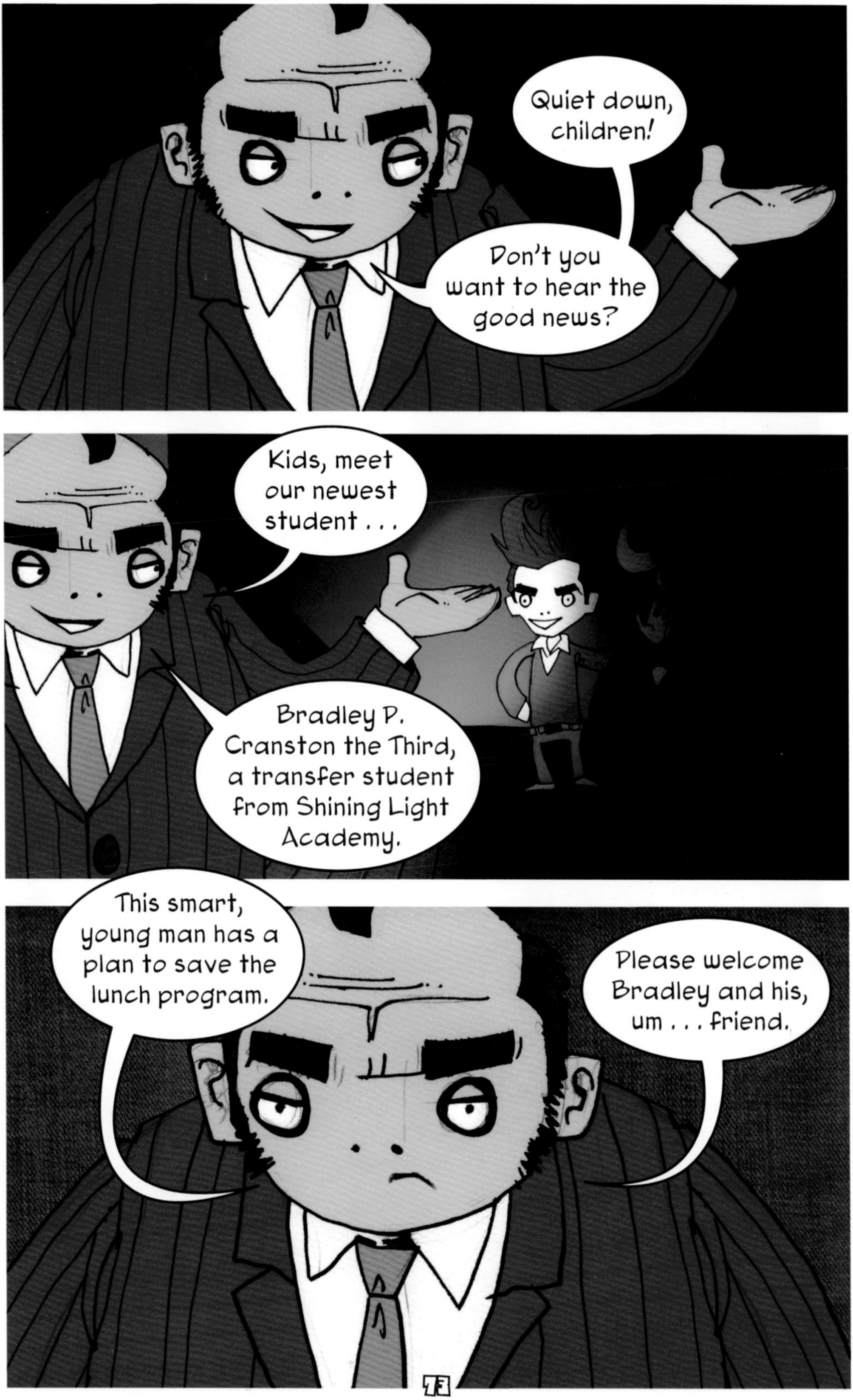
Quiet down, children!
Don't you want to hear the good news?
Kids, meet our newest student . . .
Bradley P. Cranston the Third, a transfer student from Shining Light Academy.
This smart, young man has a plan to save the lunch program.
Please welcome Bradley and his, um . . . friend.

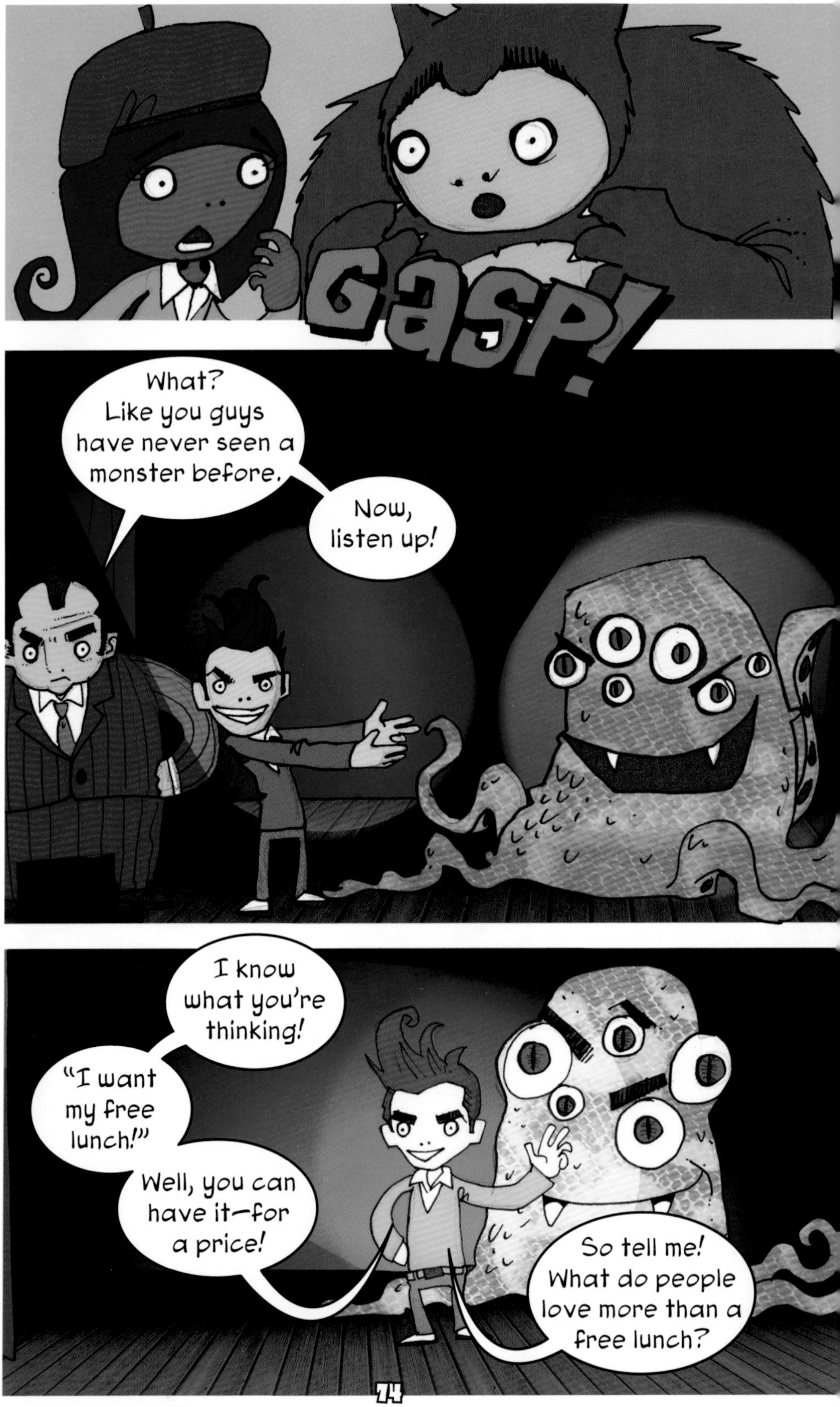
GASP!
What? Like you guys have never seen a monster before.
Now, listen up!
I know what you're thinking!
"I want my free lunch!"
Well, you can have it—for a price!
So tell me! What do people love more than a free lunch?

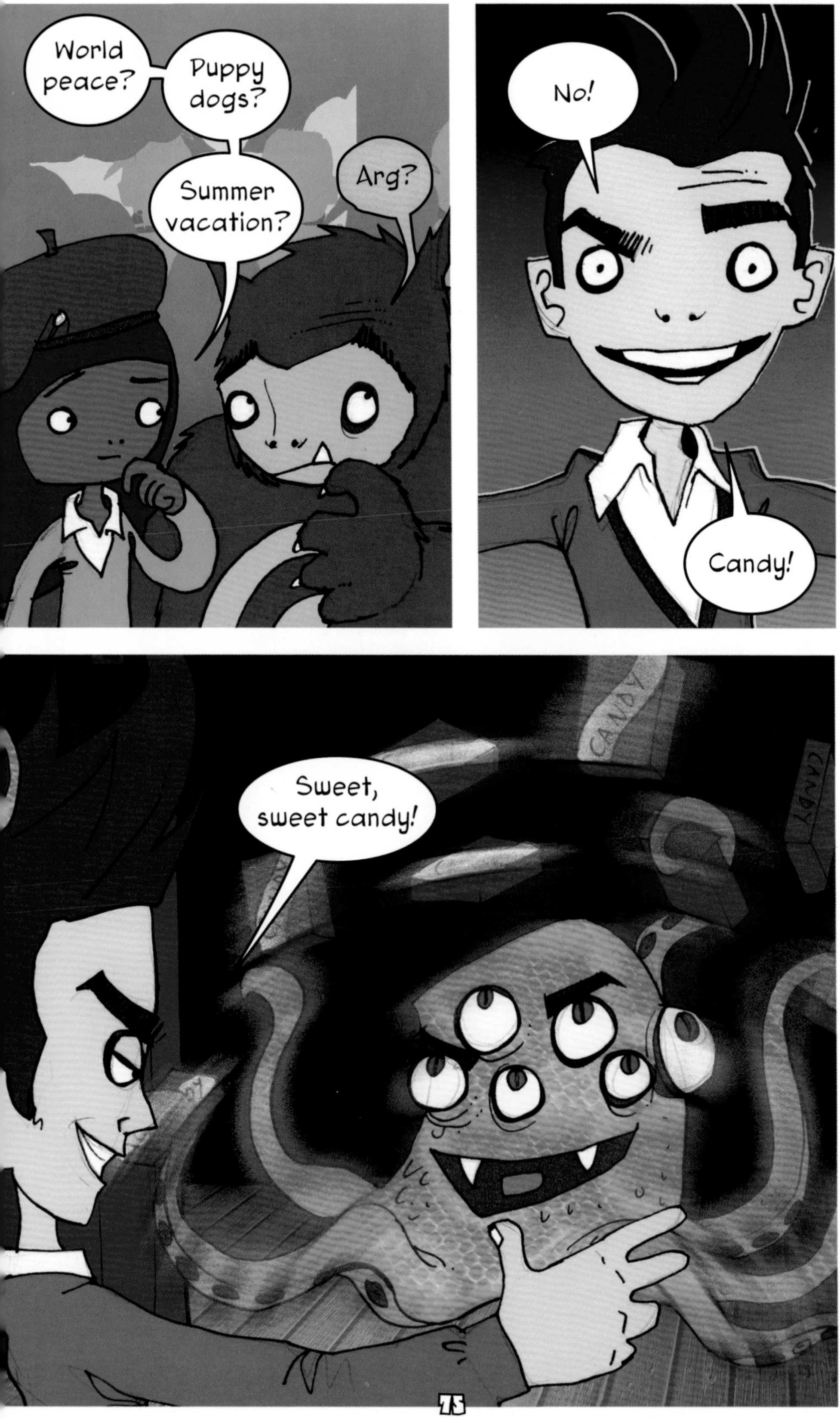
World peace?
Puppy dogs?
Summer vacation?
Arg?
No!
Candy!
Sweet, sweet candy!
CANDY
CANDY

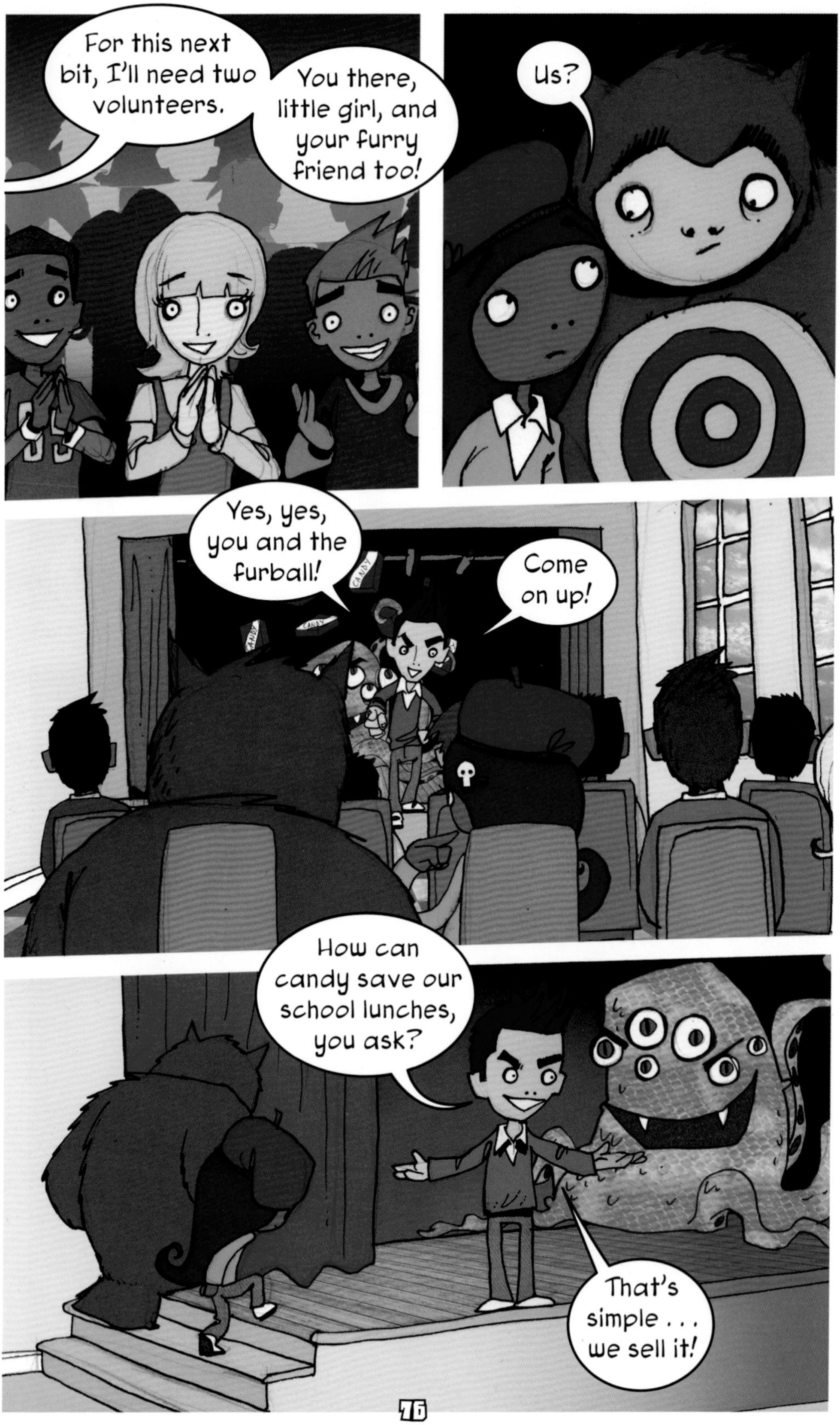
For this next bit, I'll need two volunteers.
You there, little girl, and your furry friend too!
Us?
Yes, yes, you and the furball!
CANDY
Come on up!
How can candy save our school lunches, you ask?
That's simple . . . we sell it!

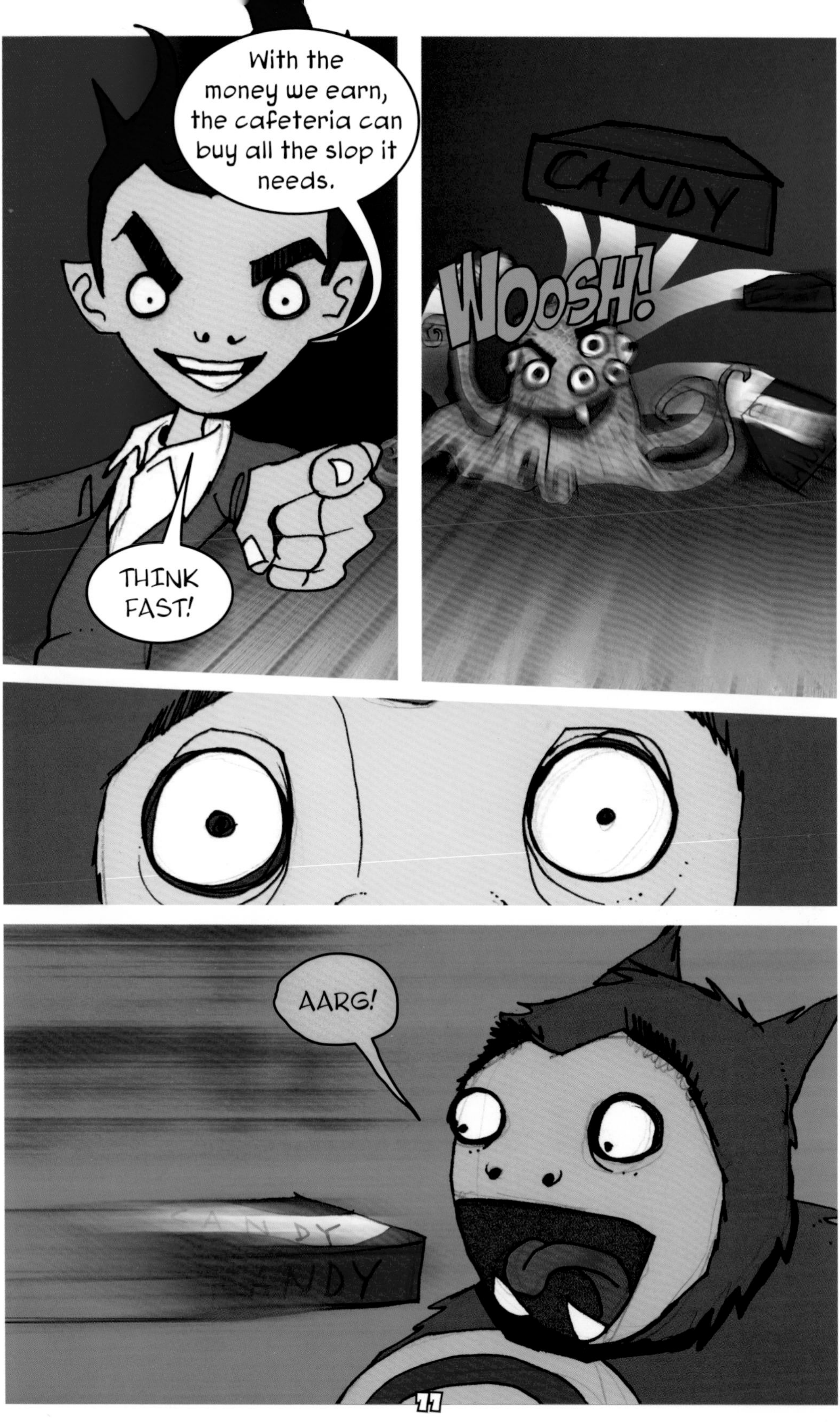

With the money we earn, the cafeteria can buy all the slop it needs.
THINK FAST!
CANDY
WOOSH!
AARG!
CANDY

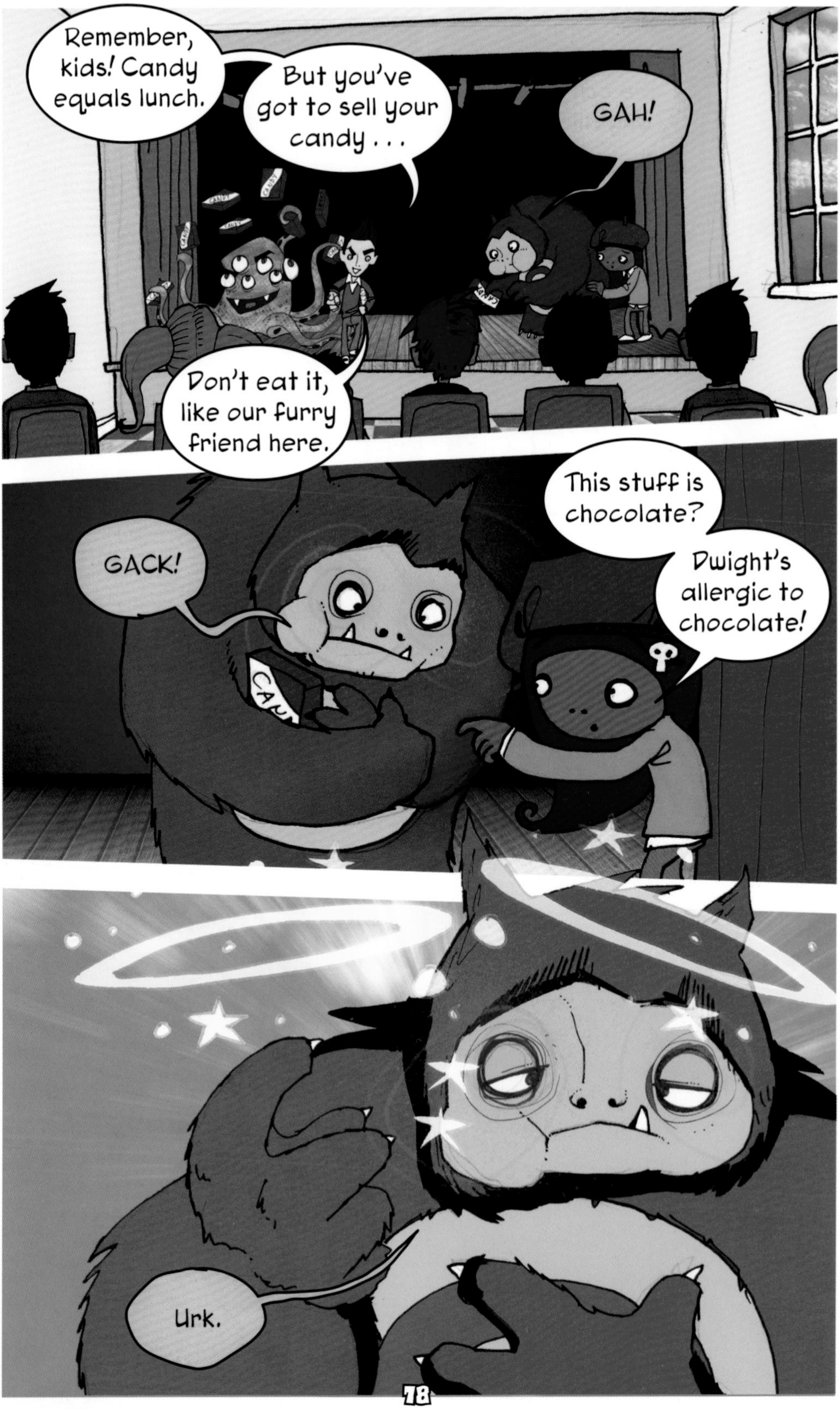
Remember, kids! Candy equals lunch.
But you've got to sell your candy . . .
GAH!
Don't eat it, like our furry friend here.
GACK!
This stuff is chocolate?
Dwight's allergic to chocolate!
Urk.

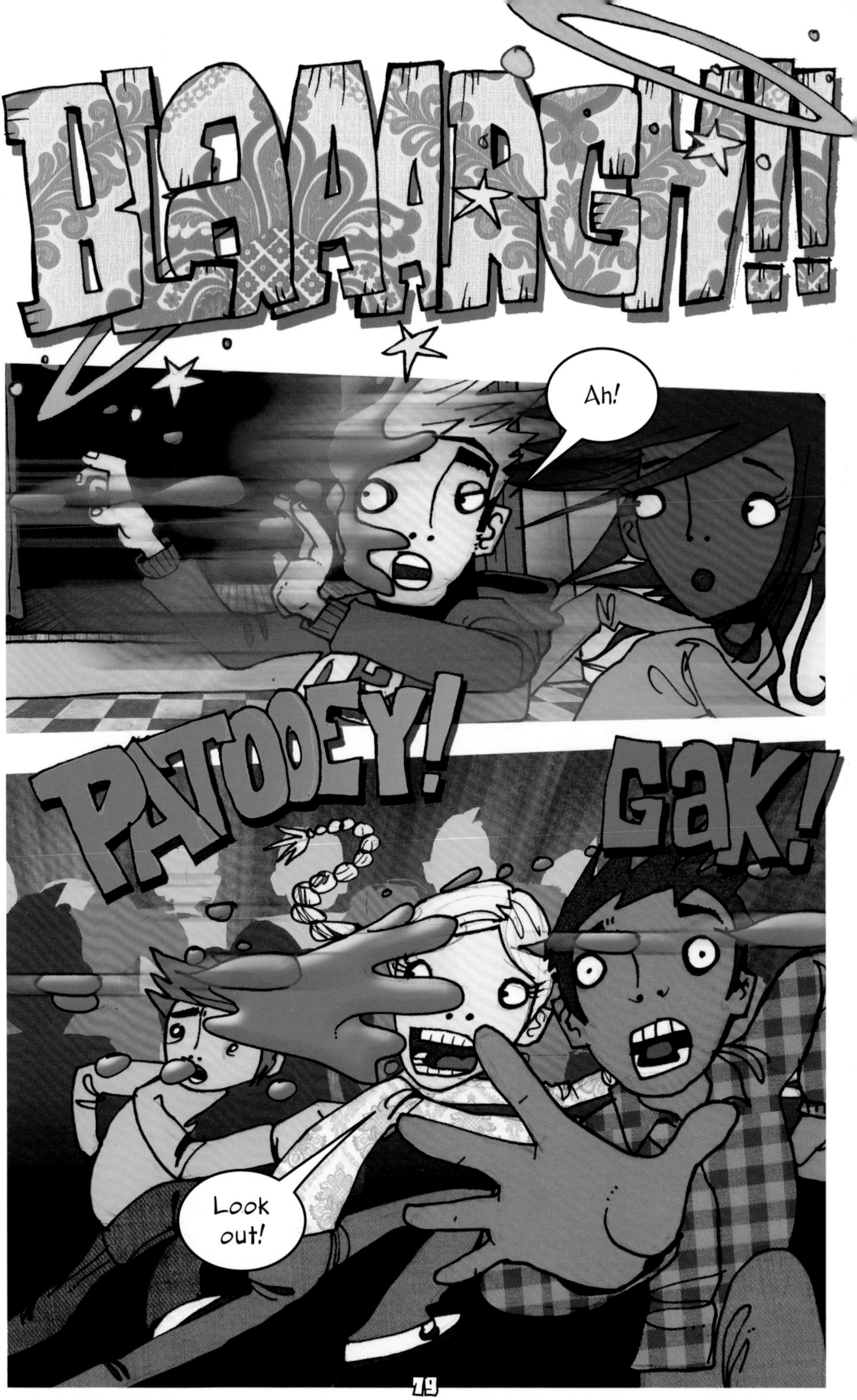
BLAAARGH!!
Ah!
PATOOEY!
GAK!
Look out!

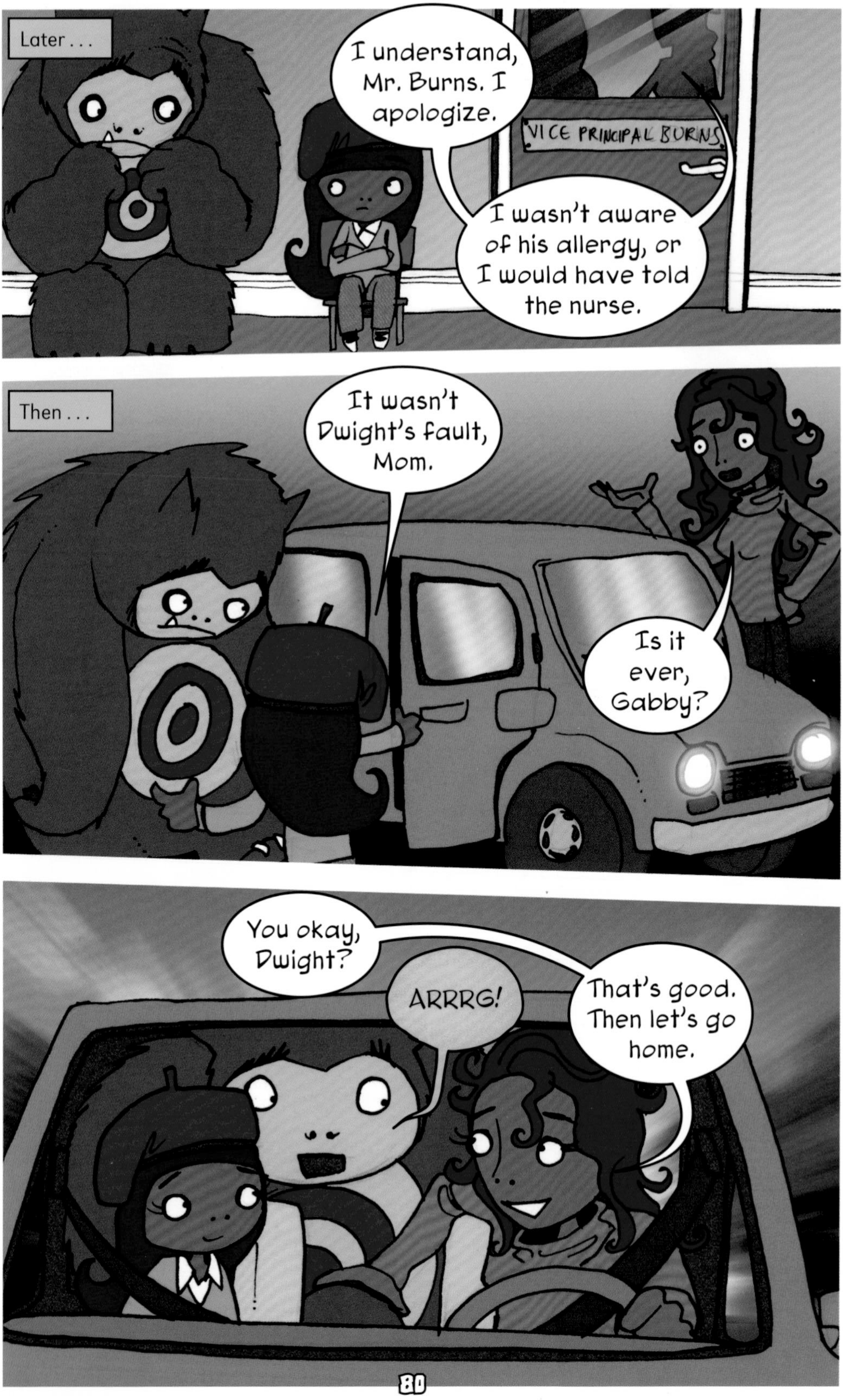
Later . . .
I understand, Mr. Burns. I apologize.
VICE PRINCIPAL BURNS
I wasn't aware of his allergy, or I would have told the nurse.
Then . . .
It wasn't Dwight's fault, Mom.
Is it ever, Gabby?
You okay, Dwight?
ARRRG!
That's good. Then let's go home.

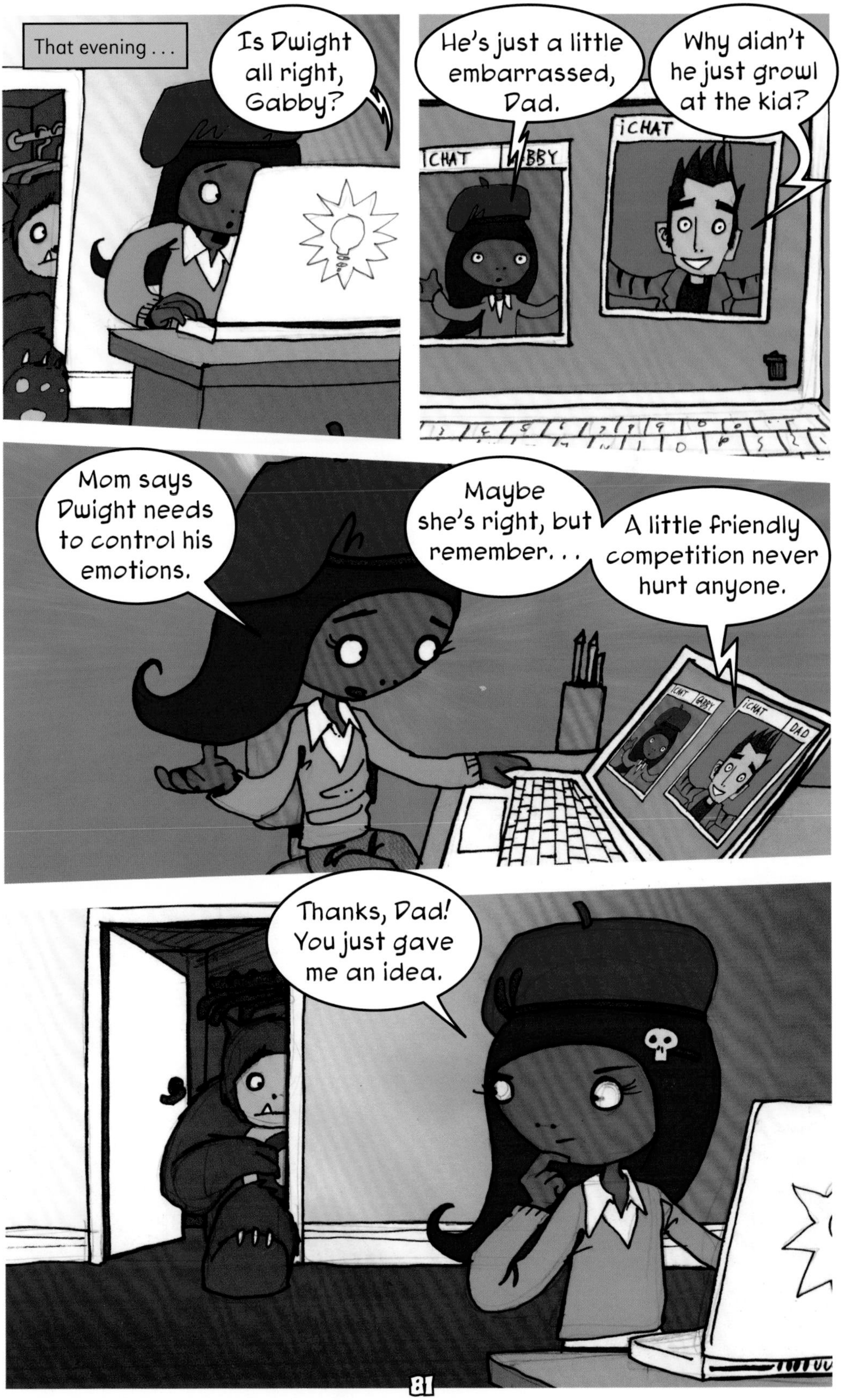
That evening . . .
Is Dwight all right, Gabby?
He's just a little embarrassed, Dad.
Why didn't he just growl at the kid?
iCHAT
Mom says Dwight needs to control his emotions.
Maybe she's right, but remember. . .
A little friendly competition never hurt anyone.
Thanks, Dad! You just gave me an idea.

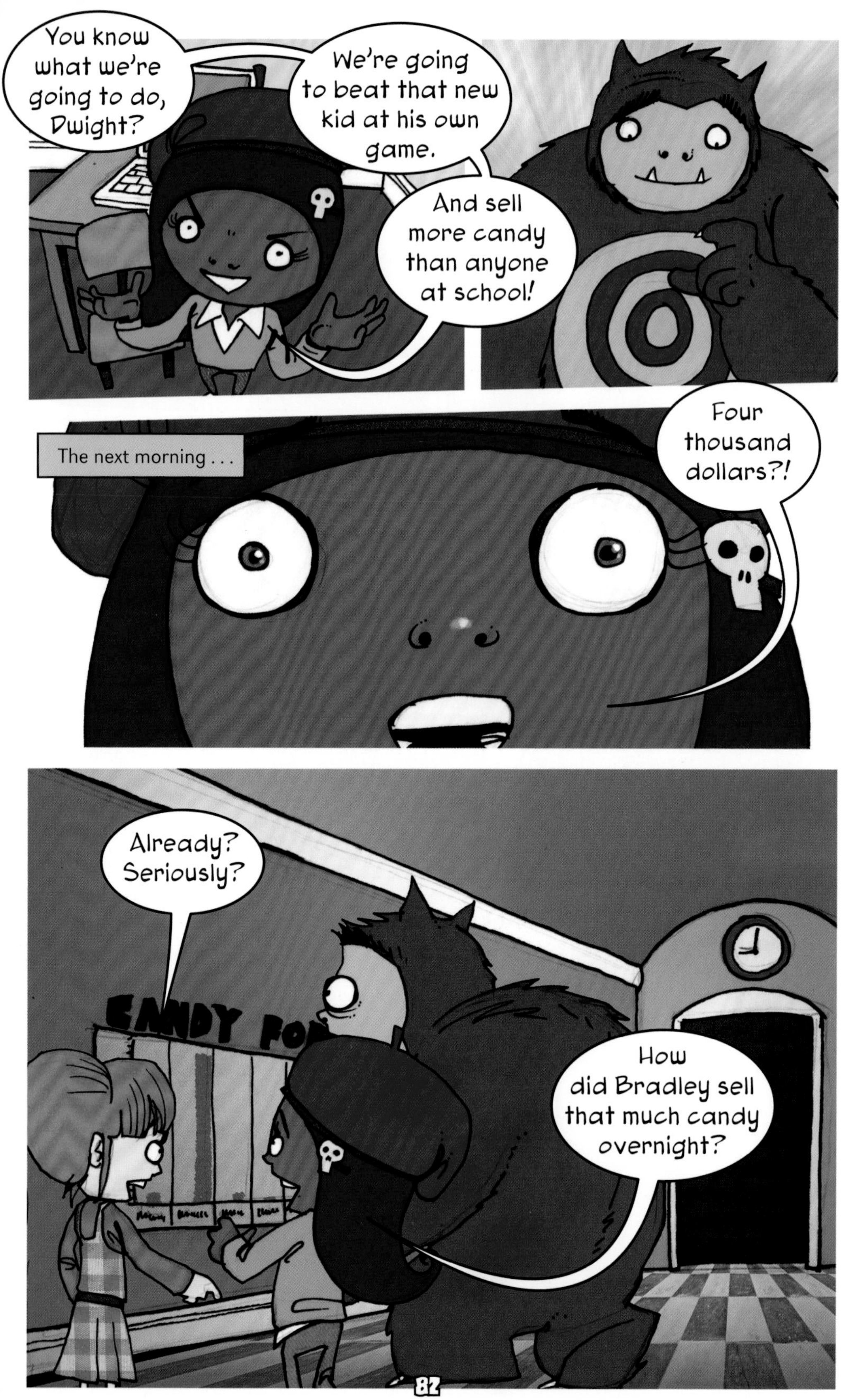
You know what we're going to do, Dwight?
We're going to beat that new kid at his own game.
And sell more candy than anyone at school!
The next morning . . .
Four thousand dollars?!
Already? Seriously?
How did Bradley sell that much candy overnight?

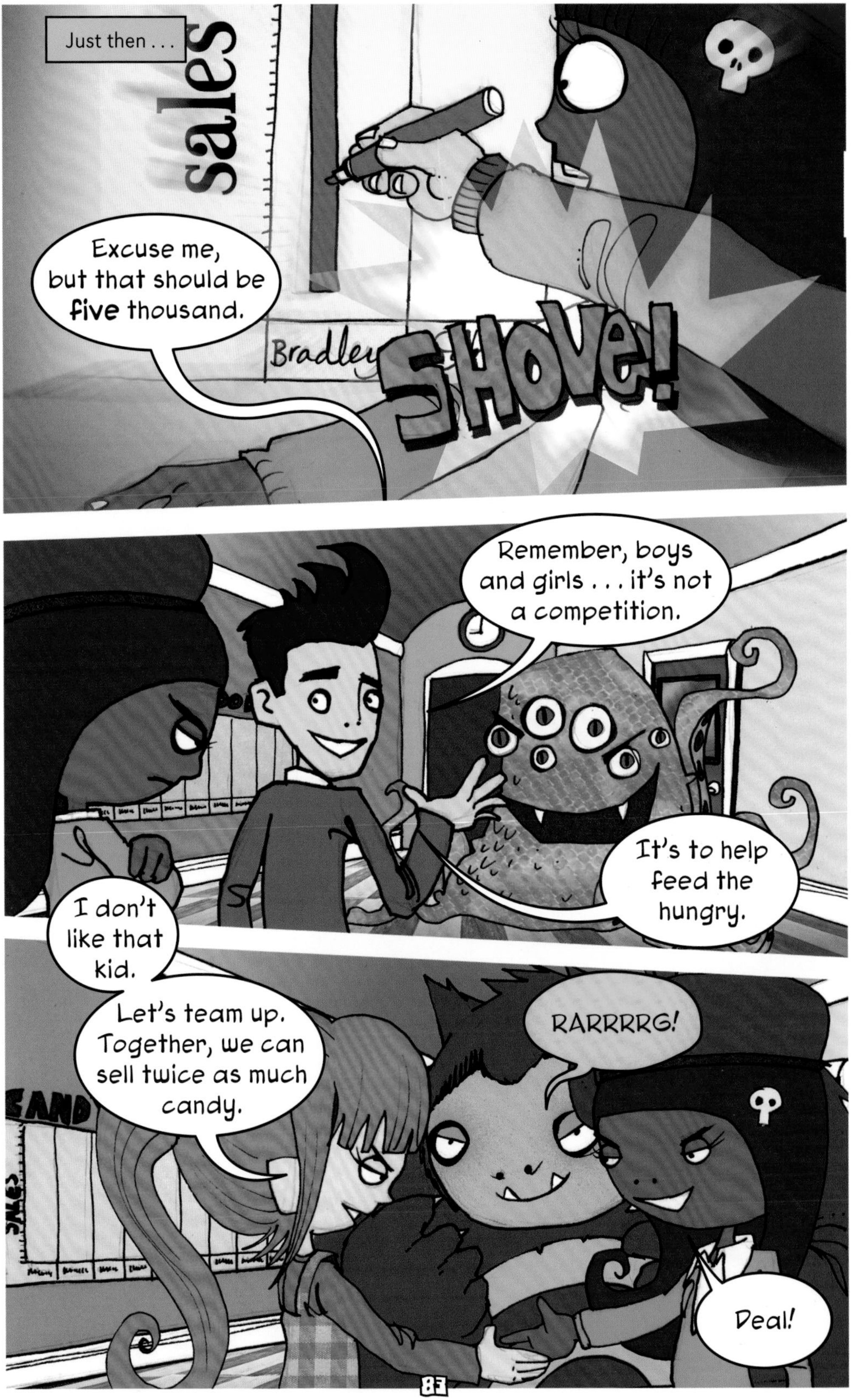
Just then . . .
sales
Excuse me, but that should be **five** thousand.
Bradley
SHOVE!
Remember, boys and girls . . . it's not a competition.
It's to help feed the hungry.
I don't like that kid.
Let's team up. Together, we can sell twice as much candy.
RARRRRG!
Deal!

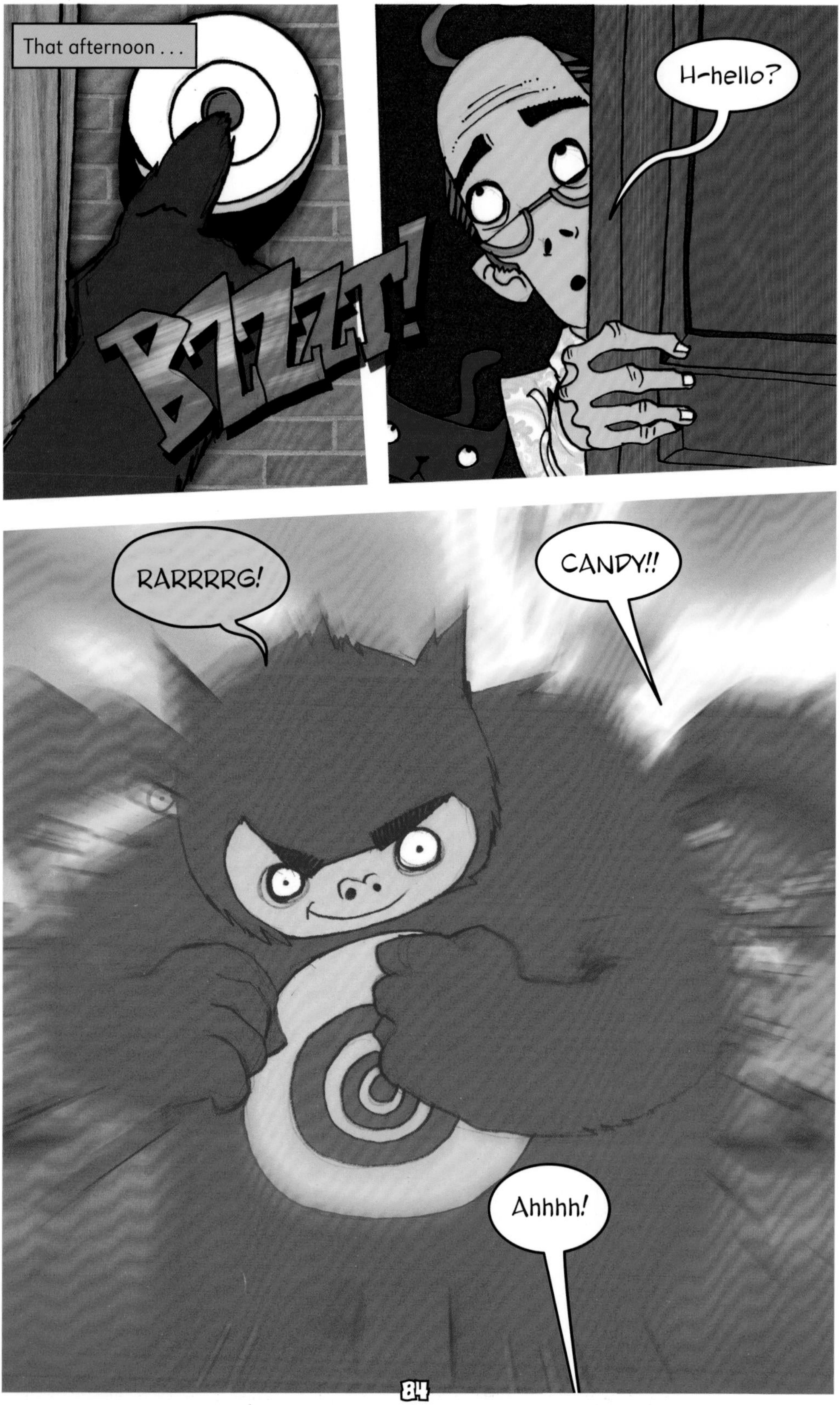
That afternoon . . .
BZZZZT!
H-hello?
RARRRRG!
CANDY!!
Ahhhh!

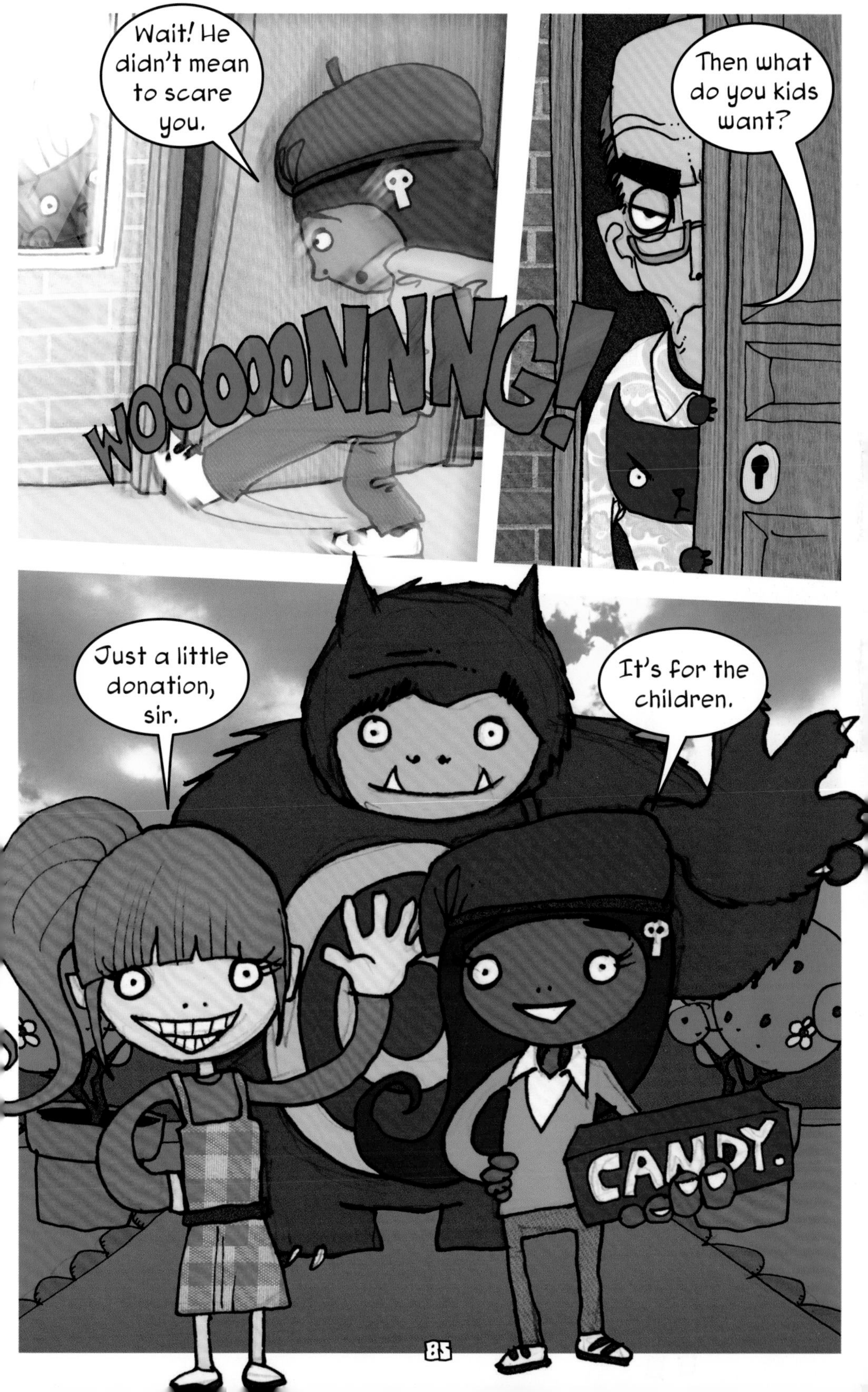
Wait! He didn't mean to scare you.
WOOOOOONNNG!
Then what do you kids want?
Just a little donation, sir.
It's for the children.
CANDY.

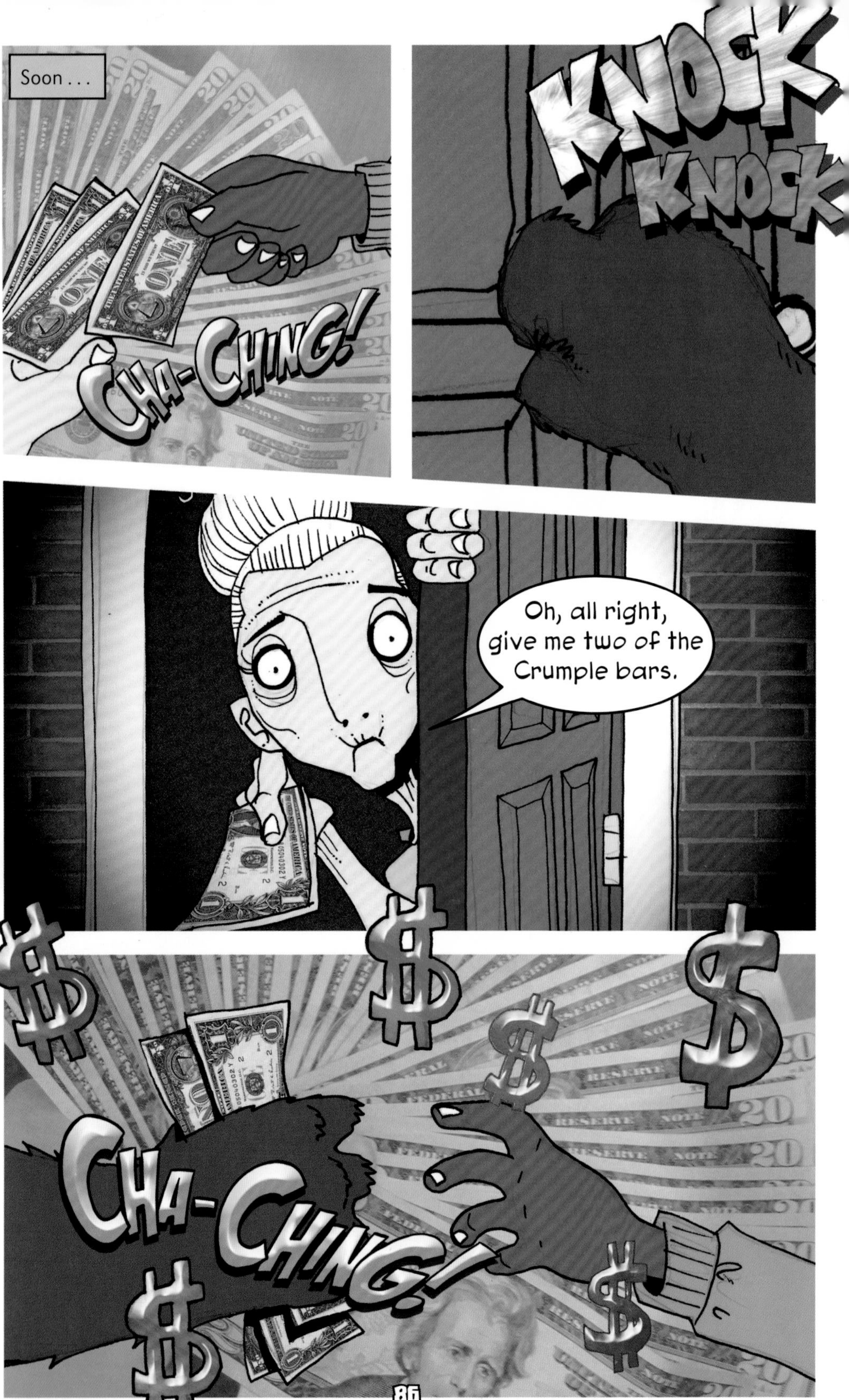

Soon . . .
CHA-CHING!
KNOCK
KNOCK
Oh, all right, give me two of the Crumple bars.
CHA-CHING!

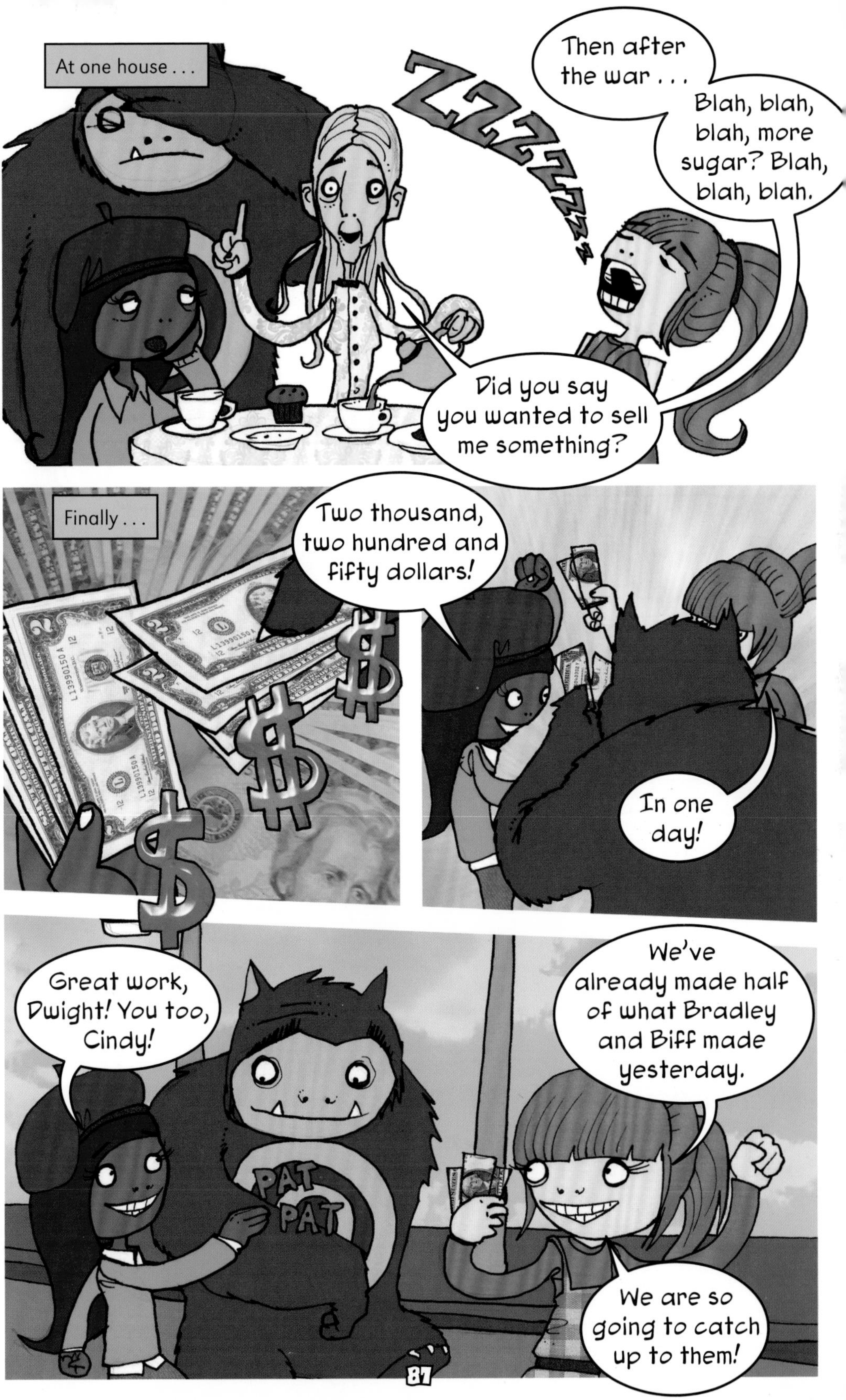
At one house . . .
Then after the war . . .
ZZZZZZzz
Blah, blah, blah, more sugar? Blah, blah, blah.
Did you say you wanted to sell me something?
Finally . . .
Two thousand, two hundred and fifty dollars!
In one day!
Great work, Dwight! You too, Cindy!
We've already made half of what Bradley and Biff made yesterday.
PAT PAT
We are so going to catch up to them!

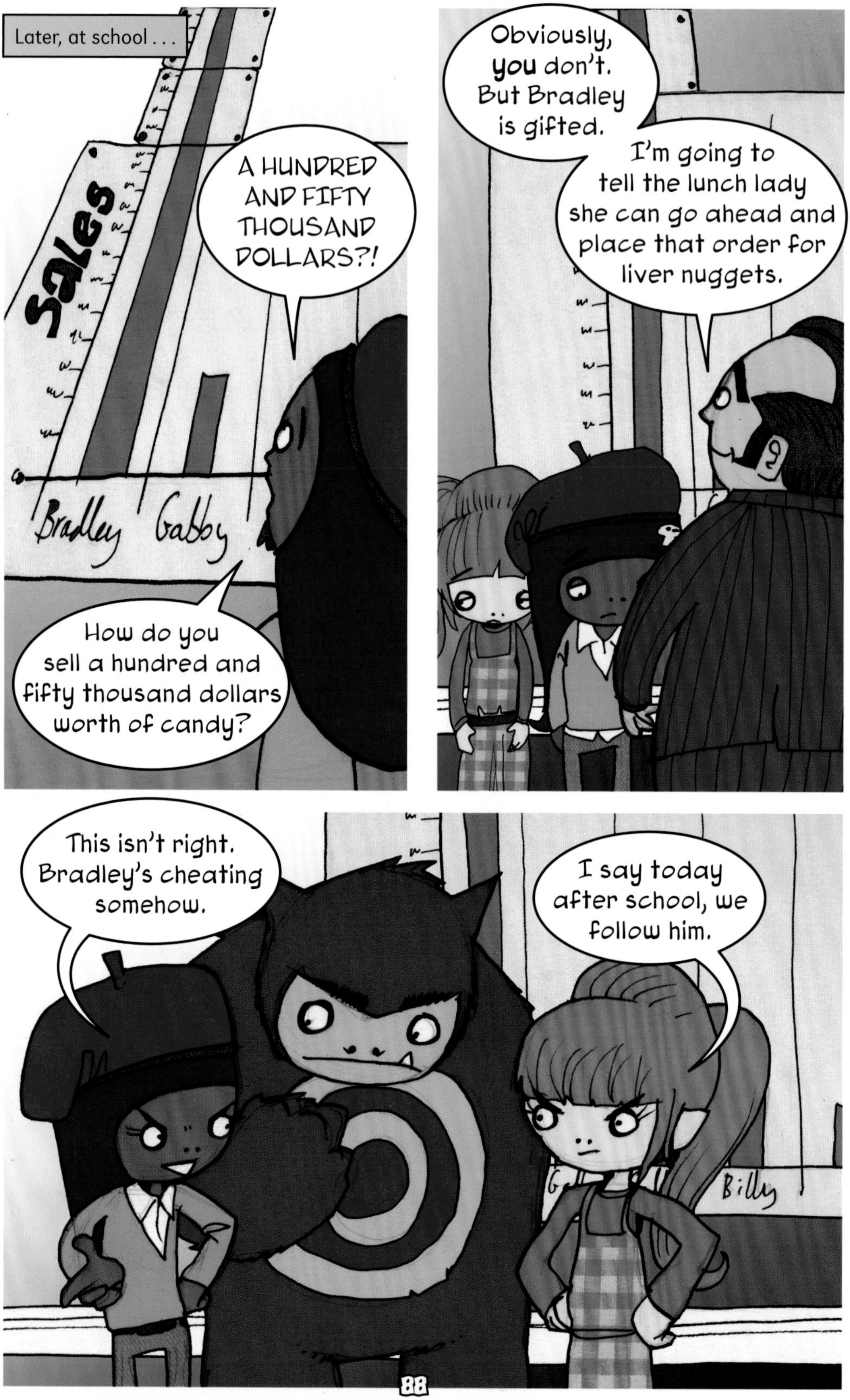
Later, at school . . .
Sales
Bradley
Gabby
A HUNDRED AND FIFTY THOUSAND DOLLARS?!
How do you sell a hundred and fifty thousand dollars worth of candy?
Obviously, **you** don't. But Bradley is gifted.
I'm going to tell the lunch lady she can go ahead and place that order for liver nuggets.
This isn't right. Bradley's cheating somehow.
I say today after school, we follow him.
Billy

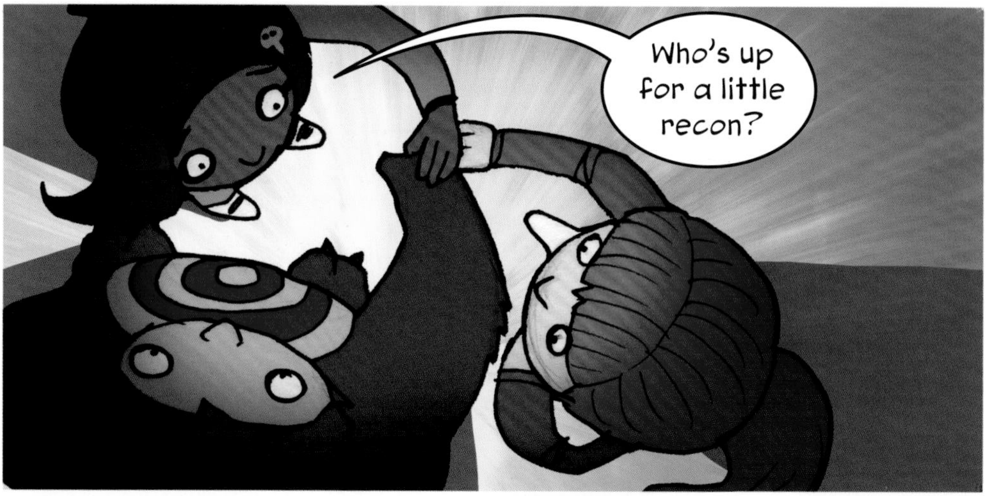
Who's up for a little recon?

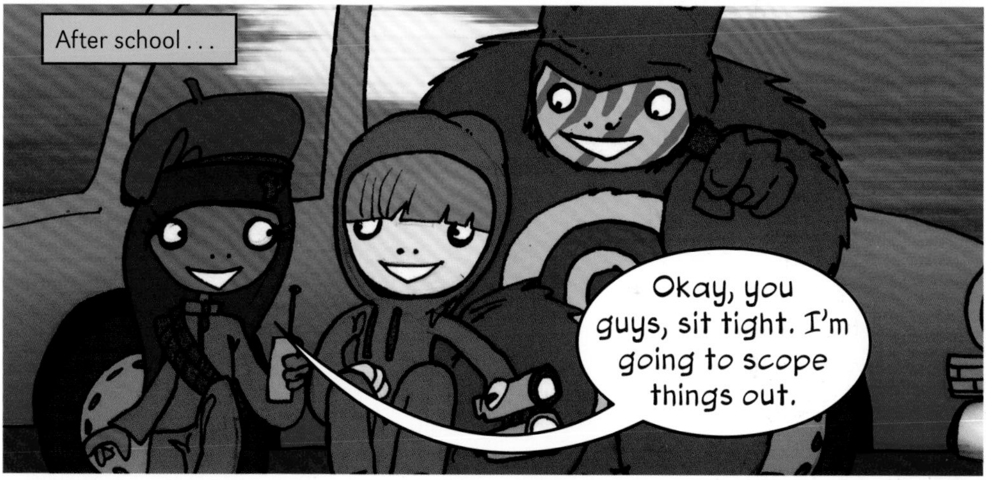
After school . . .
Okay, you guys, sit tight. I'm going to scope things out.

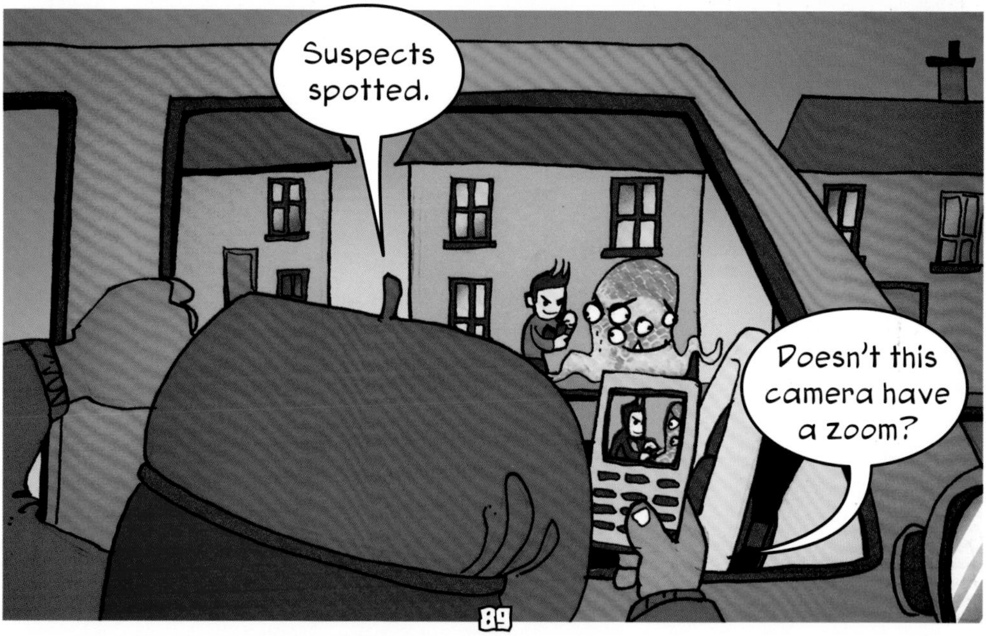
Suspects spotted.
Doesn't this camera have a zoom?

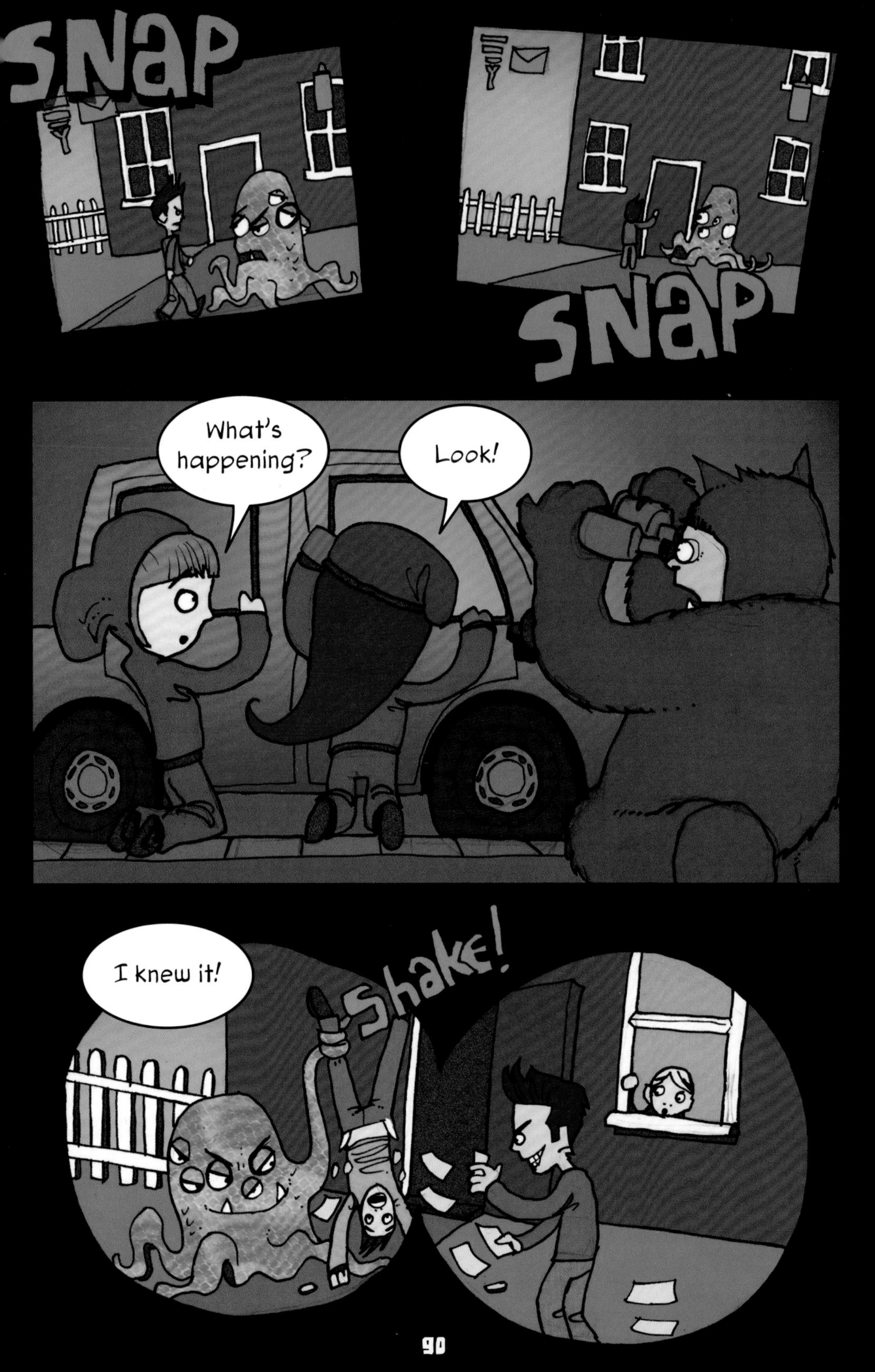
SNAP
SNAP
What's happening?
Look!
I knew it!
Shake!

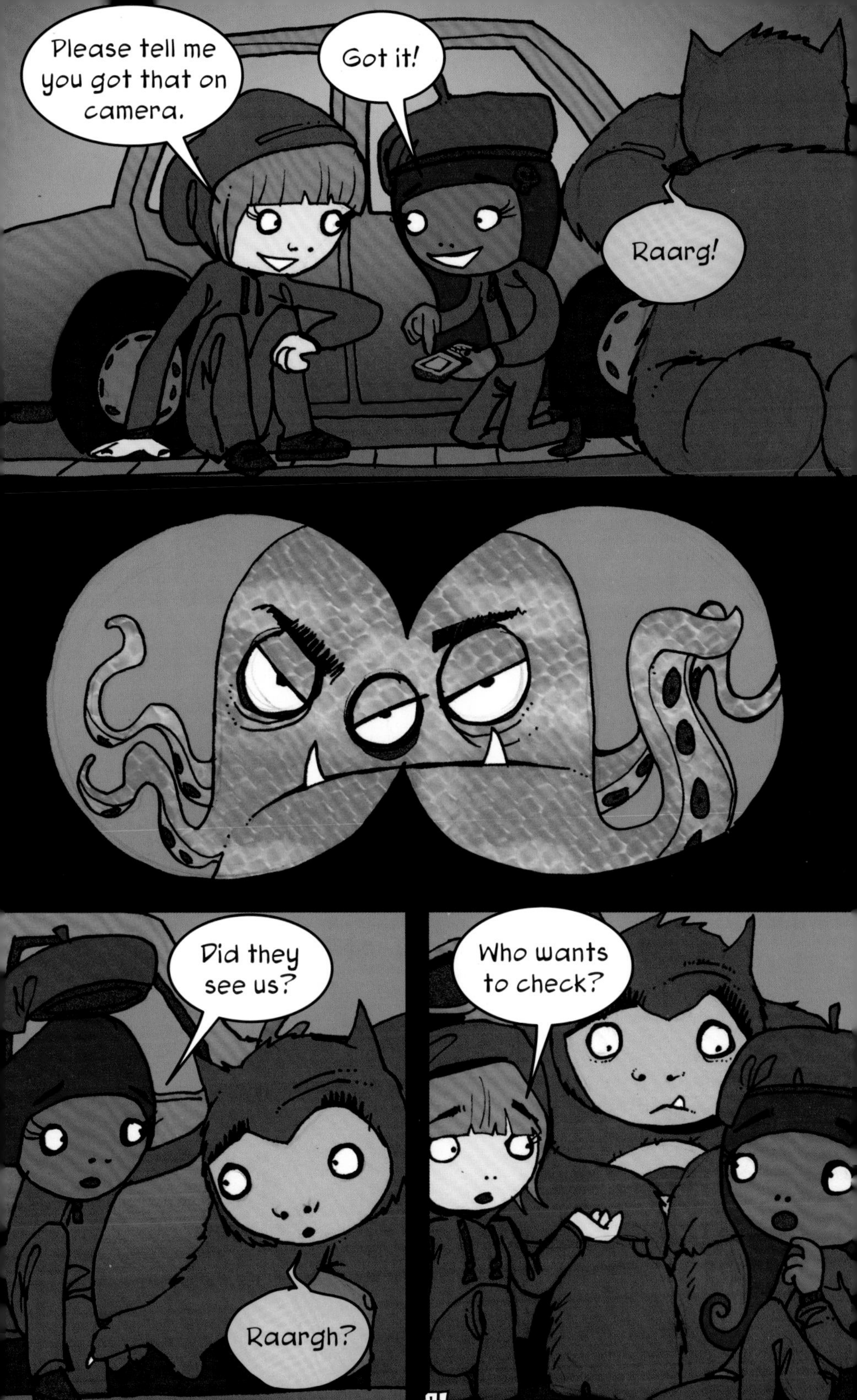
Please tell me you got that on camera.
Got it!
Raarg!
Did they see us?
Raargh?
Who wants to check?

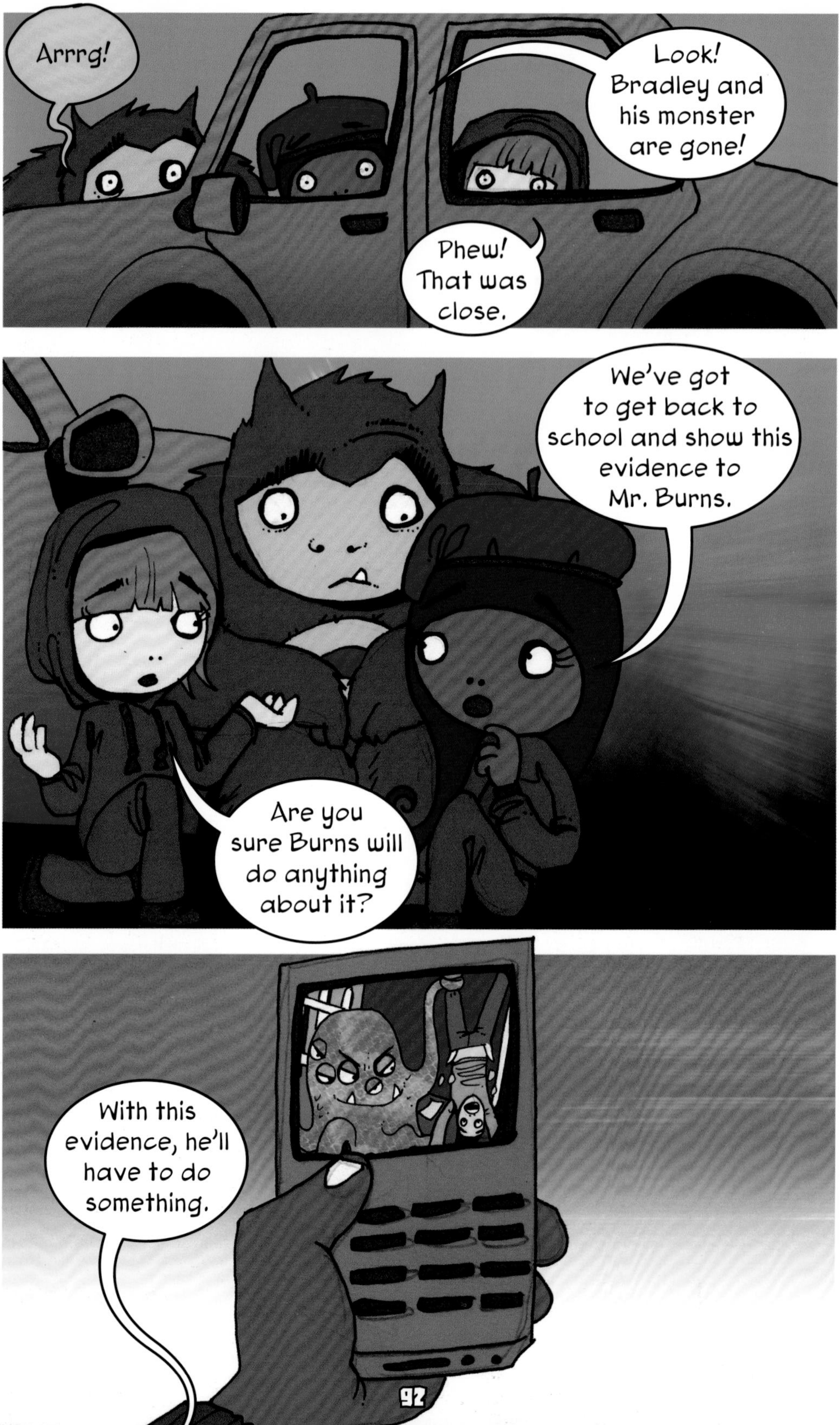
Arrrg!
Look! Bradley and his monster are gone!
Phew! That was close.
We've got to get back to school and show this evidence to Mr. Burns.
Are you sure Burns will do anything about it?
With this evidence, he'll have to do something.

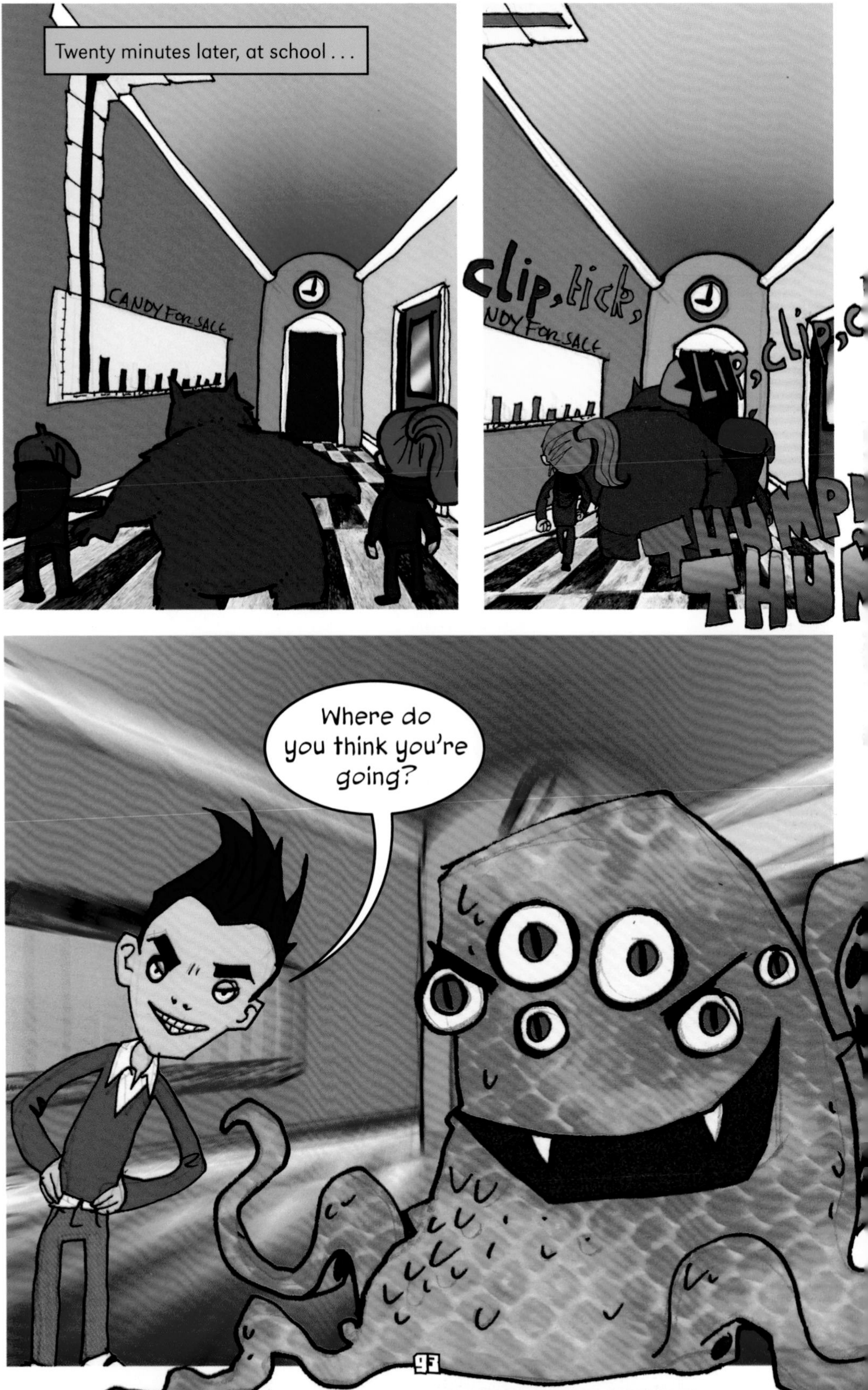

Twenty minutes later, at school . . .
CANDY FOR SALE
clip, tick,
Where do you think you're going?

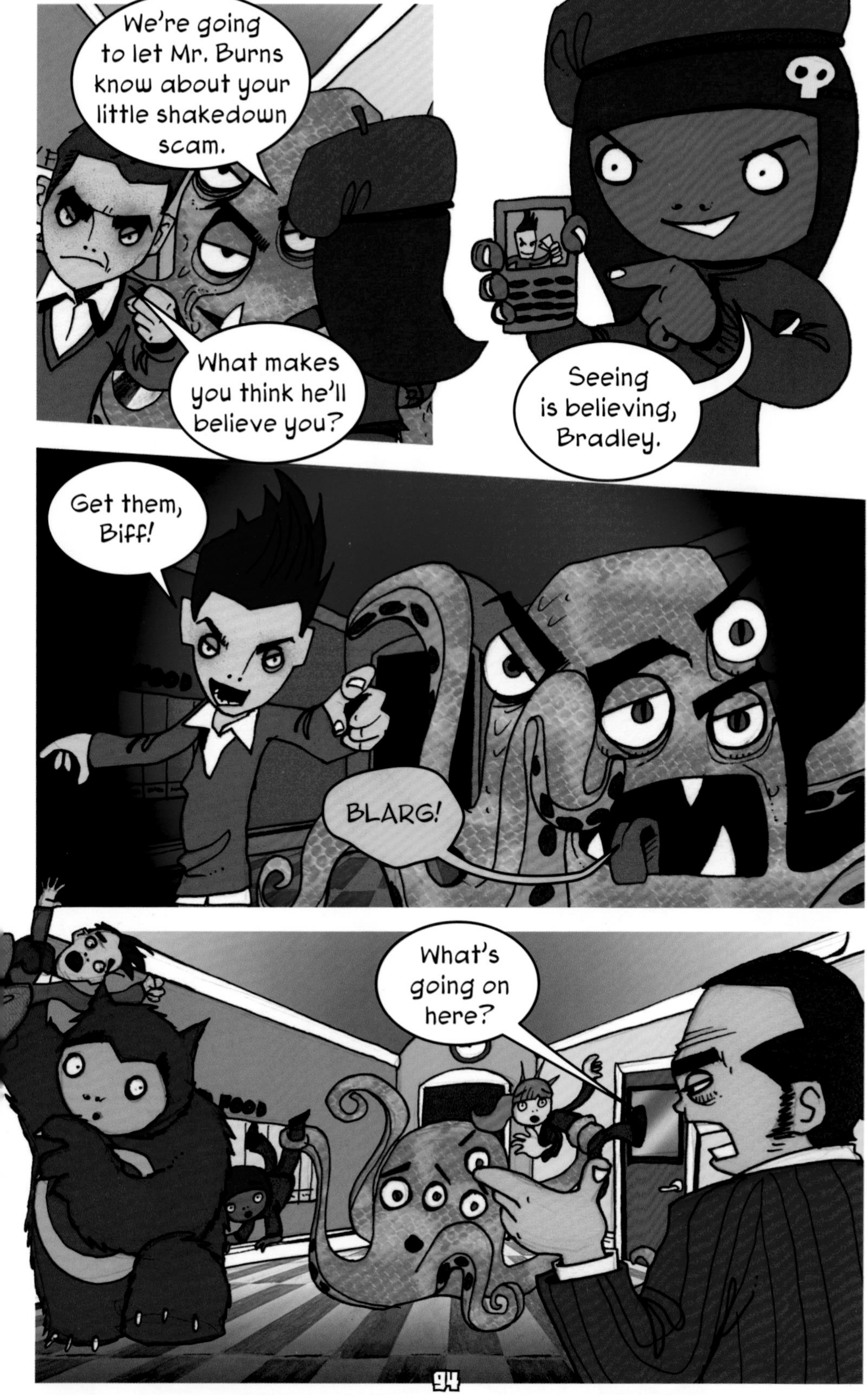
We're going to let Mr. Burns know about your little shakedown scam.
What makes you think he'll believe you?
Seeing is believing, Bradley.
Get them, Biff!
BLARG!
What's going on here?

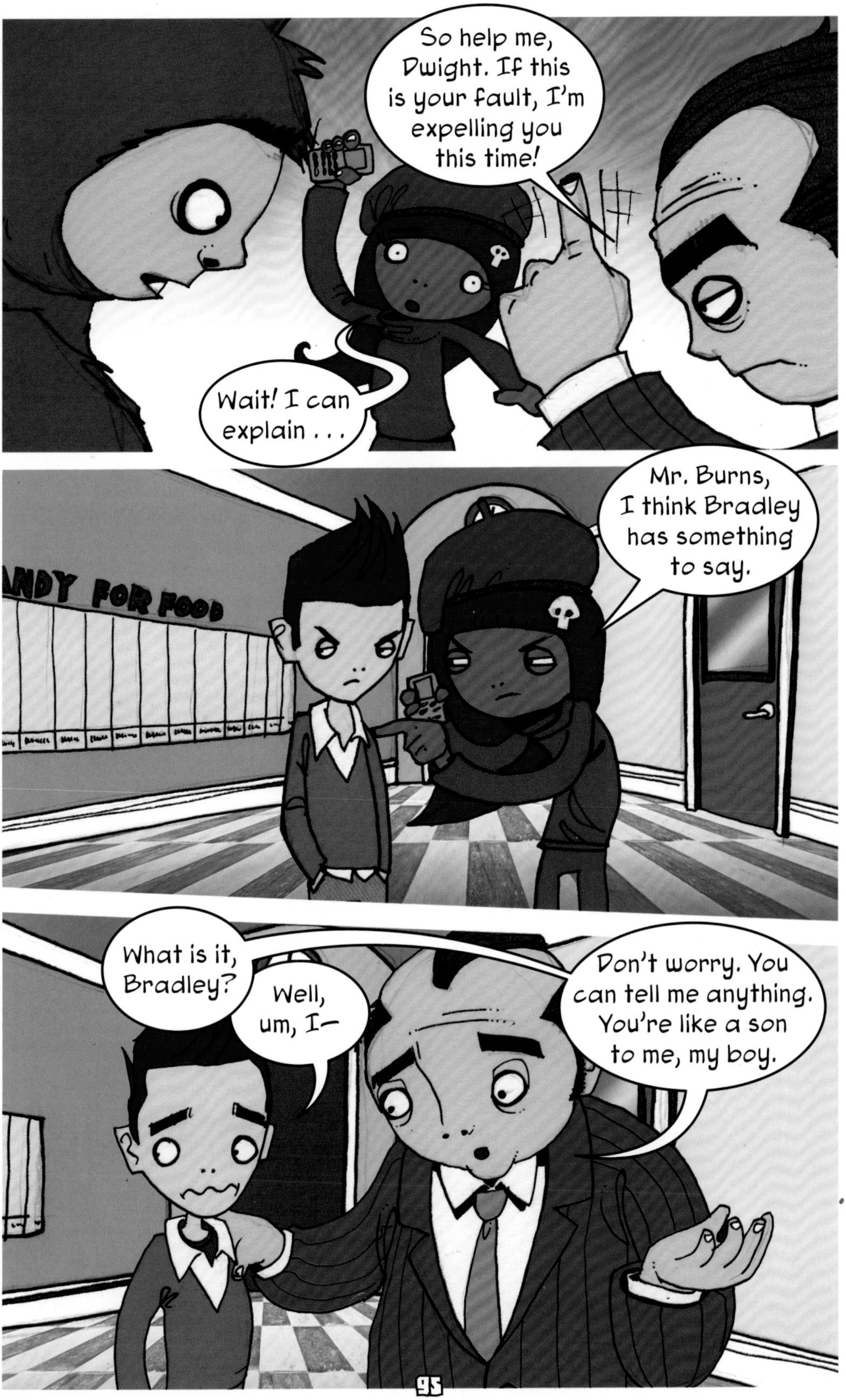
So help me, Dwight. If this is your fault, I'm expelling you this time!
Wait! I can explain . . .
ANDY FOR FOOD
Mr. Burns, I think Bradley has something to say.
What is it, Bradley?
Well, um, I—
Don't worry. You can tell me anything. You're like a son to me, my boy.

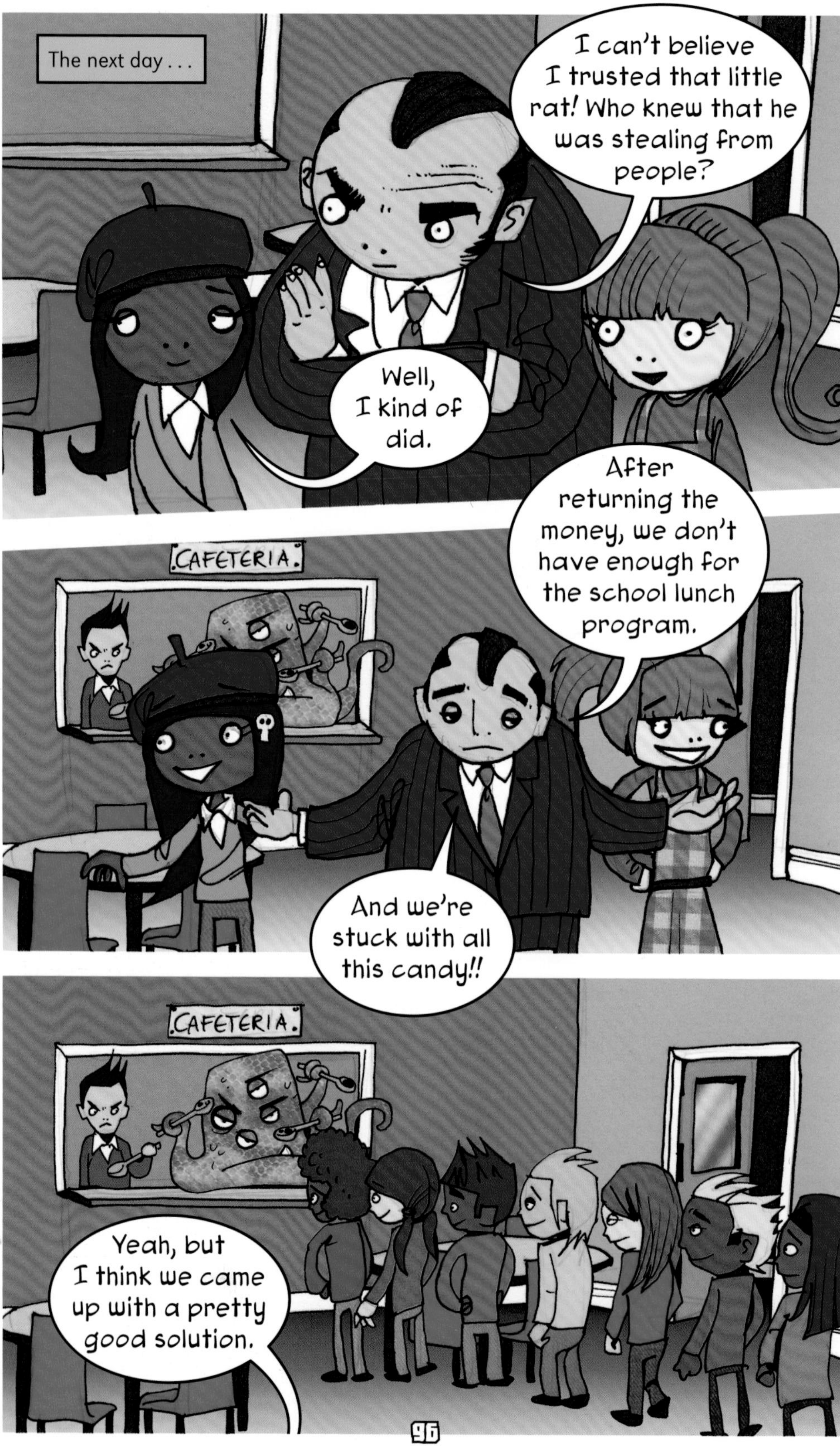
The next day . . .
I can't believe I trusted that little rat! Who knew that he was stealing from people?
Well, I kind of did.
After returning the money, we don't have enough for the school lunch program.
CAFETERIA
And we're stuck with all this candy!!
CAFETERIA
Yeah, but I think we came up with a pretty good solution.

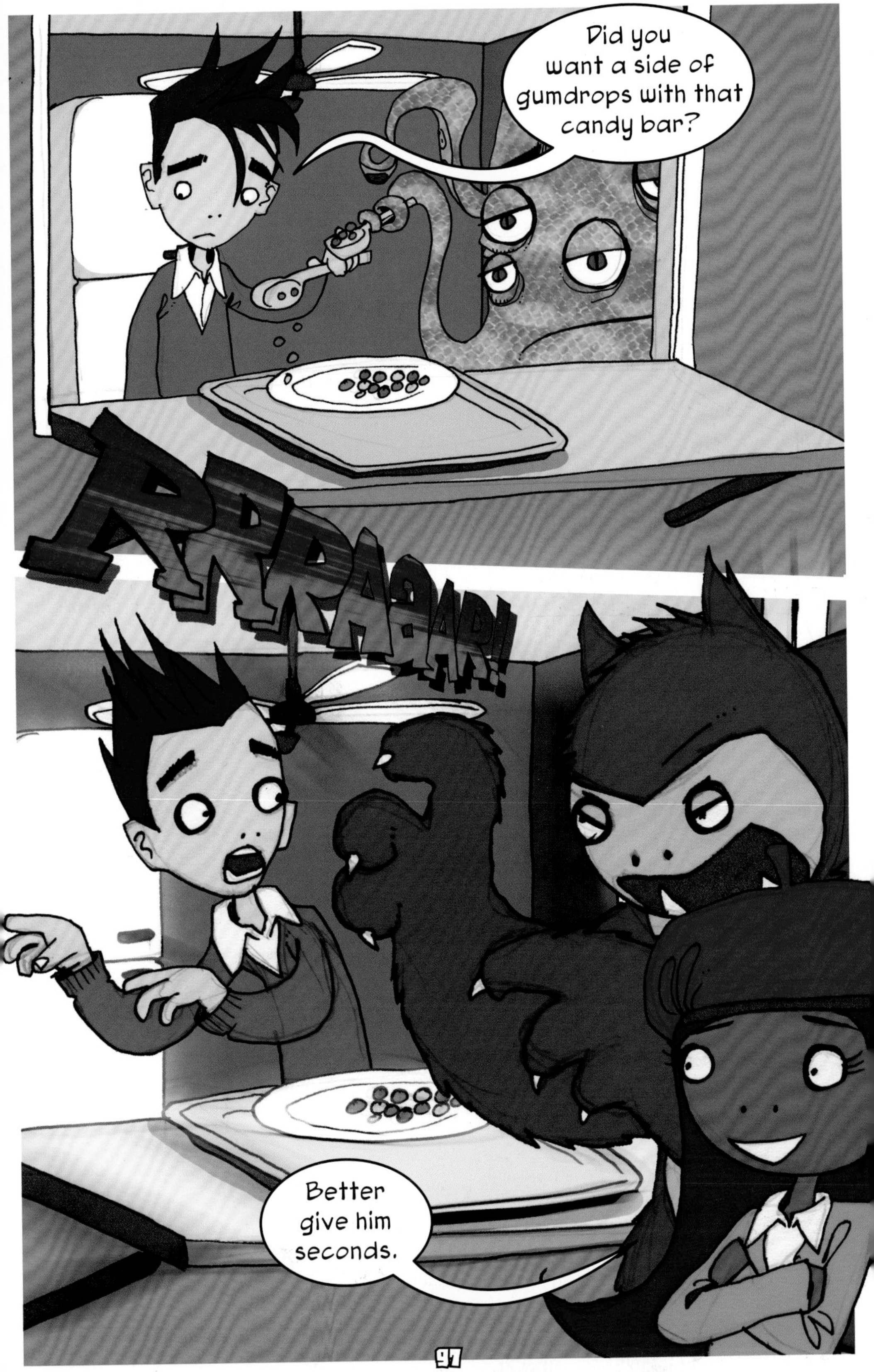
Did you want a side of gumdrops with that candy bar?
RRRAGAR!
Better give him seconds.